THE ART OF BREATHING

CALI MELLE

Cover design by TRC Designs by Cat
Edited by Caroline Palmier
Proofread by Alexandra Cowell

PLAYLIST

A Lack of Color - Death Cab for Cutie
Paper Hearts - Silver Trees (ft. Bailey Jehl)
I Feel Like I'm Drowning - Two Feet
The World At Large - Modest Mouse
Conversations in the Dark - John Legend
A Drop in the Ocean - Ron Pope
Dramamine - Modest Mouse
In My Veins - Andrew Belle (ft. Erin McCarley)
Ocean Eyes - Billie Eilish
The Few Things - JP Saxe, Charlotte Lawrence
Rules of Beautiful - Jacob Whitesides
Hold On - Chord Overstreet
She is Love - Parachute
I Will Follow You into the Dark - Death Cab for Cutie

To the mountains that have moved to make room for the stars

To O and L… this one is for you

Content Warning

Please be advised that The Art of Breathing does contain material where the characters discuss death and the main character has internal thoughts/struggles with her mortality.
This may be triggering for some readers.

Please note that none of the characters die.

Chapter One

NOT TODAY, UNIVERSE

"We aren't sure what her life expectancy is."

Imagine your life if those were the words the doctors spoke after months of testing led them to your definitive diagnosis. Imagine living your life with a diagnosis so rare that every single provider was left scratching their heads while trying to figure out how to treat you.

On the outside, I looked normal. On the inside, my body was struggling to function properly. I was diagnosed with a rare genetic mutation when I was a few months old. My mother left the hospital with what she thought was a newborn with some mild breathing issues.

Our small-town hospital never should have sent me home. They didn't have the capabilities to provide complex medical care. It wasn't until I started turning a dusky gray color while my mother tried to feed me that they realized something was seriously wrong.

I was rushed to a nearby city that had one of the best children's hospitals in the country. It was a massive research center, and it was the place I spent almost the entire first year of my life.

The majority of the smooth muscles in my body were affected by the rare genetic mutation. It severely impacted my lungs and intestines more than any of my other organs. The heart also tends to be affected with my diagnosis, but only as the disease progresses.

Unfortunately, the handful of children who had a similar diagnosis to mine had all passed away from cardiac issues before reaching adulthood. That seemed to be the last leg of the disease. Once the heart was involved, it was essentially game over.

I was fortunate enough to not have any major cardiac involvement... yet.

"Luna!" my mother called from downstairs, her voice floating up into my bedroom. Tank, my Cane Corso, lifted his head off my lap and looked to the door. "It's almost time to leave for school!"

A sigh slipped from my lips as I closed the pastel purple notebook in front of me, tucking my pen into the spiral binding. Since I spent the last few months of my senior year of high school in and out of the hospital with respiratory infections, I had been doing the majority of my schoolwork virtually. I wasn't really looking forward to going back in person for the last three weeks. I was always known as one of the sick kids—the ones who everyone constantly looked at with some hint of pity in their eyes.

All I ever wanted was to be treated normally.

Rising from the chair at the small wooden desk in my bedroom, I walked over to my closet to get dressed. I had awoken early this morning and ran through my mental checklist.

My mother had taught me to manage my own home medical care over the years, and for that I was grateful. I spent the earlier years of my life with a home nurse, and it felt like my privacy was always being invaded.

My alarm on my phone chimed, alerting me with one of the numerous notifications I had set.

I no longer had a need for the central line in my chest, but they kept it there in case of an emergency. There was always talk of one day, hopefully, being able to remove that tube, along with my tracheostomy tube, but no one knew if I would ever see that day.

I'd had a tracheostomy tube since I was a month old. It was one of the first surgeries I had as a baby, when they realized my airway was completely collapsing in on itself. It was one of the main things that had kept me alive this long—and continued to do so every day of my life.

Grabbing a syringe, I twisted it into the small balloon that was attached to the trach tube and deflated it before securing a small speaking valve onto the end of my trach. I was able to talk without the one-way valve on, but my doctor preferred I use it, as it doesn't allow for air to pass through the tube, so I was forced to breathe normally.

Even though I was born with the lungs of a ninety-year-old person with a severe case of COPD, some of my lung tissue had regenerated from the years of advanced medical care. I only had to use the ventilator now while I was sleeping or if I was sick. It was a tad annoying, but by the end of every day, my body tended to reach a point of exhaustion.

After running through my list, I rechecked my outfit in the mirror. My brown hair was as straight as a board, but I pulled it back in a French braid, leaving a few pieces framing my face. My porcelain-colored skin stood out in contrast to my hair and my deep blue eyes looked like the darkest depths of the ocean.

Today was a good day, and there was a pink tint to my cheeks. Instead of looking deathly, I only looked mildly sickly. Tilting my head back, I looked up at the ceiling and raised my middle finger in the air. *Nice try, Universe. You can take me another day.*

Readjusting the bottom hem of my shorts, I stared at the way my clothes hung on my thin frame. There was a little more definition to my body than there once was. Two years ago, I was fortunate enough to receive an intestinal transplant at the best children's hospital in the country after being in intestinal failure for many years.

No one knew the shelf life of my new intestinal tract, but I wasn't about to take it for granted. For the first time in my life, I was holding a steady weight instead of constantly losing pounds. After giving myself another glance, I abandoned my bedroom and made my way down to the kitchen where my mother was waiting. Tank followed along after me, as he was always attached to my hip.

"Good morning, sunshine." My mother smiled at me over her cup of coffee. "Good morning, Tank," she greeted my dog as he walked in beside me. Her dark blue eyes looked tired, but they always had. I don't know that I'd ever seen my mother looking refreshed and not over-stressed. "Sit down and eat. I made your favorite."

I glanced down at the table, noting a pile of French toast sitting in the center on a plate. Memories instantly flooded my mind from my seventh birthday. The doctors approved I could start trying solid foods right before my birthday. That morning my mother asked me what I wanted to have for breakfast, and I randomly asked for French toast—something I'd never had the pleasure of trying before, but always watched everyone else thoroughly enjoy.

So, she took me out that morning, just the two of us, and got me exactly what I asked for. After drowning the pieces of toast in maple syrup, I took two of the smallest bites possible. My mother cried tears of happiness that day, you would think that I won an Olympic gold medal. It was a memory that had stuck with me since then, and my mother always made me French toast when she thought I might need a pick me up.

A sad smile crept onto my face. She made enough to feed an army, but sadly, it was just the two of us who were home most of the time. Both of my brothers were in college, so I was the last kid left. And my father—bless his soul—worked his ass off as a diesel mechanic to pay for whatever medical bills insurance wouldn't cover.

Unfortunately, for my mother and I, that meant he spent long hours in the shop and was rarely ever home. We made things work, though. My mother was my rock and the constant in my life. She was the glue that held all of us together and I would literally be dead without her.

Taking a seat at the table, I speared a piece of toast with my fork and slapped it onto my plate. After putting on some butter, I poured some syrup onto it before cutting it into pieces. My mother watched me carefully as I took a small bite and chewed it slowly. Even though I had been eating for a few years now, I was always careful with the way I consumed my meals. The last thing I needed was to choke on a piece of food.

"Are you ready for your first day back?" my mother

questioned me with hesitation. She had been the one excited for me to attend in person the last three weeks. Me on the other hand—I was content finishing the year at home.

Shrugging, I swallowed my piece of French toast before meeting her gaze. "Not really. It feels like it's kind of pointless for me to go back now."

"Nonsense." My mother waved her hand dismissively. "If you really don't want to go, I won't push you to, but I think it would be good for you. You'll be graduating in three weeks. You have prom this weekend. These are the last few times you'll be seeing a lot of these people."

An exasperated sigh slipped from my lips. "I'm alright with that. My real friends are the only ones I care to see."

Melanie and Salem were my two closest girlfriends. They checked in on me and visited every chance that they could. We barely had any classes together this year, so I didn't see them as often as my mother thought while at school.

Suddenly, a horn beeped from out front promptly causing me to jump from my seat. "There's Oliver," I told my mother, offering her a smile before pushing another piece of French toast into my mouth. "Got to get to school."

"Make sure you check in with Joyce at the nurses' office when you first get there."

"Yes, mother, I know." I walked over to the front door, grabbing the multitude of bags I was required to carry with me. My backpack, medical supply bag, back up ventilator and a suction machine. I practically became a pack-mule since I could carry my own things.

The medical bag was heavy, as it included literally

everything I needed in case of an emergency, and my mother watched me with sadness in her eyes. I hated the look she was giving me right now and it wasn't a second later before she was scrambling to her feet to help me with the door.

As she pulled it open, my best friend and neighbor, Oliver, was standing outside waiting with a huge grin on his face. His sage green eyes shined back at me, and the sun poking through the clouds illuminated his inky black hair.

"Let me carry some of that," he offered, grabbing the ventilator and medical bag from me before I had the chance to refuse. That was Oliver Hart for you. The perfect gentleman who was always there to have my back. "Hey Tank," he greeted Tank as he stood beside me with his tail wagging. Oliver was one of his favorite people too.

Oliver Hart was my partner in crime. His family moved in next door when we were both three years old. After our parents met, we had our first play date and we'd been inseparable ever since. He has been by my side through every surgery, medical procedure and hospital stay. If you named it, Oliver Hart has been through it with me.

"You are so sweet, Ollie." My mother beamed at him, completely charmed by him like the rest of the universe. I mean, how could you not be? With those plump lips and perfect smile. That chiseled jawline, and those sharp features. Oliver looked like he was sculpted by the most skilled artist of all time.

"My mother says the same exact thing, Mrs. Truly." He smiled back at her, hoisting my bags over his shoulder.

"Well, your mother sure did raise a fine young man."

Oliver chuckled, taking a bow in front of her while somehow still holding my things for me.

"We should probably be going," I interjected, smiling sweetly at the two of them. "Don't want to be late for my first day back."

"Of course not." Ollie nodded. "Have a great day, Mrs. Truly."

My mother stepped up to me, giving me a hug and a kiss on the cheek before sending me on my way. It killed her every time I was out of her sight, and I understood her fear. Medical issues or not—you never knew when it was the last time you were going to see someone.

"Bye, Tank," I told my dog as I bent down and gave him a hug. Since I had a nurse at the school who was there just for me, I didn't feel it was necessary to bring in my service dog. He was a little bit of an inconvenience there, and I already drew enough attention to myself without him, but I felt bad every day I left. Tank looked up at me with his sad brown eyes and I knew he wasn't happy to be left behind.

I followed after Oliver to his black Subaru STI and paused behind him as he opened the backseat. His muscles flexed through his heather gray t-shirt as he put my things in before turning to me for my backpack. After handing it to him, I took my seat in the passenger's seat before he walked around and got in behind the steering wheel.

"I'm glad you decided to come, even if there's only a few weeks left," he offered quietly as he pushed in the clutch and released the hand brake before shifting seamlessly into first gear.

I glanced over at him as we pulled away from my house and out onto the street. "You can thank my mom."

"Well, I'll have to make sure to do that when I see her this afternoon," he replied, flashing his perfectly straight teeth at me. He directed his gaze back to the road as he took a left turn onto Main Street. "Are you excited for prom this weekend?"

A groan slipped from my lips as I tilted my head back against the headrest of the seat and closed my eyes. "I can't believe you talked me into it," I admitted as I lifted my head back up to look at him. "Are you sure there's no one else you'd rather go with? I know there were a bunch of girls hoping you would ask them."

Oliver looked over at me and the different shades of green danced in his eyes from the sunlight. "There's only one girl I want to go with, and she's sitting right beside me." He paused and winked as he held out his pinky to me. "Always and forever, Luna Truly."

My breath hitched, catching in my throat and I fought the urge to rip off my speaking valve to breathe easier. As if I hadn't already struggled to learn the art of breathing, when he said things like that, it made my lungs struggle even harder to get the oxygen that they needed.

I hooked my pinky with his. "Always and forever," I murmured back to him.

You see, Oliver Hart was my best friend and my partner in crime.

But he was also the one who my damaged heart belonged to.

Even if the feelings would never be reciprocated.

Chapter Two
REMEMBER TO BREATHE

My first day back at school was as uneventful as I could've hoped for. Which, in my case, was always a good thing. An uneventful day meant there were no medical emergencies. As far as being back around my classmates, well, it went better than I expected. I don't know if they actually missed me, but most seemed like they were happy to see me back.

Most of them were probably just glad they didn't have to attend a funeral for someone they had been going to school with for their entire lives.

There was always this weird sense of impending doom, but I wasn't the one who felt it. I had lived my entire life knowing that my expiration date was much sooner than everyone else's. It wasn't easy to accept as I entered my teenage years, but it was something that I'd come to terms with. It had just become a part of my life I didn't pay much attention to anymore.

I mean, after all, we were all going to die eventually.

On the other hand, everyone who surrounded me were

the ones who had the impending doom. Each time I ended up in the hospital, it was like everyone was bracing themselves for me to not come home again.

I was exhausted by the time Oliver carried my things back to his car at the end of the day. The movement of his driving lulled me to sleep and when I woke up, we were already at my house. Oliver leaned over through the door, his arms sliding underneath my arms as he helped me to my feet.

"I can walk, Ollie," I murmured, trying to muster the strength to push him away from me. Oliver didn't dare budge as he held onto me firmly. Once he had me steady on my feet, he slid an arm around my waist and helped me walk up to the house.

My mother was already waiting with the door held open for the two of us, and Tank was standing by her side. As Oliver walked me inside, I noticed all of my bags were already sitting in their respective spots. My heartbeat was erratic in my chest and my legs felt unsteady as he helped me into the living room and lowered me onto the couch.

"You good, Looney Tune?" His voice was soft and gentle, and it felt like a soothing blanket against my eardrums.

I couldn't fight the grin that spread across my lips as he used my childhood nickname. The smile didn't quite reach my eyes, but it was still there as it always was for him. "I'm good," I assured him, settling deeper into the couch as I took a deep breath.

Tank climbed onto the other end of the couch and rested his head on my hip. Only then did it register in my mind that air was passing through my trach without any issues.

Reaching for the end of it, I realized my speaking valve wasn't on there and instead was replaced with an HME—which stands for humidity moisture exchange. It's a small barrel-shaped piece that is connected to the end of a tracheostomy tube. It was used to add moisture to the air as it was inhaled directly into my lungs.

Another thing most people don't think about is when you breathe through your mouth and your nose, the air you inhale is warmed and there is moisture to humidify it by the time it reaches your lungs. Breathing directly through a tube, I didn't have that ease with the air that passed through it.

"Where's my speaking valve?" I questioned Ollie, feeling a little panicked. Insurance only covered one so it's not something I was in the habit of losing. It could have easily come off when I fell asleep in his car.

Ollie gives me a shy smile. "I took it off as soon as I noticed you fell asleep. I saw you had an HME in the side pocket of your backpack, so I put that on."

My heart clenched and not from anything related to my health conditions. A warmth flooded me, and I could feel the heat as it crept onto my cheeks. Oliver Hart has always been my safe place. And he would be the one to think of something like that, even though he was supposed to be focused on driving.

"Thank you," I breathed, my heart still pounding in my chest. "I really appreciate you doing that."

When I was asleep, most times I was supposed to be on my ventilator. A short car ride home wasn't that big of a deal. But if I would have slept with the speaking valve on, that could have caused some problems. With the way I struggled with a lack of breathing while asleep, I could have easily been deprived of the oxygen my body needed.

I shuddered at the thought. I had gone into respiratory arrest before and had to receive CPR on multiple occasions. The last thing I would ever want is for my best friend to have to revive me. I would want him to save my life, but I wouldn't want him to live with that trauma.

"You don't have to thank me, Luna." He smiled again, grabbing a blanket from the back of the couch before draping it over me. "That's what I'm here for."

A frown pulled down on the corners of my lips. "You're not here to take care of me. You're my friend, not my nurse."

Oliver sat down on the edge of the couch, careful to not sit on my legs. "That's not what I'm saying. But that's what friends are for—to help each other out when they need it."

I knew he was right, but sometimes I couldn't help but be stubborn. A majority of my life has been spent relying on other people to care for me. My dignity had been stripped from me at a young age. I had no control or autonomy. Now that I could do things myself, all I wanted was complete control.

Sometimes it was easy to forget I could still lean on others when I needed the support.

"Sorry, Ollie," I told him, the regret heavy in my tone. "I wasn't trying to be an ass. I just don't want you to feel like you need to do things for me."

"And I don't," he assured me as he tilted his head to the side. I watched his perfect eyebrow arch up at me. "Would you have rather I left it on and watched you turn blue instead?"

"Oliver Hart," my mother quietly scolded him from where she stood in the doorway. Her arms were crossed over her chest and her eyes narrowed at him in disapproval.

"No, mom," I interjected before she had a chance to say anything more. "He's right. I'm sorry, I should be thanking you instead."

Oliver flashed his infamous smile at me and winked. "You already did, Looney Tune. And you're welcome." He leaned over and rested his hand on the side of my face for a moment. His palm was warm against my skin, and I could feel him draining the oxygen from the room. "You get some rest and I'll see you in the morning."

And just like that, his hand was leaving my face as he rose to his feet. He smiled down at me once more before disappearing from the room. My lungs expanded as soon as I heard the front door close, and I let my eyelids fall shut as I focused on my breathing.

"Oliver is a good kid, but sometimes I want to slap him upside the head."

My eyelids lifted as I looked up at my mom. "He didn't do anything wrong. I like it when he doesn't treat me like I'm fragile."

"I know," she said with resignation in her voice. My mother had never treated me any differently than my siblings in terms of the way she parented. But the fact that I had complex medical needs, I got a lot of free passes on certain things. "Sometimes he just comes off a little insensitive with the way he talks." She paused for a moment, pursing her lips. "I hate that you both have the same dark sense of humor."

A soft chuckle slipped from my lips as I felt my eyelids

growing heavy again. "I guess that's just something trauma will do to you. There's nothing wrong with being blunt and realistic."

My mother stared at me for a moment, her expression unreadable. "Why don't you take a nap while I make some dinner? I'll grab your vent for you."

The thought made my heart sink, but I nodded. It was like a damn crutch I couldn't get through life without. As much as I hated having to use the ventilator, I was grateful it wasn't for twenty-four hours a day like it was at one point.

Unable to fight against the sleep that threatened to pull me under, I mumbled a thank you to my mother as she turned on the ventilator and hooked it up to the tube in my trachea.

I snuggled against Tank, feeling his warmth and familiar smell. The exhaustion hit me harder than it had in a while, and the whooshing sound of air lulled me to sleep as thoughts of the boy with sage green eyes who lived next door swirled around in my mind.

Chapter Three
LET'S MAKE A DEAL

My first week back at school passed by in a whirlwind. There was so much going on between everyone getting ready for prom and our graduation. By the time the weekend approached, I was in shock. I only had two weeks left before I was saying goodbye to high school forever.

Everyone had their plans to go away for college, but that was never in the cards for me. It would be too complicated for me to be able to stay anywhere but home. My mother didn't want me out of her sight, and I can't say I blamed her. The thought of going away for college never really crossed my mind because I knew it wasn't possible. But when I thought about it, it made me feel unsettled.

If there was one person who I would feel bad leaving on this earth, it would be my mother. That woman had sacrificed her entire life to care for me. At times, I felt like a burden. There were many nights I spent in the hospital, practically on my deathbed, just wishing for it all to be over. And not even for myself—but for her.

I hated the way I dictated her life without even trying to. My medical conditions ruled her life. I literally owed her everything, and sometimes I wondered if I owed her the peace of not having to care for me anymore. Not having to worry about whether or not your child was going to survive. A parent should never have to experience those thoughts and the trauma that comes along with it.

Those thoughts plagued my mind more often than I ever wanted to admit. And the only person I had ever expressed them to was Oliver. He disagreed with every single word I said. There was a part of him that could sympathize and understand where I was coming from, but he didn't believe it would make anything better. If anything, my mother would feel worse to see my demise.

Thankfully, I had the best team of doctors, with the main one dedicated to finding any way possible to extend my life. Dr. Wyn refused to treat me with palliative care. Instead, he was treating me as if there was a possible cure. After I had my intestinal transplant and there were improvements, that only made him dive deeper into his research.

The sad, hard truth was my chances of being cured, despite their endless efforts, were extremely low. A concrete cure didn't exist. They could prolong my life, but it was never guaranteed to work, and no one could even say how much time it would buy me.

"Luna," my mother's voice called from outside my bedroom door. "Are you ready? Oliver and his parents will be over any minute."

"I'll be right down," I yelled back to her, assuring her I was getting ready. The truth was I hadn't even put on my dress yet. I had done my makeup, something light and natural that made me appear more human. My stick straight hair was twisted in loose curls, but I knew they wouldn't last the entire night, thanks to the side effects from my medications.

Staring at myself in the full-length mirror that hung on the back of my door, my eyes scanned over my body. Over the countless scars from numerous surgeries. The small button shaped feeding tube that was in my stomach and the central line tubing curled around on my chest that was tucked under a clear piece of cellophane-looking medical tape. I looked like a typical eighteen-year-old girl in terms of development, but damn, I was still practically skin and bones.

I didn't know if I wanted to see Ollie right now. It felt weird in a way, and it made me more nervous than I had been in a long time. When he asked me to prom, it surprised me, but I knew if anyone was going to ask, it would be him. He was the only person who'd seen me dressed up before, but I had never dressed up to go somewhere with him as my date.

He would be leaving me at the end of the summer, and the thought broke my heart. I always knew there would come a day where we would go our separate ways, but I still didn't feel prepared for it. Oliver was the star quarterback on our high school team. He worked his ass off to get a full-ride scholarship to college playing football. The only problem—the college he was going to was six hours away.

Too far for me to ever be able to travel and visit him.

A sigh escaped me as I turned around and walked over to my bed. Grabbing the blush-colored dress, I slipped it over my head and arranged it into place. It hugged the top part of my torso before cascading into flowing chiffon that hung down to the floor. I loved the way that it looked on me, but I hated the way my stomach was doing somersaults.

My phone vibrated from where it was sitting on my bed, and I picked it up as I moved my dress and sat down on the edge of the mattress. My face lit up as I saw my other best friend's name flash across the screen. Other than Oliver, Giana Cirone was my real best friend.

None of my friends from school came close to our friendship. The only problem—Giana lived hundreds of miles away from me. I met her when we were kids after Dr. Wyn got me into some trial at one of the children's hospitals in New York. The hospital had one of these really cool saltwater aquariums built into a wall in their lobby.

My brother Eli would take me down there every day, as long as I was feeling well. That was where I first met Giana. She was recovering from myocarditis at the time. After becoming very sick from influenza, she went on to develop inflammation of her heart which required extensive monitoring and treatment. The first time we met, I tried talking to her and I thought she was just ignoring me.

It wasn't until our third time sitting side by side, watching the tropical fish floating around in the tank, that I found out Giana had suffered from permanent hearing loss. The numerous medications the doctors had her on for her heart left her without the ability to hear. And there was no way to reverse it.

GIANA

> You better send me pics from tonight. I wish I could be there to see you and Oliver.

I smiled as I read her message to myself. Giana had come to visit enough times that her and Oliver were well acquainted. Other than my mother, she was the only one who had ever questioned mine and Oliver's friendship.

LUNA

I will send you all the pics. I promise. Wish you were here!

GIANA

Don't have too much fun without me!
Love you.

LUNA

Never. Love you more.

I always wished Giana lived closer. We talked almost daily, but sometimes it just didn't feel like enough. We normally talked through texts since it was a pain to Face-Time using sign language. My abilities in ASL weren't as advanced, but I learned how to do it over the years so I could communicate with my best friend.

Without bothering to look in the mirror, I slipped my feet into a pair of silver flats and grabbed my matching silver colored clutch and slid my phone into it before exiting my bedroom. My footsteps were light against the hardwood floor as I walked down the hallway, pausing when I reached the top of the stairs.

I could hear voices from the doorway, and I knew Oliver and his parents were already here. My father's voice also drifted around, which had my heart soaring. He wasn't around as much as I wanted him to be, but knowing he was here for this meant the world to me.

Inhaling deeply, my lungs didn't quite expand like I

would have liked them too. My hand landed on the railing, and I slowly began my descent down to the first floor. Tank was at my side, walking with me. As everyone came into my view, I watched the different expressions on their faces and the way they all lit up like the sky on the Fourth of July.

My father was standing beside my mother, his arm wrapped around the tops of her shoulders. He had the biggest grin on his face and his eyes grew wet as I continued to walk down the stairs. My mother's hands were covering her mouth, tears streaming down the sides of her cheeks. The Harts both looked as happy as my parents and Mrs. Hart even had tears in her eyes.

The last one to meet my gaze was Oliver. He was standing at the bottom of the stairs in a black tux, with a blush-colored tie that matched my dress. His hands were clasped in front of his body, and he looked so grown up—not like the boy who was my best friend. I watched the way his throat bobbed as he swallowed roughly.

His eyes traveled up the length of my dress before settling on mine. Different hues of green burned in his irises, and the corners of his lips began to rise. As I reached the bottom step, he closed the distance between us, his arm outstretched for me. A smile pulled on my lips as I wrapped my arm around his.

"You're absolutely breathtaking, Luna," he breathed, his voice soft and gentle, only loud enough for me to hear.

"Look at my baby girl," my mother cried, and everyone quickly walked over to the two of us. "You look so beautiful."

My parents and Oliver's both gushed over the way the two of us looked together. My mother's gaze kept colliding with mine and every time, it seemed like she cried harder. Today was a big day for both of us. It was a day neither of us thought we'd ever make it to. But here we were.

"Okay!" Mrs. Hart clapped her hands together before motioning toward the front door. "Everyone outside for pictures!"

We were all ushered out onto the front lawn where everyone took their turn taking pictures. There were some captured of me with my parents, and Oliver with his before we got pictures taken of just the two of us together. It wasn't long before Oliver began to shut his mother down, insisting it was time for us to go.

Oliver bent his arm, offering me his elbow as he turned to face me. "Are you ready, my queen?"

A soft laugh fell from my lips. "Please. I'm nothing more than a mere peasant."

Oliver tilted his head to the side, his jaw clenching before a smile took over his expression. "Luna. You rule the goddamn universe. There is no one above you."

His words made my heart sing and just like that, it was difficult for me to breathe again.

"Wait," I let out in a rush as I slid my arm through his. "I need all of my stuff."

"Already in the car, Looney Tune," he replied with a wink.

"Do you ever not think of everything?"

Oliver flashed me his infamous smile, but there was something else lingering behind it. Something in his eyes I couldn't put my finger on. "Not where you're concerned."

Oliver walked me over to the passenger's side door, pausing as he pulled it open for me. He carefully helped me into my seat, and I looked back up at him, our gazes colliding as we shared a smile between the two of us. Oliver softly closed the door behind me as I situated myself in my seat and put on my seatbelt.

He slid into his seat behind the steering wheel before turning on his car. I glanced out the window once more at both of our families standing together in the front yard. My father stood with his arm wrapped around my mother's shoulders and the Hart's were standing in a similar fashion.

I didn't miss the tears still in my mother's eyes as I raised my hand to wave at them all before Oliver pulled the car out of the driveway. His hand leaves the shift knob, turning the music up a little bit as we cruised down the road. He made sure to put the air conditioner on low and left the windows up. I didn't know if he had done it subconsciously or if he knew I wouldn't want my hair to get messed up, even if the curls were already coming out.

"So, Luna," Oliver said, his voice cheerful as he pulled onto Main Street, which took us almost directly to the school. "Do you still have that bucket list you said you were working on last year?"

I glanced over at him, nervousness welling inside me as I raised an eyebrow. "Maybe. Why?"

"I still want to see it."

My breath caught in my throat. Last year I had pneumonia which put me in the hospital. I was going through some older journals I had after I was discharged and found a bucket list I had made when I was younger. It only felt fitting that it needed to be updated, since I had checked some of the boxes and lived past the age, I thought I would make it to.

So, I made a brand-new list—one I was still periodically adding things to. It was a much more practical list, since jumping off a cliff into water was something I'd never be able to do. I had been swimming before, but I always had to be careful to not get any water in my tracheostomy tube. Swimming underwater was something I would never be allowed to do, so that had come off my list.

When I started making my new list, I had confessed to Oliver in a medical drug induced haze I was making one. He asked to see it and I told him I would let him. When I woke up the next morning and the medication had worn off, I realized I could never show it to him. He was my best friend and there were a few things on there I wasn't comfortable showing him.

To be honest, I was more embarrassed than anything about some of them.

"I told you that there are things on there I don't want you to see," I said, swallowing roughly before wetting my lips. "There are some private things on there."

Oliver let out an exasperated sigh, playing the dramatic part he liked to do occasionally. "Fine," he practically whined while giving me his puppy dog eyes. "Show me the things I'm allowed to see."

"Why do you want to see it so badly?"

Something shifted in the air, and Oliver's face fell for a moment before he recovered. "This is our last summer before college. I think it's time we check some of them off."

I stared at him for a moment. "Are you anticipating I will die after you leave?"

Oliver's eyebrows scrunched together, and a wave of pain flashed through his eyes. "Absolutely not. I just want to be the one who does them with you. And I want us to make this the best summer ever."

My face cracked and I was unable to keep my laughter in. "I'm just kidding, Ollie." I smiled at him, but it didn't quite reach my eyes. "We both know I'm going to die eventually. Why else would I have a bucket list?"

"You know, I know we joke about it all the time, but sometimes I wish we didn't have to think about it or talk about it," he replied, the sadness laced within his quiet words.

"I know," I whispered, not fully trusting my voice as the emotion welled in my throat. "Reality is an ugly bitch, isn't she?"

Ollie glanced over at me; his perfectly plump lips pulled in a straight line. "The ugliest." He fell silent for a moment and directed his gaze back to the road as he pulled the car into the parking lot of the school. There were already a lot of cars here and students were filing into the building.

He found a handicapped parking spot since he knew I wouldn't let him drop me off at the front door, just for him to have to park toward the back of the lot. My stomach felt like there was a bundle of anxiety bugs crawling around inside as he killed the engine and turned to face me.

"I think that every five years, you should make a new bucket list."

I turned to look over at him, my eyes trailing across his features, taking in every inch that my mind already had memorized. "Don't you think every five years is a little generous?"

"Absolutely not," he retorted, shaking his head at me. "Every five years, you'll be in a different place in life so you can make a new list that matches where you're at in life. But you have to check all the boxes on your previous list before you can make a new one."

"And what if I don't get to all of them before I meet my five-year mark?"

Different shades of green swirled in Oliver's irises as he stared back at me like I'm the most difficult person he'd ever met. He knew how I was, though. There was always a little feistiness that lurked around. What else would you expect from someone who had life constantly trying to beat them down?

"I will make sure we always get the boxes checked off, Luna. Don't you worry about that."

I tilted my head to the side, curiosity building inside me. "You're leaving for college in another state this year, Ollie. You can't predict where you'll be in your life by then, so you don't have to be responsible for helping me with every bucket list I have."

"I will always be in your life. Always and forever, remember?" He said it with such a declaration, like it was never even a question. Always and forever was kind of our thing. When we were young, I made Ollie pinky promise I wouldn't get hurt when I was learning to ride my bike without training wheels. He promised me always and forever and it just stuck. It was what we did.

The butterflies in my stomach came to life as I held onto his words, and I could feel the heat creeping up my neck. My body practically switched into manual breathing, and I had to remind myself to take a breath every few seconds. Neither of us could predict the future, but hearing those words from him gave me a sense of peace I didn't realize I needed to hear.

There had always been a fear that once Oliver left for college, it would be the end of our friendship. He would move on to bigger and better things in life and never come back to me. It still wasn't a guarantee, but I knew Oliver Hart like the back of my frail hand. If he said something, I knew damn well he was going to keep his word.

"So, this summer…" he started, a smile cracking on his face as he raised an eyebrow at me. "You game for making it the best one ever and checking things off your list?"

My breath caught in my throat, but I smiled back at him anyway. "The ones you're allowed to see."

"Whatever you say, Looney Tune." He continued to smile at me as he held his hand out for me to shake. "Do we have a deal?"

I glanced down at his hand, lingering for a moment before my gaze collided with his once more. Sliding my hand into his, we wrapped our fingers around the backs of each other's hands and shook on it.

"Deal."

Chapter Four
DANCE WITH ME

The gymnasium of the school was crammed with other students. Oliver snuck my bags into one of the supply closets outside of the gym where no one would see them. I was forced to carry some of them around school with me, but while we were here tonight, I was going to try my hardest to fit in and be normal.

Different colored lights flashed around from the ceiling as the DJ played music by the stage area that they set up. The entire room had been transformed into something magical, like a fairytale. There were twinkling fairy lights and walls covered with delicate flowers in the softest pastel hues. It was like we had stepped into an enchanted forest.

Oliver held me close, his arm wrapped around my waist as he kept me tucked against his side. He walked me through various crowds of students and ignored his group of friends who were gathered around a table toward the center of the room. We moved straight over to the photo booth that they had set up over in the corner.

We stopped when we reached the line, and I glanced up at Ollie. "Didn't we get enough pictures earlier?"

A laugh slipped from his plump lips. "Those were the most generic things ever. Plus, those were memories for our parents. *These* are memories for us to have."

I smiled up at him as the line began to move and we followed behind until it was our turn. Oliver slid his hand from my waist, dropping it to my hand as he let me step into the booth first. His palm was warm against mine and his fingers held me close. My heart was in my stomach, and it was pounding with such force as we both stood in front of the camera.

We looked at the small basket of different props before looking at each other. The curtain was drawn shut behind us and it was just the two of us. All of the sudden, something began to count down and it pulled us both from the moment of our close proximity.

"Shit," Oliver muttered, reaching for a fake mustache from the basket. He grabbed a crown and tossed it to me. "It's going to take the picture without us being ready."

Laughter bubbled from my lips as Oliver crammed in the small space against me to be able to fit into the screen for the picture. It flashed in front of our eyes before showing a preview of the image. We were caught mid-action—me attempting to hold the crown on my head as Oliver held the mustache to his neck since he couldn't reach his nose in time.

We broke out in laughter together, and Oliver tossed the mustache back to the basket before repositioning the crown on my head. He straightened it as he wrapped his arm around the tops of my shoulders, pulling me flush against his side.

The camera flashed again, and we both looked over at the screen to see the preview. That one had my heart fluttering as my stomach did somersaults. In the picture, Oliver was staring down at me like I was the sun that shined through the clouds on the darkest days. I was looking up at him like he was the only thing I could ever see.

My heart soared as we both stared at it. I was too caught up in the moment, my mind barely registering the sound as it began to count down from three again. Oliver's arm was still wrapped around me, and his breath was warm against my cheek as he let out a shallow exhale. He pressed his soft lips to my cheek and my eyelids fluttered shut as warmth flooded my body.

The camera flashed again, and his lips lingered before he pulled away. My eyelids lifted and my cheeks were burning hot from the mixture of feelings that flooded my body. In the years Oliver and I had been friends, we hugged, but we'd never kissed. Not even on the cheek like this.

I looked up at him for a moment and his green eyes met mine with a fire burning deep inside them. He cleared his throat and shifted his weight nervously as a smile pulled on the corners of his lips. We both turned our eyes back to the screen, and I swear that my heart was going to beat out of my chest as I looked at the picture of the two of us.

It was one I would be saving for the rest of my life. I was torn between the two. The one taken before was a sweet moment, but this—this was something I had never experienced in my life.

Oliver pulled his arm from my shoulders and slid his

hand into mine. His fingers intertwined with mine and he led me out of the photo booth and back out into the real world. Prom was happening all around us and neither of us even realized while we were tucked away in our own little corner of the universe.

"Did you want anything to drink or eat?" Oliver asked me as we walked past some tables of food and drinks.

"I'll just take a water," I told him, and he grabbed two from the table before handing one to me. With my hand still in his, I didn't want to pull it away to bother opening up my water, instead, I held onto him as he led me through the crowd that was gathered on the dance floor.

We walked over to the table where Oliver's friends were seated. They were all guys from the football team, and they knew Oliver and I were best friends. They kind of embraced and accepted me like an extension of him. Although, I'm sure if it weren't for him, none of us would really be friends. They had reached out when I was in the hospital different times, but no one ever reached out to hang out with me except for Vivi and Salem.

Two seats were saved for us at the table, and Oliver pulled his hand from mine as he moved my chair out for me to sit down. Setting down my clutch and water bottle, I tucked my hands around the backs of my thighs to fold my dress with my legs as I sat down. Oliver scooted my chair in before taking his seat.

"What's up, man?" Dylan, one of Oliver's friends slapped his hand and they did some little handshake thing.

The rest of the guys all greeted us, and Dylan and Oliver broke out into a conversation about college. They were both going to Dupree University, so they would be there together in the fall. Part of me was jealous. I wasn't allowed to leave for college, so I was stuck attending the community college that was only twenty minutes from my house.

While I tuned the guys out, my eyes surveyed the gymnasium until I came across my two friends. Salem and Vivi were standing toward the left side of the room, talking to each other as they swayed their hips along to the music. I told them I would see them here, and I knew neither of them had dates, so I wanted to spend time with them, too.

Reaching out for Oliver, I wrapped my hand around his forearm to get his attention. He looked over at me, a wave of concern washing over his eyes as they bounced back and forth between mine.

"Is everything okay, Luna?"

I nodded, smiling at him. "I'm going to go see Vivi and Salem." I paused, releasing his arm as I pointed over to where they were standing. "I'll just be over there with them."

Oliver smiled back and nodded. "Don't disappear on me."

"Never." I winked at him as I rose from my seat.

Oliver watched me carefully, studying my movements as I pushed my chair back under the table. Even with the carefreeness between the two of us, Oliver was always cautious and careful. He entertained my off-the-wall ideas and wanted me to have my independence… but he never wandered too far away from me.

I left my bottle of water and clutch at the table and when I was halfway to the girls, I found myself wishing I would have brought my drink along with me. They both spotted me as I moved closer to them, their faces lighting up brightly.

"Luna!" Vivi exclaimed as she quickly embraced me. She moved away, her hands still on my shoulders as she looked me up and down. "Girl, you look amazing!"

Salem hugged me after Vivi released me. "Seriously, you're stunning. I'm so glad that you came."

"Where's Oliver?" Vivi questioned me, looking over my shoulder as if she'd find him standing directly behind me. "You guys came together, right?"

I nodded, smiling at her. "He's over with some of his friends. I saw you guys over here and wanted to come see you."

"We weren't sure if you were still coming, but we're so glad you did!" Vivi practically yelled over the loud music. She stared at me for a moment, her gaze lingered longer than I liked. It wasn't often I felt it from my friends, but every once and awhile, it was hard to ignore the concerned look in their eyes. "How are you feeling?"

There it was. That stupid question I loathed with a passion. Such a loaded question, at that.

"Good," I smiled at her, brushing away the irritation I was feeling inside. "I've been feeling a lot better since I got out of the hospital."

"That's always good," Salem interjected, saving me from Vivi's stupid questions. "We're just glad you came back for the last few weeks. Can you believe we're graduating soon?"

I shook my head at the two of them as they stood in front of me. In a way, it felt like we were all growing further apart. They were my two best girlfriends, but they were also going to be leaving after summer was over.

There had been some distance between the three of us recently, but I wouldn't be the one to bring it up.

"Our last summer together," Vivi said with a sadness in her voice as she pulled Salem and I in for a group hug. "We have to make sure we spend as much time as we can together since none of us will be at the same college."

"Of course," Salem agreed with her, hugging both of us tightly. "I'm going to miss the two of you so much."

I nodded along but remained silent as their words floated around in my mind. I never really questioned our friendship until this moment. It had occurred to me before that we were all living separate lives, but neither of them knew what it was like to be in my shoes. To be tied down the way I was. I would never be able to experience life like they could.

I didn't want to be the one who held them back from doing anything.

"I actually have a really busy summer, but we need to get together before you both go away," I told them, not letting on to my lie. I didn't have a busy summer, except for spending it with Oliver. He was the one person on the planet who didn't look at me like I might shatter into a million pieces, even if he did express his concerns and proceeded with caution.

"Excuse me." His voice broke through our little group hug. We all stepped away from one another, turning in his direction. Oliver was standing there with a bashful smile on his face. "May I steal my date from the two of you?"

Salem and Vivi both smiled at Oliver, completely captivated by his charm like the rest of the universe. I couldn't blame them—there was something about him that was impossible to resist.

"Of course," Vivi offered. "We'll catch up with you later, Luna."

The two of them disappeared into a crowd of people, leaving Oliver and I standing facing each other. The lights that flashed around the room mixed in his irises as his eyes bounced back and forth between mine. Suddenly, they began to dim, and the upbeat music switched into something slow and sensual.

Oliver held his hand out to me. "Dance with me."

I swallowed hard over the emotions welling inside me and nodded, slipping my hand into his. Oliver laced his fingers with mine, his palm warm against mine. My heart was in my throat, and I was stepping into unknown territory. I had never danced with anyone before.

Oliver led me out onto the dance floor, and we found an open spot where we blended in with everyone else. He released my hand, our gazes colliding as he closed the distance between us. He slid his hands around my waist and laced them together against the small of my back.

My body was pressed flush against his and I lifted my arms, wrapping them around the back of his neck. He smelled like the ocean, and I inhaled deeply, savoring the scent. Turning my head to the side, I rested my cheek against his chest and listened to his heart as it hammered inside his chest.

I let him lead, swaying out bodies back and forth as we danced together to a John Legend song. I was careful to make sure I didn't step on his feet, even though all we were doing was rocking back and forth while slowly spinning in a circle. This may have been my first time, but I watched enough romance movies that showed people dancing.

"Thank you for coming with me tonight, Luna," he said softly, his chin resting against the top of my head. "You're the only one I wanted to share this moment with."

Lifting my head from his chest, I turned to look up at him. Oliver's green eyes were filled with emotion and felt like they were burning holes through mine as he stared directly into my soul. "Thank you for bringing me, Oliver."

"I meant what I said," he murmured softly, his breath smelling like fruit punch. "I didn't give a shit about anyone else who was waiting for me to ask them. You're the only one I want to be here with."

My heart crawled back into my throat, and it felt like I was starving for oxygen. Our surroundings completely dissipated, vanishing into the background. The only thing that mattered was Oliver's hands around my waist and the way our bodies were moving together. That, and the way I was lost in the depths of his green irises.

"This was one of the things on my bucket list," I admitted, my voice quiet and thick with emotion.

"Coming to prom?" he questioned me, tilting his head to the side in curiosity.

I shook my head and swallowed roughly. "Dancing with someone."

Oliver fell silent and his eyebrows pulled together slightly as a mixture of emotions washed over his eyes. It wasn't often his expression became unreadable, but in this moment, I wanted to see inside his mind. I wanted to read his thoughts.

"I'm glad I was your first."

I stared back at him as I struggled to catch my breath.

"Me too."

Chapter Five

SUNSHINE AND GUILT

The soft whooshing sound of the air from the ventilator filled the room as I slowly peeled open my eyes. Tank nuzzled his head against my thigh, and I reached down to pet his head. I stared up at the ceiling of my bedroom for a moment, listening to the machine as it switched into a different mode. It was a newer style of ventilator, so it delivered breaths depending on what the patient needed.

When I was sleeping my body would sometimes forget to breathe, and that's when the vent would kick in and do the job for me. Now that I was awake, it no longer served a purpose since my body had begun to do all of the work. I slowly sat up and swung my legs over the edge of the bed before rising to my feet.

I unhooked myself from the machine, turned everything off and went about my morning routine. It was ingrained in my brain and a part of my everyday life. It was like second nature, and I didn't really pay it much attention as I went through the motions. Since it was Sunday morning, I didn't bother getting changed and headed downstairs to the kitchen in my pajamas.

My mother was already down there, and I paused in the doorway as I watched her hovering by the stove. She flipped the eggs in the pan in front of her before turning around and noticing me.

"Good morning, sunshine and good morning, Tank." She smiled at me and my dog. She was looking thinner than she had in the past and her hair was pulled back in a low ponytail. I hated the way she looked like she was aging faster than she should be. She was only in her forties but life with a sick child had really taken a toll on her. "Grab a seat at the table and I'll bring breakfast over."

I wasn't really hungry, but I wasn't about to argue with her. I couldn't do something like that when she worked as hard as she did to ensure I was properly taken care of.

"Where's Dad?" I questioned her as I took my seat and poured myself a glass of water. There wasn't a plate sitting at his seat and it made my heart sink.

"He had some work he had to attend to this morning. Since he took the day off yesterday, he told them he would come in today to finish the project he was working on."

That was life for my father. The poor man worked six days a week just to make ends meet. Even though my mother was the one who usually stayed at the hospital with me while I was sick, he had exceeded his limit on personal days. He took off work, whenever he was able to, to be with me as well, and thankfully his employer was understanding of our life.

Since he was off yesterday to see me go to prom, now he had to work today to make up for it. It was just another thing that made me regretful for my life. I could see the strain it had put on our family over the years, and I couldn't help but feel like a burden in moments like this.

"He'll be home by lunchtime," my mother assured me when she saw my facial expression. I had broken down before in the past and expressed these feelings to her. She could read me like a book, and I know it was written all over my face right now.

"Okay," I responded, my voice quiet and hesitant. "I feel bad he had to go in today just because he was off yesterday."

"Such is life, sunshine." My mother offered me a sad smile. "He wouldn't have missed yesterday for the world, so the tradeoff is completely worth it. How was prom? I know you were tired last night, so we didn't really get to talk about it."

I couldn't fight the smile that consumed my lips. "It was amazing."

Memories flooded my mind and my heart soared high through the clouds. It was possibly the best night I ever had. Oliver and I spent the night dancing to the different songs that came on and when I couldn't keep up, he escorted me back to the table to rest.

"I found these pictures with your stuff," she told me, handing the three photos from the photo booth to me. My eyes met hers while taking them from her. Her eyes glistened and she hastily wiped a tear away as it fell down her cheek. "Happiness looks good on you, sunshine."

"That's all everyone wants in life, right?" I asked her, my gaze dropping down to the photos in my hand. I mentally made a note to take pictures of them to send to

Giana later. My stomach began to do an entire gymnastic routine as the feelings from last night hit me in a rush.

"That's what everyone deserves," my mother replied quietly. The emotion was thick in her words, and it settled in the air between us. "Are you happy, sweet girl? I know life hasn't been the easiest, but I want you to be honest with me."

I lifted my eyes back to hers, watching her as she sat down in the seat next to me. "I am. I really mean that," I told her truthfully. "But sometimes, I can't help but feel like I'm a burden to everyone around me."

My mother reached toward me and took my hands in hers. "No one thinks that, Luna. You are a blessing in all of our lives, and we would be lost without you. Everyone has to make sacrifices in life and as a parent, I wouldn't imagine it any other way."

"I'm sorry for everything I've put you through." My voice cracked around the words as tears pricked the corners of my eyes. Guilt overwhelmed me and I fought hard against it. "No parent should have to go through life wondering when their child is going to die."

"Luna Mae." My mother's voice was stern, and she squeezed my hands lightly. "There is nothing you should ever apologize for. None of this is your fault."

Tears streamed down the sides of my face, and I didn't bother to hide the emotion as it tore through my body. "If I wouldn't have been born, you never would have had to go through all of this."

My mother's face contorted, and she shook her head at me as her own tears mimicked mine. "If you wouldn't have been born, our lives would have never been blessed the way they have been with you. You are my greatest joy in life, and I don't want you to ever feel anything but good about that. We've had a lot of misfortune, but so much to be thankful about."

"I know," I responded as I pulled my hands from hers and wiped the tears away from my face. "Sometimes I just feel really bad about it all."

"I can understand that, but don't for once think we aren't grateful for you. I would do it all over again if we had to, Luna."

My gaze dropped down to the photos in my hand again. They captured the perfect moment—just two carefree teenagers at prom. No medical supplies in the background and nothing apparent except for the small tube poking out from the center of my throat. The happiness written on my expression is all I want to feel and for everyone around me to feel.

"The two of you looked good together last night," my mother said as she looked at the pictures with me. "Oliver really is a great kid. You're lucky to have a friend like him."

"I know," I agreed with her, feeling the emotion building again. "It just sucks he'll be leaving at the end of the summer."

My mother reached out to me, sliding her hand under my chin as she tipped it up to look at her. "That boy will never stray far from you, Luna. Even though he's leaving for college, he'll always be tethered to you."

"How do you know that?" I asked her, feeling the fears of losing my best friend even though her words were supposed to assure me.

I watched her as she lifted herself from her seat and smiled down at me. "Your mother might know a thing or two," she said with a wink. "Just look at the way he's looking at you in those pictures, if you don't believe me."

He looked at me like I was the only thing that mattered in the world.

"Have the two of you talked about what you're doing this summer?" my mother asked as she grabbed the food from the stove and brought it over to the table. "I'm sure Oliver has something up his sleeve to keep the two of you busy."

I swallowed roughly, smiling up at my mother as she sat back down. "We're actually going to work on checking off some things from my bucket list. Oliver insists we complete the entire list by the end of the summer."

My mother smiled back at me, although there was a sadness to her voice. I had never mentioned my bucket list to her before this moment. "Of course he did." She paused for a moment, her eyes desperately searching mine. "I didn't know you had made a bucket list."

"Oliver thinks I should make a new one every five years. But I'm not allowed to make a new one until I check all the boxes from the previous list."

Her tongue darted out as she wet her lips and nodded at me. "I like that idea a lot." There was still a lingering sadness, but I didn't entertain it. People who were perfectly healthy made bucket lists too. They weren't just reserved for people with a terminal illness.

"He wants this to be the best summer that we've ever had."

My mother smiled back at me. "There's no doubt in my mind he won't go to the ends of the earth to make sure it happens."

I smiled back at her, letting her words settle in my soul

as she excused herself from the table for a moment. I watched her walk out of the room, but my mind was elsewhere. Lost in the boy who lived next door with the green eyes.

The one who would always make sure that my dreams came true—no matter what.

Chapter Six

The last two weeks of my senior year of high school passed by in a blur. They went faster than I wanted them to and now we were finally at the day that really counted. It was time for graduation and to say goodbye to all of the people I spent the past thirteen years with. In a way, there was a sadness that hung heavily in the air that day, but at the same time, there was a shimmer of hope.

I had reached another milestone we were never sure I would get to experience. My parents had already seen both of my brothers graduate from high school, but that was expected with them. My life was so precarious, and we were constantly dealing with the uncertainty of the future.

But here we were. We finally reached the day, and no one knew it, but it was an item I had on my bucket list.

To most people, something this simple wouldn't seem like a big deal, let alone something you would dedicate a spot to on your list of things you wanted to do before you die. To me, this was huge. It was bigger than anything I had ever accomplished in life. And I was ready to start the next chapter, even if no one could predict what that would look like.

I shifted my weight on my feet as I stood in line. My gown felt like it was suffocating my body as it hung heavily on my shoulders. It was a hot day for the beginning of June and the lightweight sundress I had on underneath wasn't helping to cool my skin.

A bead of sweat rolled down the back of my neck, and I readjusted the loose curls around my shoulders. I listened as our superintendent called Oliver's name and watched as he began his walk across the stage. The crowd of students and people who were in attendance went wild. Oliver was loved by so many, and it made my heart swell to see him getting the acknowledgment he deserved.

He was so much more than a smiling face and a kind person. He was quite literally everything. He was the one person who gave me hope in the world around us and in humanity itself. That there were people out there who genuinely cared, who could see past all the medical equipment and disabilities.

Tears filled my eyes as I watched him receive his diploma and shake the hands of the different teachers and the principal standing at the end of the line. It wasn't every day you got to watch your best friend graduate high school. He worked his ass off to get to where he was, and I was so excited for what was to come in his future—even if it meant we weren't going to be spending every waking moment together.

They went through the rest of the line until they finally reached my name. My stomach felt like it was going to fall to the floor and my heart pounded erratically in my chest as my name was called out through the microphone. Counting my steps, I was careful as I took each one across that stage. It felt like an eternity under the hot sun that hung above in the sky.

My lungs were screaming at me, as if they weren't getting the oxygen they so desperately needed. It was partially due to the heat, but more so because of my anxiety. This was it. It was like closing the last page to a book and having no idea of what to expect now. School had been a normalcy in my routine for years. I didn't like not knowing what to expect next.

By the time I collected my diploma, my surroundings came crashing back down around me. Instead of the buzzing sound in my ears, I could hear everyone cheering loudly for me. I could hear my teachers and everyone congratulating me as they shook my hand. The leather diploma cover felt strange in my palm, and I paused as I reached the end of the stage, glancing out at my parents in the crowd.

Even though this piece of paper was for me, the whole day was really for them. As much as I wanted to celebrate the milestone for myself, it was something they deserved to celebrate for themselves. They were the two people who had kept me alive and ensured I had everything I needed to make it this far in life.

Even with the odds stacked against us.

I found my seat in the front row that faced the stage. Vivi was seated to my right, since our last names came right next to each other in the alphabetic order we followed. She looked over at me, a huge smile on her face.

"We did it, girl!" She held her hand up to mine for a high five.

I slapped it, smiling back at her. "We made it to the finish line."

And now our lives were about to go in completely different directions. I already knew I would be losing my friends after this day and I was okay with it. I completely understood and knew it was a part of life. The one thing I refused to accept was losing Oliver like this too. He's the one person I was terrified of losing the most.

They made it through the remainder of the names on the list and each diploma was handed out to the students in our graduating class. After everyone was seated, the superintendent congratulated our class as a whole. As if on command, everyone rose to their feet and grabbed their caps. We all tossed our hats to the sky while other students cheered and carried on. I tilted my head back, watching as all of our royal blue hats flew up toward the bright white clouds that stood out in stark contrast in the background.

We couldn't have asked for a more beautiful day for a celebration like this.

After everything was over, we all gathered around with our families. My mother and father greeted me with their warm, embracing hugs. Both of my brothers, Eli and Jackson, surprised me with their attendance. I wasn't expecting to see them here and when they both swept me up into their arms and swung me around, it felt like everything was finally the way it should be.

Each of us were separated by two years. Jackson was the oldest at twenty-two. He just finished his undergraduate and was off to grad school this fall for his master's in psychology. Eli was twenty and I was eighteen. We were all close growing up, but after they both went off to college, we didn't see them as often.

It hurt my heart, knowing how close we once were, but it was all in the nature of the beast and the circle of life. They were building new lives in the new cities they lived in. And I was still stuck in Dansbury, where I would most likely spend the rest of my days.

There was a part of me that was a tad jealous. My brothers never treated me like I was any different from the two of them, but the reality was that I *was* different. I didn't have the joy of just experiencing life like they got to. I was too busy trying to survive it.

"We're so proud of you, little Luna," Jackson said as he put me down on my feet. His hazel eyes shined back at me. Our mother had blue eyes and our father's eyes were hazel. Jackson had more of a golden, green color, where Eli and I were blessed with our mother's beautiful blue eyes.

"I'm so glad both of you were able to come," I told my brothers as I took a step back from the two of them. I was beginning to sweat profusely from the hot sun pounding down on us. Undoing the buttons of my gown, I shrugged it off my shoulders, and my mother took it from me.

"We wouldn't have missed it for the world." Eli smiled at me, his voice soft and gentle. He was always the quieter of the two. He was much more reserved, and it was hard to tell what was going on in his head most of the time. But if Eli had a soft spot for anyone, it was for me.

As we were gathered, the Harts came walking over to us. My gaze collided with Oliver's and his entire face lit up. He broke out into a jog, running ahead of everyone as he barreled straight toward me. He slid his hands under my armpits and lifted me into the air as the lilt of his laughter rolled across my eardrums.

A giggle slipped from my lips, and I kicked my legs slightly as he spun me around before setting me down on the ground. His hands fell down to my waist, and I tilted my head up to look into his sage green eyes. "We did it, Looney Tune!"

"Can you believe it?" I laughed, smiling back at my best friend. "We actually made it through four years of high school."

Oliver's smile cracked slightly and a wave of emotion washed over his gaze. "I always knew that we would."

There was a heaviness in his tone and the air around us grew thick with melancholy. Regardless of the good things that happened, the graveness of the situation always had its way of showing its ugly face through the sunshine.

"Who's ready to go get this party started?" Mrs. Hart asked from behind us, her voice breaking through the somberness that hung between us. She planned a joint graduation party for Oliver and me at their house. My mother had invited our family and friends, and it was supposed to be a huge thing.

Part of me wasn't really interested in having to entertain and see everyone, mainly because I was mentally exhausted from the day. I couldn't let everyone down, though. I needed to put on a happy face and be grateful for this day and everyone around us.

"We still have a few hours, Penny." My mother laughed at her. "I think we're going to head home so Luna can rest for a little bit and then we will be over before the party starts."

I glanced over at my mother, silently thanking her with

my eyes. It was like she always knew what I needed without me even having to say it. The heat had taken a toll on me, and the anxiety that riddled my body wasn't helpful either. My lungs needed a break and I needed to take a nap before being active the rest of the night.

Mrs. Hart stepped up to me with a bright smile on her face. She reached out, her palm soft as she placed it on the side of my face. "Go get some rest, Luna. We'll be waiting for you when you're ready." She paused for a moment, her chin bobbing slightly as her eyes grew damp. "I'm so proud of you."

She pulled me in for a hug, embracing me tightly as if she were afraid I would simply slip through her arms like sand. We broke apart and she took a step back before standing with Ollie and her husband. The three of them said their goodbyes to us before disappearing through the crowd. I didn't miss Oliver as he glanced at me once more over his shoulder, offering a small wave before he was gone.

"You ready to go home, Luna?" My mother questioned me as she wrapped her arm around the tops of my shoulders. "You can take a nap and get ready for the party."

I glanced over at her. "Thanks, Mom."

"Always, sunshine."

She began to lead me back to the parking lot, to where our car was. My brothers and father followed behind us, all of us in a comfortable silence and lost in our thoughts. By the time we were pulling out of the parking lot, I could feel my eyelids growing heavier. I popped the speaking valve off my trach and held it in my hand as I rested my head against the window.

It didn't take long before my breathing began to slow

and the darkness was pulling me under. When my body was exhausted, there was no way for me to fight it. And sometimes, I was honestly tired of fighting. It felt like that was all that I ever did, almost as if there was no reprieve from it. It was either fight or die.

I wasn't ready for death, so I fought with every ounce of strength I had, but sometimes I had to give in to the exhaustion. And when my body needed to rest, I had no choice but to listen.

Chapter Seven

THE BEAUTY OF LIFE

When I awoke from my nap, I changed into something a little more comfortable. I settled on another sundress, but it was one that reached my ankles. After sliding my feet into a pair of flip flops, I headed downstairs to see what everyone was doing.

My mother and father were sitting in the living room together, watching a movie. It wasn't often I got to see them spend time like this together. Neither of my brothers were with them, so I lingered in the doorway, watching the two of them from a distance as they laughed at the TV.

They both looked so carefree in the moment, like they had nothing to worry about except for what they were watching. I loved that for them and wished they had more time like this together. Most days, my father was exhausted after he got home from work and would fall asleep before they even made it up to bed.

I missed seeing the two of them like this together.

"Are you spying on them?" Eli whispered as he stopped beside me and rested his arm on my shoulder.

I swallowed hard over the emotion that was thick in my throat. "They look so content. They're always so stressed and I never get to see them like this."

"They're stressed because they care, Luna. You know, they could have given you up if they didn't want the responsibility, but they didn't."

His words felt like a blow to the chest. Like he reached inside my rib cage and drove his fist directly into my heart. "Sometimes, I wish they would have."

"That's pretty fucked up," he muttered under his breath, his voice matter of fact. "None of us would change the way our lives have been. Stop being so damn negative about it and be grateful for having people who care this much about you."

"Don't tell me how to feel, Eli," I whispered to him, tasting the venom on my tongue. "You don't know what it feels like to be in my shoes."

"No one knows what it feels like to be in anyone else's shoes but their own." He tilted his head, a ghost of a smile playing on his lips. "That's the beauty of life. We just get to live on our own and make the best out of it."

"What about them, though?" I questioned him as we both turned our attention back to our parents. "Don't they get to enjoy their lives sometime?"

Eli is silent for a moment.

"What do you think they've been doing this entire time?"

"I'm sorry," I apologized to him, my voice quiet and layered with guilt. "These past few weeks have been emotional and I've been letting them drag me down."

"Well, stop it then. You're our sunshine and none of us like cloudy skies. Don't let the loud negative thoughts dim the light that shines down on our world."

Eli removed his arm from my shoulder and gave it a squeeze with his hand before he left me alone to watch our parents. His words continued to ring in my head as I lingered in the doorway for a few more minutes before I finally entered the room.

My mother, with her supersonic senses, somehow noticed my presence and turned around to face me. A smile pulled at the corners of her lips and my father turned off the TV as he glanced over at me.

"How was your nap?" my mother questioned me, her voice warm and comforting like a baby's blanket.

"It was good." I smiled back at her. "I feel refreshed. Like I can conquer the night now."

Both of my parents rose to their feet and headed in my direction. My father looked at me thoughtfully and it made my heart constrict. He was never a man of many words, but he didn't need them. He had a way of speaking with his expressions.

"I'm sure the Hart's are waiting for us," he said softly as he smiled at me and wrapped his arm around the tops of my shoulders. "What do you say we all head over there and crash the party?"

My phone vibrated in my hand and I glanced down to see that it was Giana calling. I looked back to my parents. "It's G. Can I talk to her quickly and then we'll head over?"

"Of course." My mother smiled brightly. I slipped out from under my father's arm and stepped into the other room as I answered her call.

Giana's tanned face showed up on the screen and she had the biggest grin on her face as she waved at me. There was so much commotion in the background, but her sole focus was on me right now. Her bright blue eyes shined and I wished we were able to celebrate with each other.

Your mother sent me the video from your graduation ceremony, she signed after setting the phone down in front of her.

I did the same and propped it against the backsplash in the kitchen.

I wish we would have been able to celebrate together, I signed back to her.

Giana frowned for a moment. *Sometime over the summer? I know you and Oliver have big plans,* she said with a wink as she wiggled her eyebrows at me.

I gave her the middle finger just as her brother's face appeared in the frame next to hers.

"Luna!" Nico said, his voice loud and filled with excitement. "Congratulations on your graduation!"

I was surprised to see him with her. I had met Nico while we were in the hospital, and since Giana and I had grown as close as we did, our families were well acquainted. I hadn't seen either of them since their mother passed away last year. We celebrated Nico getting drafted into the NHL and then a few short months later, we were mourning the loss of the rock in their family.

"Hey, hot shot." I smiled at Nico. "How's the professional hockey life treating you?"

Nico shrugged. "Spent the past season proving my worth, but I'm really hopeful I'll get the call."

I smiled back at him. Nico worked hard playing hockey

to get to where he was now. "There's no doubt in my mind at all that you will get the call."

Giana tried to shove her brother out of the way. The two of them laughed and the sound of Giana's laughter made my heart swell. Since she had lost her hearing when we were kids, it wasn't often she let her real voice be heard. The times I had actually heard it were few and far between.

"Well, it looks like I'm getting kicked out of this conversation. Hopefully we'll see you soon, Luna!" Nico said with a playful grin. His bright blue eyes matched his sister's, along with their dark hair.

"Bye Nico!"

Sorry about him, Giana signed to me as she rolled her eyes. *He's annoying as hell.*

What brother isn't annoying? I replied back to her, and we both smiled. My mother appeared in the doorway and tapped at her wrist. I turned back to Giana. *Sorry, G, but I have to go. Oliver's parents are having a party.*

Text me later, Giana told me before adding she loved me and ended the call.

I turned back to my parents who were both waiting and offered them a smile. "Sorry, she just wanted to congratulate me on today."

My mother smiled as I walked over to them. "Emilia would have been so proud. I can't believe Giana graduated last week. And did I hear Nico's voice too?"

I nodded at her. "It sounds like things are going really well for him with hockey."

"He's one hell of a player," my father chimed in. "I always knew Nico Cirone would go places."

There was a soberness that settled around us as all our

thoughts drifted to Giana and Nico's mother. It hadn't been an easy two years for them, and a part of me had struggled with survivor's guilt since Emilia passed away. Her cancer came quickly and it wasn't long before she lost her battle. I should have died a long time ago, yet here I still was.

Life didn't make sense.

"Okay, enough of this." My mother's voice broke through the silence as she clapped her hands together. "We have two amazing kids we need to go celebrate."

My father smiled at me; his expression filled with pride. "Let's head over to the Harts before they send out a search team."

The three of us walked out of the kitchen together and my mother paused at the bottom of the stairs before calling up to my brothers. They both came down immediately, and we headed over to Oliver's house together as a family.

It was in these moments I missed all of us being under the same roof together. Who knew how much time we would have like this? The thought was one that troubled me constantly, but I didn't want to hold my brothers back from living their lives. They had every right to experience it to the fullest.

When we got over to the Harts house, the party was already in full swing. A few of my aunts and uncles greeted us as soon as we walked through the gate that led into the backyard. The blades of grass tickled the bottoms of my feet as they slipped between my feet and flip flops. There were more people than I expected, but this was everything Oliver deserved. He deserved to be celebrated.

After briefly speaking with our family members, I

slipped away when I caught Oliver's gaze from across the lawn. His parents were sitting at one of the tables seated near the patio attached to the back of their house. We had spent so much time playing in his yard as children, it would always hold a special place in my heart.

Mrs. Hart had strung fairy lights between the trees and the house and it illuminated in the darkness of the night. Music played from the surround sound speakers they had hidden around the patio area. As I walked past her, she smiled brightly at me, raising her hand to wave.

I waved back to her, feeling like I was in some sort of a dream. None of the people around me really mattered at that moment. I wanted to get to my best friend because he was who I really wanted to celebrate with. We made it through all these years together and our time together was running out faster than I wanted.

It was like watching the sand in an hourglass drain from the top to the bottom. Yet, it was as if it was moving in fast forward. It was draining, five grains of sand at a time instead of one.

"Luna." Oliver beamed at me, his voice a stark contrast to its hoarseness. "I was beginning to worry you weren't going to come over."

"You're not going to get rid of me that easily, Oliver Hart," I reminded him with a wink.

A mixture of emotions flickered in his eyes, but it quickly washed away as he held one hand out to me. "Come with me."

Sliding my hand into his, I let him lead me away from the party. As we walked around the back of their shed, I knew exactly where he was taking me. We reached the massive oak tree in the back corner of the yard, both of us tipping our heads back to look at the treehouse Mr. Hart built for us when we were younger.

Oliver glanced over at me, a soft smile played on his lips as he slipped his hand from mine and motioned to the wooden ladder that hung from above. "After you, my queen."

A soft laugh escaped me and I rolled my eyes at him. "You're going to inflate my ego if you keep calling me your queen."

"That's the plan, Luna." He winked at me as I grabbed hold of one of the prongs on the ladder. "Even after you realize I'm speaking the truth, I will never stop reminding you of what you really are."

My breath caught in my throat, leaving me breathless for a moment. If I didn't know Oliver the way I did, I would think he's just a smooth talker. The type of guy who tells you the things you want to hear. But that's not Oliver Hart. He tells me the things I *need* to hear.

My lungs decided to cooperate and I sucked in a deep breath before I began my ascent up the ladder, toward our own little slice of heaven we created together. It was dark inside as I crawled up through the hole in the middle of the floor. Oliver was right behind me and walked past me to reach the battery powered lights we had hung across the ceiling.

I dropped the hatch over the opening in the floor and Ollie lit up the treehouse with the lights. My eyes traveled around the space, a feeling of nostalgia filled me as I looked at the posters we hung up many years ago. On one side were the boy band ones I hung, and on the other were all the football related ones Oliver hung.

"Jeez, we should maybe update this place, don't you

think?" I questioned him with a smirk as I dropped down onto one of the bean bags we had. We each had our own, along with some pillows, blankets, and extra cushions from their old patio furniture.

Ollie sat down on the other bean bag chair with an inquisitive look on his face. He tilted his head to the side. "Now why would we do that? It's like a history museum here… the history of our childhood."

His words warmed my heart, and I couldn't fight the smile that pulled on the corners of my lips. He was right. Even though it was outdated, it had different pieces from when we were growing up. Oliver's comic books were stacked in one corner and the young romance novels I read were stacked right beside them.

"You're right," I agreed with him, nodding thoughtfully. "We used to spend so much time up here when we were kids. I feel like we haven't been up here in so long."

"Which is why we're back here now. This is our place, Looney Tune, and no one else's."

Someone from the party called for Oliver, and I glanced out the window to see his mother walking around. "I think your mom is looking for you. Maybe we should get back to the party."

Oliver's hand was warm as he wrapped it around my wrist and pulled me back to my bean bag chair. "Nope. I don't care about the party, and she can bother me later. Right now, this is our time, in our place."

A soft laugh fell from my lips. "Whatever you say. When she gets mad because she couldn't find you, that's your fault."

Oliver pursed his lips and sighed as he rose to his feet. I watched him as he walked over to one of the windows and pushed open the wooden shutter before yelling out to his mom to tell her we were up here and we'd be down in a little bit. He pulled the shutters closed and the hinges creaked from wear and tear before he took his seat next to me.

"What are we doing up here, anyway?"

"I know you better than anyone else, Luna," Ollie reminded me with a smirk. "You'd rather be up here and away from all the people down there."

I shrugged dismissively, even though he hit the nail on the head. "Yeah, you're right."

"And I want to talk about your bucket list," he added, completely catching me off guard as he rolled onto his side on the chair to face me. "Summer starts tomorrow, so what's first on our agenda?"

My eyes widened as I stared back at him. "I didn't bring my list with me," I all but choked the words out. I still hadn't written a revised version for him to see, but I would do that later tonight.

"Luna, you have a better memory than anyone I know," he admitted, his eyes shining back at me. I watched the way his shirt hugged the muscles in his back as he turned away. My mouth suddenly felt dry and I swallowed roughly, trying to not study him, but I couldn't tear my eyes away.

Oliver rolled back to face me with a notebook and a pen in his hand. His gaze collided with mine as he caught me watching him. A look of amusement danced in his eyes and he raised an eyebrow at me as the warmth spread up my neck and across my cheeks.

Being the perfect gentleman he was, he didn't call me out on it.

"Tell me what was on your list and I'll write it down now."

I swallowed again, wishing I had brought a water bottle with me. My list had a few personal things but I could leave them out. All I had to do was tell him the other things on the list. "Okay, but one thing," I told him, my voice low with warning. "You're not allowed to laugh at any of them."

"Deal." He smiled, nodding as he held out his pinky finger to me. I slid mine through his and we linked them together, shaking before we broke apart. Oliver positioned his pen on the paper and began to write as I read out my list.

LUNA'S BUCKET LIST

1. ~~SLOW DANCE WITH SOMEONE~~
2. DRIVE A BOAT
3. RIDE ON A FERRIS WHEEL
4. ATTEND A WEDDING
5. GET A TATTOO
6. SEE THE WORLD
7. GO ICE SKATING
8. SLEEP UNDER THE STARS
9. GO ON A BLIND DATE
10. SEE THE OCEAN

I watched as Oliver finished writing the last one before he looked up at me. His sage green eyes collided with mine and there was a hint of sadness in them. It wasn't the expression I was anticipating from him. Most of the items on my list seemed juvenile and I was worried that he would judge me for them.

"They're stupid, aren't they?" I questioned him, waving my hand dismissively as though none of it really mattered.

Oliver shook his head and his throat bobbed as he swallowed hard. "None of them are stupid, Luna," he assured me, his voice hoarse and thick with emotion. "Each and every single one is perfect."

"Why the long face, Ollie?" I questioned him, refusing to ignore the way that he was looking at me with a dampness in his eyes.

"Sometimes it just hurts, you know?"

His words caught me off guard and my breath caught in my throat as I tilted my head to the side. "What hurts?"

"The fact that you don't get the simplicity in life and these other assholes take everything they have for granted."

It felt like a ton of bricks had landed on my chest. He spoke nothing but words of truth, and if only he knew how often that thought crossed my mind. I had spent a lot of my life sitting on the sidelines, watching the world around me continue to move as if I were stuck in my own personal purgatory.

As a child, I watched the kids at the playground get into arguments while they played tag. All I had wanted was to have the option to get tagged by another kid, but I struggled to walk up a flight of stairs without being completely breathless.

I couldn't fault anyone for not realizing they had a lot more to be thankful for. You can't judge someone from the outside when you don't fully know what is going on in their lives or their own internal struggles.

We were all on our own journeys in life, some of them just looked a little different than others.

"You can't be mad at them for it, Oliver," I told him, my voice soft and gentle as I reached out for his hand. His skin was warm against mine and it was seeping into my veins. "They don't know what they're taking for granted because they've never been without it."

His jaw clenched and he laced his slender fingers through mine. I watched him carefully as he squeezed his eyes shut, his chest rising as he inhaled a deep breath. When he lifted his eyelids, there was nothing but torment that filled the depths of his green irises. "It's just not fair, Luna."

"We don't get to choose what is or isn't fair," I reminded him as the corners of my lips lifted into a sad smile. "That's just the beauty of life."

Chapter Eight
NOTHING SHORT OF THE SUN

"Where are we going?" I asked Oliver as he drove us past the city limits of the small town we lived in. He picked me up first thing this morning with the promise of a surprise. It was officially the first day of summer and he was adamant on getting started on checking off my list.

Oliver glanced at me from the corner of his eye before he looked back to the road. "If I told you, that would only ruin the surprise."

I shrugged with indifference. "You know it doesn't have to be. You could just tell me and it wouldn't ruin a thing."

"Sorry, tuna." Oliver smirked at me as he used the nickname I despised. "You're just going to have to wait until we get there."

"Did you forget what I said the last time you called me tuna?"

Oliver pulled his car onto the highway and reached for

the gear shifter as he increased the speed. "You told me you wouldn't be friends with me anymore if I did it again."

"I meant what I said," I told him as I gave him the most serious look I could muster.

He glanced over at me with an eyebrow arched. A ghost of a smile played on his lips and his expression cracked as he chuckled. "Luna, we were like ten. Plus, I wouldn't let you get rid of me that easily. I'm like a cockroach, I keep coming back."

I scrunched my nose up at him. "Please don't ever refer to yourself as a cockroach." I laughed softly. "You're giving cockroaches a bad name by doing that."

Oliver gasped dramatically as he slapped his hand against his chest, just above his heart. "You wound me, Luna Truly."

"Maybe," I responded with a shrug. "But you need someone to keep you humble. You'd be lost without me."

It was meant to come out as a joke, but the air between us suddenly shifted.

Oliver's expression transformed and he glanced at me with a look of torment and sadness in his eyes. "I would be." He fell silent again for a moment as he reached into the back of the car and grabbed a blanket from the back seat. "Why don't you get comfortable? We still have about half an hour until we're there."

"Thanks," I murmured as I took the blanket from him and laid it across my lap. I wasn't tired, but I was thankful for Oliver changing the conversation to something different. There was just one last thing I wanted to address with him. "Can I ask something of you?"

"Anything for you, my queen," he said softly as he

flashed me his perfectly straight white teeth. They were the kind only orthodontists could produce. Oliver went through having braces and even headgear at one point. I'd never forget how goofy he looked with that metal contraption on his head.

"I don't want any heaviness this summer," I admitted quietly as I tucked my hands underneath the blanket. "Just happiness. Sometimes, I just want to be able to forget it all, you know? The darkness feels like it consumes my life some days, and I want the summer to just be about the two of us."

"If you want light, then I will bring you nothing short of the sun."

Ollie's words reached inside my soul as they entangled themselves in the fibers of my heart. Warmth spread through my body and I was unable to fight the grin that pulled on the corners of my lips.

He said he would be lost without me, but it was the complete opposite.

My life would be nothing without Oliver Hart.

I settled back into my seat, and Oliver turned up the music as he drove us farther away from town. My eyelids fell shut at some point. When I opened them again, we were pulling up a stone driveway. The gravel was loud under the tires as we entered the parking lot and found a spot. Sitting up straighter in my seat, I looked out the window, and saw the glistening water of the lake.

"Stillwater Lake?" I questioned him as I turned back to look at him.

Oliver turned off his car and looked at me. Mischief danced in his eyes and a ghost of a smile played on his perfect lips. "Are you ready to drive a boat?"

I glanced out the window at the boat rental shop before looking back at my best friend. "Hell yes."

He abandoned me in the car as he hopped out and slammed his door shut. He moved at lightning speed, opening my door before I had the chance to do so myself. I looked up at Ollie as he pulled it open and held out his hand to me. My breath caught in my throat and I had to remind myself to breathe, as I slid my hand into his.

His palm was warm against mine, his fingers fitting perfectly between my own. "We'll grab your bags after we get the boat."

"Okay," I whispered, not fully trusting my voice. My brain was being torn in two different directions. I was hyper aware of how close he was and focused on how our hands felt pressed together. I was also stuck in manual breathing, having to remind myself to take a breath. He seemed to have that effect on me lately and suffocating never felt this good before.

Oliver led me to the small shop and pushed open the door, holding it open for me. The bell that hung from the top of it rang as we stepped inside. "Do you want any snacks to take with us?"

"I'll be right with you," a gruff voice called out from somewhere in the back.

I looked up at Oliver, shaking my head. "I'll be okay. Maybe we can find somewhere to get lunch on our way home?"

"That sounds like a perfect idea," he said grinning down at me.

We walked past the aisles that had some dry grocery items before we reached the front counter. A guy stepped through the door behind the counter with a grim look on his face. He looked to be in his early twenties—tall and tan with an athletic frame. His dark brown hair was a mess of tousled waves that hung just above his eyebrows, a contrast to his clear blue eyes.

"What can I do for the two of you?"

Oliver shifted his weight on his feet. "I called yesterday evening about renting a boat for a few hours. It should be under Oliver Hart."

The guy turned his attention to the computer on his right. I watched him as he clicked the mouse a few times and his eyes scrolled the screen. "Yep. It's right here and I see you already prepaid. I just need your ID to scan it and for you to fill out some paperwork before I can let you take it out."

"Perfect," Oliver responded to him as he reached into his back pocket with his free hand. He let go of mine momentarily as he pulled out his ID and handed it to the guy. I stood there silently as he filled out the paperwork while his ID was being scanned. I didn't want to make it known I was going to be the one driving the boat since I still hadn't even gotten my driver's license. There's no way they would legally let me drive a boat with only a learner's permit.

"All right," the guy said as he tossed the paperwork onto the other side of the counter. "I'll take you out to the boat and get you set up."

Oliver and I followed him out the back door. Realization dawned on me and I halted as soon as my sneakers hit the gravel. Oliver stopped beside me and gave me a questioning look. "What's wrong?"

"My bags," I murmured softly, not wanting to draw too

much attention to us since the guy didn't even notice we stopped.

"Shit," Oliver muttered. "I'll go get them and meet you down by the boat if you wanna follow him down to it."

I nodded, and Ollie quickly broke out into a jog, heading back to the car. My eyes traveled over to where the guy was and I began to walk after him. He wasn't walking very fast and there was a slight limp in his left knee with every step he took. It piqued my interest. Given that he was relatively young, it took me off guard.

It didn't take me long to catch up to him. As I fell into step beside him, he looked down at me before looking behind me. "Where'd your friend go?"

"He went to get our things from the car," I told him, and he nodded. Curiosity had its claws in me and I was suddenly intrigued by this guy. Given my own disabilities, whenever I met someone else who fell under the same umbrella, I was always curious. "What's your name?"

He turned his gaze back in front of him as we continued to walk toward the docks. "Vaughn," he replied gruffly.

"Are you from here, Vaughn?" I asked, attempting to make small talk. I didn't know what was taking Ollie so long, but I wasn't going to stand here in silence with this stranger. The least I could do was get to know him.

"Yes and no." He shrugged. "My hometown is a few hours away, but my parents have a house here on the lake and own the shop."

"That's pretty cool," I told him, smiling as we stepped onto the dock and walked over to one of the boats. "Oliver and I live about forty-five minutes away, although I've never actually been here before."

Vaughn stared at me for a moment, as if he was studying me. I expected some sort of judgment from him, but there wasn't a single drop that lingered in his eyes. Just a simple look of curiosity. "It's like a slice of heaven here. I hope you enjoy your time out on the boat."

"I hate to ask this..." My voice trailed off as I paused for a moment, shifting my weight nervously on my feet. I lived a life of having to take every precaution possible and the thought of being out on the open water had me a little nervous at the moment. "If there happened to be an emergency, how long does it usually take for responders to get here?"

I heard Ollie's footsteps as he caught up to us. Vaughn already had the boat pulled out with the engine running while we were waiting for Oliver to return. I glanced over my shoulder, flashing him a small smile. He was quick on his feet, with all of my bags in tow.

"Are the two of you planning on moving onto the boat?" Vaughn asked, but there wasn't any humor in his voice. He was definitely different from most people I had met in my life. Usually, I received sympathetic stares or people simply would avoid looking at me. Vaughn was the opposite. He seemed to lack a filter and wasn't afraid to look.

"These are all of her medical supplies," Ollie offered, his voice quiet as his gaze flashed to mine. He took the liberty of speaking for me, but I couldn't be mad. It could potentially be a liability if something happened and the owner of the boat wasn't aware. "It wouldn't be smart of us to not bring them."

"Of course." Vaughn nodded, his lips terse. "Sorry, that was insensitive of me." He stopped for a moment, his crystal blue eyes flashing to mine. He inched closer as Oliver was loading my bags onto the boat. "Usually takes EMS about five to ten minutes to get here."

I stared at him, silent for a second. Emergency medical services would be helpful, but they wouldn't be who we really needed in the event of an emergency. "What about ALS?" I questioned him. *Advanced life support.*

Vaughn's jaw clenched and his throat bobbed as he swallowed. "About the same amount of time."

"Thanks." I nodded, offering him a small smile. "Can't be too prepared, right?"

A harsh laugh slipped from him. "I wish I would have been more prepared. Wouldn't have had a knee injury that ruined my entire hockey career."

I wanted to ask him more about what happened to him, but that would have been rude. My mother had taught me better than that, and after all the weird looks I had gotten in public, I knew better. It wasn't my business, and Vaughn was merely a passing character in the story of my life.

"You ready, Luna?" Oliver questioned me from where I was standing on the dock. I turned around to face him, a smile on my lips. Vaughn's footsteps grew quieter as he left the two of us to our little adventure.

I climbed onto the boat and headed over to my best friend. "I was born ready."

"Yeah, I doubt that." Oliver laughed, as he innocently pulled me onto his lap. "I'll drive the boat out to the center of the lake and then you can take over."

I could feel his warmth beneath my legs and it was seeping into my soul, mixing with the marrow in my bones. Oliver was everywhere and I was consumed by him. His scent invaded my senses and I closed my eyes, feeling his arms around me as he grabbed the steering wheel to the boat. It just felt right—like this was exactly where I belonged.

We were best friends, but he was more than that to me.

He would always be more to me…

Chapter Nine

BE FEARLESS

Oliver waited until we were far enough away from the shop where Vaughn wouldn't be able to see us before he wrapped his hands around mine and lifted them to the steering wheel. His warmth was still seeping into my soul and I felt my focus becoming a struggle.

Oliver Hart was the sole distractor and I had never experienced this with him before.

Over the past few years, I had noticed my attraction for him growing deeper. It was like our friendship had shifted within the past few weeks, and now I was sitting on his lap while he was showing me how to operate a boat. It was completely innocent, yet I couldn't fight my heart as it threatened to beat out of my chest.

"I don't think I can do this, Ollie," I told him, raising my voice over the sound of the engine. "It just doesn't feel natural."

Oliver's breath was warm against my ear as he leaned forward. "You've got this, Luna," he encouraged me as he guided one of my hands to avoid the wake from another boat. "It's just like driving a car."

"There aren't any waves on the road," I deadpanned, which earned a soft chuckle from my best friend.

"Touché," he said, his breath tickling my skin. "I'm right here with you. I promise I'm not going to let anything happen to you."

My hands began to sweat as I clutched the steering wheel until my knuckles turned white. I started to regret adding this to my list and was questioning my ability to do so. It didn't feel natural, the way so many outside factors determined the boat's movement through the water. The engine and mechanical parts only did so much. I had no control over what the water beneath us decided to do.

"Just breathe, Luna," Oliver breathed in my ear as he began to stroke the backs of my hands with his thumbs. "Inhale and exhale, over and over. I got you."

He didn't stop, as he counted along with my breathing until I calmed down. His words were like silk against my eardrums, sliding against them and tangling themselves in my soul. He had this uncanny way of chasing my worries away when they refused to leave on their own.

"Why am I freaking out over this?" I half laughed, half choked out the words.

"Because it's something new. It's not your safe little bubble you're used to," he murmured as he continued to ease my worried mind. "Doing something new is always scary, but it's about conquering your fears. Make this boat and this lake your bitch, Luna Truly."

I laughed at Oliver. His words made no sense—I couldn't simply make them my bitch, but the sentiment was there. He wanted me to be fearless, and with him I felt superior. Like I was riding on a cloud and I could conquer anything with him at my side.

I sucked in a deep breath and let it out. "Okay." I nodded, swallowing roughly. "I got this."

Oliver lifted his hands away from mine and I instantly noticed his absence. His palms were warm as he rested them on my thighs and gave me a reassuring squeeze. He was the literal rock in my life—the glue that held me together when life threatened to tear me apart.

I never had much control over what happened in my life, but Oliver was always there to remind me of the things I could control. He couldn't help the unpredictable factors, so he made sure he could with everything else.

He was my anchor. The one who made sure the tumultuous waves of life didn't pull me out to sea.

My hands gripped the steering wheel, and I squinted my eyes against the harsh sunlight as I slowly maneuvered the boat around the lake. There weren't any boats near us so I didn't have to worry about the wake. The water was calm, and *I was doing it.*

"You're doing great, Luna." Oliver smiled against my ear. "Drive it over into that small cove over there," he said as he lifted his hand and pointed his finger to the left.

Following his instruction, I turned the wheel and drove the boat across the lake. My lips were spread wide with a grin I was no longer able to fight. We weren't going very fast, and I watched Oliver's hand land on the gas as he began to push it forward.

I glanced at him over my shoulder, my stomach fluttering as the boat began to pick up speed. He winked at me as he wrapped his other arm around my waist, holding me firmly against him. I trusted Ollie with every breath of my life. He wasn't reckless and I knew he wouldn't lead me astray. He would never put me in a dangerous situation, not if he didn't feel I was safe.

The boat carried us across the water, my onyx colored hair whipping around in the wind. It was such a freeing feeling, being in control as it felt like we were doing the impossible. The boat jumped around from different waves we hit, but I was able to keep the wheel straight.

We were cruising across the lake and it felt like we were floating through the sky. I had never been on a plane to know what that actually felt like, but I imagined it to be something similar.

A laugh slipped from my lips and tears sprang to my eyes as I was overcome with emotion. I didn't believe in myself when it came to trying new things, but once again Ollie proved me wrong. He challenged me, even when I was terrified.

"There's my fearless Luna." He chuckled against my ear as he slowed our speed when we reached the cove. He dialed it back until we were barely moving and killed the engine as we began to coast into it.

I spun my legs around until I was sitting sideways on his lap. My body turned to face him and his green eyes collided with mine. He smiled brightly, his perfect white teeth showing as his grin crinkled the corners of his eyes. His dark wavy hair was a tousled, tangled mess and his cheeks were tinted pink.

"I did it, Ollie." I smiled at him, a sense of pride building inside me. My heart pounded erratically in my chest and my stomach began to do somersaults as my eyes bounced back and forth between his. "I didn't think I could actually do it."

A wave of emotion passed through his irises. Oliver's arm was still wrapped around me, but it was around my back now. I had a heightened sense of awareness of how close he was and his warm hand wrapped around my waist. "I always knew you could."

"I couldn't have done it without you," I whispered, not fully trusting my voice with the way he was looking at me. I couldn't quite put my finger on what was washing over his expression, but it was different. He had looked at me like this before, but it was fleeting.

They were all moments of us being closer than we should have been. The moments where the lines of our friendship appeared to be blurred. In the photo booth. Dancing at prom. The treehouse on graduation night.

"You're right." He smirked as he lifted his eyebrows and nodded. His expression transformed into a playful one and his tone was lighter, more carefree. "They wouldn't have rented you a boat with just your learner's permit. So, you literally couldn't have rented a boat without me."

Our laughter danced across the lake, and I shook my head at him, rolling my eyes. "You're impossible, Oliver Hart."

"Yeah, but you love me," he retorted with a wink as he lifted me from his lap.

I followed behind him as he grabbed a bag I hadn't noticed he'd brought along. Oliver spread out an entire lunch he packed for us. He helped me onto the floor of the boat, making sure I was comfortable before he handed me a sandwich.

Even as our day on the lake came to an end, I couldn't get his words out of my head.

Oliver let me drive the boat back to the center of the lake before he took over and drove us back to the dock. We handed it over to Vaughn, who still had me wanting to know his story and the reason for his limp.

Oliver drove us home, but he made sure to park his car in my driveway instead of his own. He helped me into the house before he carried all my things in for me. I was too tired to fight him or I would have insisted I help. It had been a long day and my body was completely worn out.

But as I tucked myself into bed that night, my mind was still circling back to Oliver on the boat.

Yeah, but you love me…

His words held more weight than gold and he would never know.

I could never let him know the truth about how I felt.

Even if Oliver Hart could love me, it would just be a cruel joke against him from the universe. He would outlive me, as I would expect him to. It would be one thing to break someone's heart because of a failed relationship but it was entirely different if the broken heart came from someone's death. There's no way to heal a wound that deep.

It was bad enough that one day, Oliver would have to bury his best friend.

I wouldn't let him bury the person his heart belonged to, too.

Chapter Ten

DOG DROOL AND INK STAINS

After our day on the boat, something felt different between Ollie and I. It was difficult to explain because I'd felt my feelings blossoming for him for quite some time, but it just felt different. He was a gentle, kind soul. He was always concerned about my well-being and very attentive to how my body was handling the stress of what we were doing.

He pulled me onto his lap to drive the boat and it surprised me. It wasn't the first time we'd been close, but the way he held me had awoken something deep inside me. It gave me a weird sense of hope, yet I knew things could never grow into anything more between us.

That hope had to be extinguished immediately. Oliver had an entire life ahead of him; one he hadn't even started yet. I was dead weight and would only continue to weigh him down until I was gone. I wouldn't do that to my best friend. I would never burden him with my feelings because I knew Oliver better than anyone else in the world and I knew what he would do with that information.

He would rather lie to make me happy than break my heart because of his own feelings.

...

I was sitting on my front porch with my mother, soaking up the rays of sun, as I waited for Oliver to come pick me up. He made sure to tell me our plans ahead of time—well, maybe not with what the day would hold, but more so the summer.

He knew how easily my body became fatigued, so he didn't want to exhaust me. Oliver said every two days we would work on checking off an item on my bucket list. And that was at the minimum. I didn't expect him to spend every day with me, but the past two days he hung around the house with me while my body regained some of its energy.

Yesterday, we spent the day inside laying around and watching movies. It was just like old times, like when we were kids. We made popcorn and a bed of pillows and blankets on my living room floor. I tried to ignore the times he held my hand or wrapped his arm around my shoulders and pulled me in to cuddle with him.

We could never be more than friends so there was no sense in reading into it.

Plus, it's not like it was anything new with the way Ollie acted with me. He was my partner in crime and we were best friends. That's what best friends did, right?

Today was a brand new day, and I woke up feeling completely refreshed.

"What do you and Ollie have planned for today?" my mother asked me as she sipped her hot cup of coffee. She was home yesterday, and I didn't miss the way she smiled at the two of us together. She never dared to speak anything of it, but she noticed it.

"I have no idea," I told her with a smile on my lips. "He likes to keep me on my toes and doesn't like telling me before he comes to pick me up."

My mother smiled back at me. "How things have changed," she said with a look of amusement dancing in her eyes. "Oliver used to be the worst with surprises. Do you remember when your father and I got you Tank, and Oliver completely ruined the surprise?"

I glanced down at my massive dog lying on the floor by my feet. My parents had gotten me Tank as a service dog. Oliver and his parents knew about it because they kept Tank for a few days until my birthday. It was my eighth birthday and my parents wanted it to be a surprise.

Oliver kept it to himself for about thirty-six hours before he broke down and told me. He was just too excited and since we shared everything with each other, he thought it was okay. I still remember him sneaking me into their laundry room and showing me the brindled puppy sitting there.

No one could be seriously mad at Oliver for it, and it didn't make getting Tank any less special. He was always by my side, from that day on. Tank wasn't exactly happy when Oliver took me out on the boat and he wasn't allowed to come along.

Tank lifted his head as Oliver began to walk up the walkway to our front porch. A smile pulled on the corners of my lips as I watched him approach us.

"Hello, Ollie." My mother smiled at my best friend.

"Good morning." He smiled back at her before his gaze collided with mine. "Hey, Luna."

"Hey," I said quietly as I fought a shy smile. Every now and then this would happen. I would suddenly find myself feeling shy around him and I knew it was from my feelings I buried deep inside. "What's on the agenda for today?" I asked, attempting to recover from my awkwardness.

Oliver smiled brightly, the dimples in his cheeks on full display. "Now, Luna. You know it's supposed to be a surprise each time."

"Funny you say that," my mother mused, the playfulness heavy in her tone. "Luna and I were just talking about when you ruined the surprise with Tank, and now you're so adamant on surprises."

"Hey! That's not even fair!" Ollie exclaimed as his words were followed by laughter. "I was eight years old, okay? It felt like I was getting a puppy too, and do you know how hard it was to keep it a secret for as long as I did? I was too excited to keep it from Luna any longer."

My mother laughed, and I couldn't fight the giggle that escaped me. "I know, Oliver," my mother told him. "We're just giving you a hard time. No one holds it against you."

"Hmm, it seems like you do if it's still getting brought up ten years later," Ollie threw back with a joking tone. There wasn't a cruel bone in that boy's body. Oliver couldn't be mean to anyone even if he tried. Although, I had seen him stick up for me on a few occasions, but that was just him being protective, not mean.

"Are you ready to go?" I asked Oliver as I rose to my feet. "I'm ready to see what item we're checking off today."

"Let's do it." Oliver smiled. "I'll grab your things. Grab Tank's leash… he can come with us this time."

I glanced over at my mom and she shrugged. She had no idea what we were going to be doing today any more than I did. Oliver disappeared into the house and quickly reappeared as he carried my bags out to his car. I stepped inside and grabbed Tank's leash which really caught his attention.

"You want to go for a car ride?" I asked him as I patted the top of his head. Tank attempted to spin around in a circle but with his huge body, he looked as graceful as a pregnant cow. I laughed and waved to my mom as I walked out to Oliver's car with my dog on my heels.

I let Tank into the backseat and climbed into the front passenger's seat before Oliver closed my door for me. It didn't take long before he was sliding in behind the steering wheel and we were pulling away from the house. I didn't question where we were going because I knew what his response would be.

I would find out when we got there.

Even though Tank was sitting in the backseat, he positioned his massive head between the two of us. Drool dripped from his lips onto Oliver's shoulder as he tried to smell the side of his head.

"You're lucky I love you and that damn dog." Oliver laughed softly. "He drools like no other animal I've ever met."

My heart soared at his words but I had to calm myself down and bring myself back to reality. Oliver did love me, but not in the way I wanted him to. And I had to constantly remind myself every time he said something like that.

I simply laughed along with Oliver as he drove us into town. He pulled down a side street and into a small parking lot before he killed the engine. I wasn't familiar with where we were and I turned to look at him with a questioning look on my face.

"Nope." He shook his head as he pressed his index finger against my lips before I had the chance to ask. "You'll find out soon enough."

An exasperated sigh slipped from my lips, and Oliver winked at me before he got out of the car. I glanced back at Tank who was staring at me with his tongue hanging out of his mouth. "I don't know what we're going to do with him, boy," I told him, laughing to myself as Tank just looked at me like he didn't understand a word I was saying.

After getting out of the car and securing Tank with his leash, the three of us began to walk down the street. There were different stores all around, all of which I had never been inside before. As we reached the one on the corner, I lifted my gaze up to the sign.

Inked Flesh.

I gasped as I looked over at Oliver. "We're getting tattoos?!"

Ollie smiled back at me. He simply nodded and slid his hand into mine as he led me through the front door. We stopped at the front desk where a girl with bright purple hair looked up the appointments Ollie booked. A guy named Harrison came out and called both of us back. He was big and burly, covered in tattoos and piercings with a wizard-like beard.

"Your dog isn't going to eat me, is he?" he questioned the two of us as we walked over to him with Tank in tow.

"Tank's harmless," Oliver assured him, as he squeezed

my hand and smiled. "He's a specially trained service dog. No need to worry about him at all."

"Good shit." Harrison smiled at the two of us. "That's pretty fucking cool. Having a big ass scary dog like him to be a service dog."

I smiled down at Tank. "He's the best one I could ask for."

We followed Harrison back to his work station and Oliver had me sit down first. Harrison turned his attention to me. "So, what are we doing today, pretty lady?"

"I want to get "Remember to Breathe" in a script font along the inside of my forearm."

Oliver squeezed my hand and smiled. Harrison studied me with his eyes for a moment before nodding. "We can do that. Let me get some things set up and a stencil and if you like it we can get started."

I watched Harrison as he busied himself getting all the equipment set up. He showed me different scripts on his iPad, and I picked one out before he wrote my little quote in it and printed it out. After we decided on the placement and size, he got started. Oliver held my hand the entire time, even though I didn't need him to.

Since it was my first tattoo, I didn't know what to expect, but it didn't hurt as badly as I thought it would. It was more of an annoying, burning sensation. After all of the medical procedures I had over the years, it was nothing. And before I knew it, my tattoo was finished and he was wrapping it up to protect it.

I got up from my seat, thinking we were leaving, but instead Oliver took the spot I was sitting in. I looked down at him with a look of amusement. "You're getting a tattoo, too?"

Oliver nodded. "Yep. It only seems fitting."

I excused myself for a moment to go take Tank outside to give him a drink of water. I always carried around a collapsible bowl and a bottle of water, but with the mess he usually made, it was better if I took him outside. When I got back in, Harrison had already started on Ollie's tattoo.

It didn't take long for him to finish, and I walked over to him to see what it was before Harrison covered it. In the space on his hand between his thumb and forefinger there was a cursive L carved into his skin.

My breath caught in my throat and my mouth went dry. As I lifted my gaze from his tattoo, Oliver was already watching me with emotions rapidly washing over his eyes. He got my initial tattooed into his skin. It was a permanent part of him now, just like he was a permanent part of me.

"Do you like it?" he questioned me, his voice soft and gentle. There was a hesitancy to his words, like he was afraid of what I might say.

I stared into his sage green eyes, lost in the moment with him. "I love it."

"So do I." He smiled, but there was so much left unsaid...

Chapter Eleven

JUST ENJOY THE RIDE

"**W**hat's on the agenda for today?" I asked Oliver as he took a seat at the kitchen table. It was midmorning and he didn't look like he was dressed to go anywhere, so it left me feeling a little confused. Oliver promised we were checking things off my list every few days, but it didn't appear like he had anything planned for today.

Oliver lifted his gaze to mine. "Today is going to be a little different. I don't have anything planned for us until later this evening."

I tilted my head to the side and glanced down as Tank licked Ollie's hand. "Are you going to tell me what we're doing later?"

"Nope," Oliver said matter-of-factly with a smile on his face. "You should know I'm not telling you anything beforehand, Luna. You're just going to find out when it's time."

Light laughter fell from my lips and I shook my head at

my best friend. "You know you can't always keep me in the dark."

Oliver tilted his head to the side, a ghost of a smile playing on his lips as he stared directly into my soul. "I think I'll be the judge of that. You gave me free rein to handle your bucket list this summer, so I'll do as I see fit."

"Fine," I agreed with an exasperated sigh. "I'll stop asking."

Oliver smiled at me as he lifted his glass of orange juice to his lips. "It's about damn time."

"Do you want me to make you guys some breakfast?" my mother asked as she strolled into the kitchen. It's a habit of hers I wished she would break. At some point she would have to stop taking care of me like she did.

"I had cereal before Ollie came over," I told her with a smile glancing at Ollie. I was trying to branch out with more independence and I could tell my mother wasn't sure how to handle it.

Oliver smiled at me before he looked at my mother. "I'm good, Mrs. Truly, but thank you."

Always the polite gentleman.

My mother nodded at the two of us, and Tank padded over to her to get a quick pet. "The two of you don't have plans until later this evening, right?"

I glanced at my mother, cocking my head sideways as I raised an eyebrow. "You know what we're doing?"

She shook her head, a smile on her lips and she laughed softly. "Nope. I know nothing." She raised her hands as she began to walk over to the two of us and placed a list on the table in front of me. "Can the two of you run to the store for me then? I just need a few things."

Directing my gaze to Oliver, I looked at him, but he

was already picking up the list and smiling at my mother. "Of course."

"Thank you!" She beamed at the two of us and winked at me before she disappeared from the room again.

Oliver abruptly got up from his seat. "You want to go now?"

"I'm still in my pajamas," I reminded him as I glanced down at my slippers. I still had one of Oliver's old t-shirts he gave me years ago and red flannel pants on. "Can you give me a minute to get ready?"

"Always, Luna." Oliver nodded as the corners of his lips lifted. "I'll always wait for you… as long as you need."

My breath caught in my throat as his words hung heavily in the air. Without another word, I got up from my seat and quickly exited the kitchen with Tank hot on my heels. I didn't pay any attention to my dog and had to stop in the hallway to catch my breath.

I glanced down at the healing tattoo on my forearm. *Remember to Breathe.* Sometimes it felt like it was easier said than done. Everything between Oliver and I had always come easy, but I was finding it harder and harder to breathe around him.

And it wasn't because of the physical condition of my lungs.

It was because of the metaphorical condition of my heart and what Oliver Hart was doing to it.

WITH ONE HAND ON THE STEERING WHEEL AND THE OTHER ON the gear shifter, Oliver drove his car with ease down the street as we headed deeper into town to the store. Tank was in the backseat with his head hanging out the window.

"What's on her list?" I asked Oliver as we pulled into the parking lot. Usually, my mother did her own shopping but every once in a while she asked us to do it for her, so this wasn't anything out of the ordinary.

Oliver shrugged. "It's a bunch of random stuff." He handed me the list and I scrolled over it with my eyes as he found a parking spot and turned off the engine of the car.

"Oliver," I said his name with a declaration as I looked over at him with my lips pursed. "This is hardly even a grocery list. There's like, three things on it."

He shrugged again. "Must be important things she needs." He pushed open his door and climbed out before I could get another word out. Tank panted from the back seat and I quickly jumped out.

"We get Q-tips from the medical supply company, so no, that's not something urgent." I paused, planting my hands on my hips as Oliver grabbed my emergency bag but left the rest of my equipment in the back seat. "Vanilla extract?" I continued, my voice filled with disbelief. "And coconut milk. Come on, Oliver. What is this, really?"

He looked me dead in the eye, his poker face on as he held his hands up like he had no idea. "She made the list, Luna. Ask her."

"The two of you are up to something and I'm going to find out what," I told him as I opened the backdoor for Tank and held onto his leash as he climbed out.

Oliver laughed softly. "Stop overanalyzing everything, Luna. Just enjoy the ride, regardless of how minuscule it may seem at times."

He threw the strap of my bag over his shoulder and strolled over to me, holding his hand out to me. As if it were second nature, I slid my palm into his and laced our fingers together before we began to walk toward the store. Ollie didn't rush me and we took our time together as we walked through the store and collected the things from my mother's list.

Oliver was always patient and never in a rush. He never led and he didn't follow. He simply fell in step beside me, always there with a shoulder to lean on whenever I needed it.

When we arrived back at my house, my mother wasn't even around to receive her small shopping bag from us.

"I'll be back over later, okay?" Oliver told me, with a hint of mischief in his eyes.

I narrowed mine at him as I walked through our front gate into the yard and let Tank loose. "This is all fun and amusing to you, isn't it?"

Oliver lifted an eyebrow. "Something like that. I like that you have no idea what's coming next, even if you're the one who created the list." He paused and absentmindedly raked his teeth over his bottom lip. My stomach did a somersault as my gaze dropped to his mouth. "Be ready around seven."

Heat crept across my cheeks and I felt embarrassed as I lifted my eyes back to Oliver's. There was a fire burning in the depths of his green irises, and I watched his throat bob as he swallowed hard. "What do I wear?"

"You could wear a burlap sack and you would still look beautiful, Luna." His voice was low and the corners of his mouth lifted slightly. "Wear whatever you're comfortable in."

Oliver winked, leaving me on that note as he let himself back through the front gate and disappeared into his house next door. I stood there for a moment, his words playing over in my mind. My cheeks were growing sore from the way I couldn't stop smiling.

Leave it to Oliver to say something sweet, leaving me confused at the same time. He didn't give me much to go off and I had no idea what to wear. Something comfortable might not be the best suited for whatever plans he had up his sleeve.

I waited until six o'clock to get ready, even though I had been obsessing over the thought of it all day since Oliver left me. I tried to heed his advice and just simply enjoy the ride. But how could I enjoy the ride if I didn't know whether or not a dress was an appropriate outfit?

After pulling my hair back into a low bun, I applied a small amount of makeup and slipped into a baby blue sundress. It had small flowers dispersed across the fabric and it didn't make me look quite as pale as I actually was.

Perfect Oliver was always on time and the doorbell rang at seven o'clock on the dot, just as I was slipping my feet into a pair of ballet flats. With the summer evenings being a little cooler than the days, my body struggled to stay warm with my subpar circulation.

My heart pounded rapidly in my chest, and I grabbed a sweater from my closet before making my way down to the front door. As I pulled it open, Tank shoved his massive head through the opening and pushed the door as Oliver laughed on the other side.

My eyes widened and my stomach felt like it was in the Olympics as I took him in. He had a dark blue collared shirt on, with khaki shorts and a pair of boat shoes. "You told me I could wear a burlap sack and you show up looking like we're going to the country club?"

Oliver laughed again and simply shook his head at me as he bent his arm and held out his elbow for me. I looked at him, puzzled as I cocked my head to the side.

"Don't we need to take my stuff?"

Oliver shook his head again. "Come with me and you'll see."

Curiosity got the better of me and I slid my arm through his and fell in step beside him as we walked down the stairs. Confusion laced with curiosity as he directed me through the grass and we walked through the yard, rounding the side of the house.

Oliver stopped and the air left my lungs in a rush as I took in everything that he had set up. There was a large heather gray blanket spread out on the grass with a few different baskets arranged on it. The side of the house was lit up by the projector Oliver brought over and had propped up on a stack of buckets by the fence.

I released Oliver's arm, taking a step toward the blanket as the soft sound of classical music tickled my eardrums. There was a picture of a map displayed from the projector.

"What is this?" I asked him, my voice barely audible as I turned around to face him.

Oliver's sage eyes softened. "Number six on your list. You wanted to see the world and since I can't take you to do that, I wanted to bring it to you."

My throat swelled with emotion and the corners of my eyes burned. "Ollie…" My voice trailed off.

He stepped toward me, sliding his hand into mine. "The world deserves to be seen by someone like you, Luna." He pulled me onto the blanket, kicking off his shoes before he moved to sit on it, pulling me along with him. "Let me show it to you."

Chapter Twelve

CLOUDS OF COTTON CANDY

I t all felt so surreal.

Folding my legs under me, I smoothed my dress out while Oliver pulled out his phone and changed the music. It switched into a soft melody that was accompanied by a woman singing in French. He lifted his gaze to mine, his green eyes shining back at me as a smile spread across his lips.

I watched him carefully as he grabbed the small remote for the projector and pressed a button on it. It flipped the picture on the screen, and I looked over at the side of the house, watching as it shifted into a video that began a tour of France.

Lifting my hands to my mouth, I caught my own gasp and my heart rattled inside its cage as I watched the beauty unfold in front of me. From the corner of my eye, I caught Oliver grabbing one of the baskets and as I glanced over at him, he was pouring each of us a glass of wine.

"Wine from Paris, France," Ollie said softly as he handed me the glass. I glanced up at the screen, watching as it continued with its video tour and the music playing in the background. "And some cheese to go with it," he told me as he passed me a small plastic container with cubes of cheese.

"How did you manage to pull all of this off, Ollie?" I questioned him as I slowly sipped my wine. It had a tart flavor, one that lingered on my tongue with a tingling sensation. It warmed my throat as I swallowed it, but it did nothing to calm my emotions. "Where did you get all of this stuff?"

Oliver smiled at me and winked. "I have my ways, Looney Tune."

He scooted closer to me on the blanket, his shoulder brushing against mine as he lowered his mouth to my ear. "Paris would be the first place I would take you to in France. I'd hold your hand as we strolled up and down the streets. We'd visit the Louvre Museum and of course, we'd see the Eiffel Tower."

Oliver leaned forward, pulling out two small croissants from the first basket. He placed one on a napkin and handed it to me before situating himself right beside me. His warmth radiated against my skin and every nerve ending in my body felt like it was on fire.

"We would have to eat the best pastries before taking a tour of the countryside. That's where the wine would come in, so I guess I served the food backward."

I quickly chewed the bite of croissant I just took before responding. "It's all perfect, Ollie. Everything about this is more than I ever could have imagined."

Oliver turned his head to look down at me, his eyes slowly searching mine. He lifted his hand, his fingers brushing against my lip as he brushed away a flaky piece of pastry from my mouth. His expression was unreadable and his hand lingered, his thumb slowly stroking my bottom lip.

At that moment, I felt the oxygen draining from my lungs. They screamed in protest, my body reminding me I needed to take a breath before I started to shift into a state of oxygen deprivation.

He tore his gaze from mine, his hand abandoning my face as the music changed and the video from the projector shifted to a new country. And just like that, the moment was gone, even though the remnants of it hung heavily in the air around us.

Oliver continued to take me on a tour through Europe, handing me different foods from each country. The music perfectly shifted with each video that played through the projector. The entire thing was flawless and exceeded any expectations I could have possibly had.

The sun had already set and the chill was settling into the air around us. Oliver began our tour through South America as we traveled the beaches of Brazil. He looked over at me as I wrapped my arms around myself to chase away the coldness settling in my body. I watched him as he grabbed my sweater and another blanket.

He helped me put on my sweater and he rose to his knees, wrapping the blanket around my shoulders. Oliver moved behind me, stretching out his legs on either side of mine as he pulled my back against his chest. A sigh slipped from my lips as I rested my head against his chest and felt his warmth envelope me as he wrapped his arms around my body.

"I don't think I planned the food accordingly..." His voice trailed off, his breath warm against my ear. "I thought I had all the countries covered but I just realized the only thing I have left is dessert from Mexico."

A soft laugh vibrated in my chest. "It's fine, Ollie. This is more than I could have ever imagined and I am so grateful to you for taking the time to do this for me."

Oliver tightened his arms around me as he pressed the side of his face to mine and we both stared at the video on the side of the house. "I wish I could actually show you the world, Luna. I wish I could give you so much more than this."

"Oliver," I started, my throat feeling like it was coated with peanut butter. "You've already given me more than I could ever want."

He nuzzled his face against the side of mine, his chest expanding against my back as he inhaled deeply. "I just want to give you the entire fucking world." He paused for a moment, his breath sweet and warm against my cheek. "You deserve everything."

My heart pounded erratically in my chest and my breathing grew shallow as I turned around in his arms to face him. I was taking a risk, putting both of us in this position, but I was finally taking Oliver's advice. I wanted to enjoy every step of the journey I was on.

"Luna," he murmured, his eyes staring into my soul as he brought his hands up to cup the sides of my face. "Luna, Luna, Luna."

The videos stopped playing at some point, and I was still sitting between Oliver's legs as he stroked the sides of my face with his thumbs. My heart crawled into my throat and the air around us was palpable with tension. His eyes kept dropping to my lips before finding my gaze again.

"I really want to kiss you right now," he admitted, his voice cracking around his words. "Is that okay with you?"

His words caught me off guard. I had been dealing with my own feelings for Oliver for so long, but I never allowed myself to believe that maybe he felt the same way. I swallowed roughly over the lump lodged in my throat. It could be that we were both just caught up in the moment right now, but I wasn't about to turn down my first kiss... especially with Oliver Hart.

I nodded as my eyes rapidly bounced back and forth between his. "I've never been kissed before."

"Good." Oliver smiled, even though he already knew that. "I always wanted to be your first..."

His voice trailed off as he inched his face closer to mine. My eyelids fluttered shut and I swear my life flashed before my eyes. My heart was an erratic mess and Oliver's breath was warm against my mouth as he dipped into my space.

His lips were soft, silky and sweet like clouds of cotton candy as he pressed them to mine. Neither of us dared to move and my lungs screamed in protest as I held my breath. After a few moments passed, Oliver slowly pulled away, a sigh escaping him as he pressed his forehead to mine.

Silence settled around us as I struggled to catch my breath. Oliver didn't let go of me and kept his forehead to mine until my breathing grew even and as regular as it could be.

"Thank you, Luna," he whispered as he lifted his head from mine. I watched the waves rolling against the shores of his ocean eyes.

I stared at him, my eyebrows pulling together in confusion. "For what?" I questioned him. He had no reason to be thanking me for anything.

"For being the best part of my life."

And just like that, my heart kicked into overdrive again. There wasn't a single flaw in Oliver and I had loved him for as long as I could remember. But in that very moment, I knew there would never be room for anyone else in my heart.

My heart would always belong to my best friend, even if he didn't have the slightest clue.

"You're the best part of my life too," I admitted, my voice quiet as I didn't fully trust it at that moment. I couldn't fight the yawn forcing its way out and I quickly brought my hand to my mouth to cover it.

Oliver chuckled softly. "It's been a long day. Let's get you inside so you can get some rest."

We pulled apart from each other and Oliver rose to his feet, extending his hand for me to take. He lifted me up with him and as I stood up, the exhaustion really began to kick in. It was as if Oliver could sense it and he slid one arm behind my back and the other under my legs as he scooped me into his arms.

A gasp escaped me as he lifted me into the air and began to walk toward my house. "You don't have to carry me, Ollie," I whispered to him as I reveled in his warmth. "I can walk."

"I know you can," he said matter-of-factly as he paused to open the front door and walked us inside, kicking the door shut behind him. "But there's no reason you have to when I can hold you in my arms instead."

He warmed my soul with his words, and I relaxed against him, resting my head against his shoulder as he carried me upstairs into my room. My mother and father were nowhere to be seen and I was thankful. It felt like an intimate moment I didn't want either of them seeing.

As we reached my bedroom, Oliver walked me over toward my bed before he set me down. My feet hit the floor just as Tank pushed his way through the door. Oliver lowered me to my feet, his hands gripped my waist until he knew I was steady.

Tank pushed his way between the two of us and Oliver chuckled as he took a step back. He watched the two of us as I patted Tank's head, letting him know that he was a good boy. As I turned my attention back to Oliver, I was suddenly overcome with so much emotion as the entire night replayed in my mind.

"Thank you for all of this, Ollie. Everything tonight, everything this summer... I don't know how I will ever be able to repay you for making this as special as you have."

Oliver stared down at me, a mix of emotions washing over his eyes. "You never have to repay me, Luna. I want to give you everything I possibly can."

"You're the best person I've ever met," I told him, stepping into his space as I wrapped my arms around the back of his neck. "Thank you for being you."

Oliver's hands found the small of my back as he pressed my body against his for a moment longer than he normally would before we broke apart. A crooked smile played on his lips. "Why does it feel like you're saying goodbye to me? I showed you the world and now you're done with me for the summer?"

"I'm not going anywhere," I assured him, the lie tasting bitter on my tongue. It wasn't a lie in the moment, but neither of us could ever predict the future. And one day I would be leaving this world without him.

I forced a soft laugh to lighten the mood. "Our summer is far from over."

"Good." He smiled down at me before he leaned forward and pressed his lips to my forehead. "Sweet dreams, Luna."

"Goodnight, Oliver," I told him as I watched him turn to leave my bedroom.

He paused in my doorway, turning back to look at me once more. "I hope you dream of me," he said quietly before he disappeared into the hallway, leaving me alone with my thoughts as he took the oxygen from the room with him.

Chapter Thirteen
WE DON'T GET TO CHOOSE

Oliver kissed me.

I didn't know whether I was living in a dreamland or reality anymore. I lifted my fingertips to my lips as I stared back at myself in the bathroom mirror. My cheeks were tinted pink and my blue eyes were bright. It was as if Oliver breathed life into me.

I always imagined my first kiss with Oliver, and that came nowhere close to what had actually happened between us. He gave me the world tonight and I was floating on a cloud of euphoria. It was a boost of dopamine I didn't know I needed.

My heart pitter-pattered in my chest as I thought about what would come next. Was I supposed to pretend like it didn't happen? Is that what Oliver wanted? Things weren't supposed to get messy and clouded between us and now I felt like I was in unfamiliar territory. I didn't want our friendship to change but there was definitely a shift… one I wasn't sure we would ever be able to come back from.

After brushing my teeth, I slipped into my bedroom to get ready for bed. My mother walked in just as the shrill beep from my ventilator echoed through my room. She stood in the doorway, her lips fighting to conceal the smile that threatened to take over her face.

"How was your night with Ollie?" my mother questioned as she walked over to me. She sat down on the bed next to me, her hands reaching for the vent tubing.

Lifting my chin, I gave her more access to connect it to the small tube near the base of my neck. The warm air rushed into my lungs and the machine began to read my own breathing. It was in an assist mode where it didn't constantly breathe for me. It would deliver a breath if my own wasn't deep enough or if my body happened to miss one.

"It was good." I smiled at her, feeling the warmth creep across my cheeks. It was a strange feeling. Even though it was just a kiss, something about it felt forbidden. I wanted it to be our secret, and I didn't want anyone else to know.

My mother tilted her head to the side as I scooted toward the headboard and pulled the covers over me. "What's that face about?"

I laughed softly and shook my head. "Nothing."

"I'm glad the two of you had a good night. Did he come in with you? I thought I heard someone in here."

I nodded. "Yeah, but he was only up here for a few minutes."

My mother let out a weird sigh and it shifted the mood. Her eyes were slightly wide and she sucked her lip between her teeth before releasing it with a pop. "I know when you were younger we had the sex talk, but we didn't really go as in depth as we probably should have."

I stared back at her, completely mortified. "Mom, we don't have to do this."

Her face softened, her skin wrinkling around her eyes as she chuckled. "With how close you and Oliver are getting, I think maybe we should."

"Mom." The word came out as a plea. This was not the conversation I wanted to have with my mother, and now I couldn't help but wonder if our security cameras caught our kiss. "I went to high school with other kids. I know enough about sex and protection that we don't have to talk about this. Plus, Oliver and I won't be doing that, like, ever."

She stared at me for a moment and chewed on the inside of her cheek. I watched the emotion wash over her expression and her eyes grew damp as she looked at me with only a tenderness that a mother could offer.

"Honey, you're old enough to make those decisions yourself." She paused and sniffled as her chin quivered. "I was never sure if we would get to this point in your life."

The grave reality of her words hit me like a ton of bricks. "I know," I whispered, my voice barely audible over the whooshing sound of the ventilator. There were so many moments in my life spoiled by the uncertainty of my future. My mortality made things more significant than they needed to be.

And sometimes, I hated it. I just wanted to be normal and experience things like everyone else. I wanted my first time having sex to not feel like it was a major milestone that needed to be celebrated or cried over. I could only understand how my mother felt about it all to a certain degree.

"I don't mean to be emotional about it, Luna." She

laughed lightly as she brushed away her tears. "I'm happy we're here. There were just so many times it was hard to tell what the future would hold."

"I know, Mom," I told her, the tenseness mixing with my tired tone. "I've been living this life the entire time."

She stared at me for a moment, shock apparent in her expression almost as if I slapped her. She rolled her lip between her teeth, shifting uncomfortably on my bed. It wasn't often I brought it up because I didn't want to diminish her feelings and experience at all, but sometimes I couldn't help with the irritation that festered inside.

No one else experienced my life from my point of view except for me. Neither of us knew what life was like for the other.

"I'm sorry, Luna," my mother apologized, her voice gentle. "That was insensitive for me to say."

I shook my head at her. "No, it's just our reality. I've been here through all of it and I know how precious each moment is. Sometimes, I just wish this wasn't the life we were living."

Her expression was strained. "I wish it wasn't, either. You don't know how many nights I laid in bed questioning everything, begging into the void for the universe to just let you live a normal life. But then I realized, we don't get to choose the life we live. All we get to choose is how we live it."

Her words were like a punch to the gut. My breath caught in my throat, causing me to choke before the ventilator censored I was having an issue and delivered the breath for me. There was so much weight to those two simple sentences. I had been spending my time trying to enjoy the ride but there were moments like this when I let things bring me down.

"You're right, Mom," I told her, my eyes searching hers as a smile pulled on her lips. "I choose to live it in every way possible."

"Good, Luna." She smiled back. "That's all I want for you. To live a full life and one without regrets. I want you to experience everything possible. Just because our reality is a little different from others doesn't mean that you can't live too."

"You and Oliver sound alike." I giggled as I nestled deeper into my pillow. "He's always telling me to just enjoy the ride."

My mother rose to her feet and leaned over, pressing her lips to my forehead. "Oliver's a special one, honey. And I couldn't be more thankful for a light like him in your life."

"Goodnight, Mom," I said as I rolled onto my side and tucked my arm underneath my pillow. "I love you."

"I love you more, Luna. More than the moon loves the stars."

With that, she disappeared from my room, leaving me alone with my thoughts of my evening with Oliver. I had to tell Giana. I had been updating her about all of our summer adventures. I grabbed my phone from my nightstand and promptly sent her a text.

LUNA

G, I'm freaking out.

GIANA

What's wrong? Is everything okay?

I smiled. My stomach flipped. I couldn't believe what had happened. It had to have been a dream.

LUNA

Oliver kissed me.

Giana wastes no time responding.

GIANA

I JUST DIED AND WENT TO HEAVEN.

OMG. I NEED ALL THE DETAILS GIRL.

I laughed out loud. Exhaustion was settling in my bones.

LUNA

Tomorrow?

GIANA

You better call me first thing or I'm driving to Vermont.

A soft laugh escaped me and I locked the screen on my phone before putting it back on my nightstand. As I let my eyes fall shut, all I could think about was my evening with Oliver. The most perfect moment ever. My mind drifted to the last words he spoke to me before he left.

"I hope you dream of me."

As I closed my eyes and felt the sleep slowly creeping in, I knew exactly what my dreams would consist of that night.

The green eyed boy from next door who held my heart in his hands.

THE NEXT MORNING, I WOKE UP TO A TEXT FROM OLIVER asking if he could come over to talk. We didn't discuss what our plans were for the rest of my bucket list after our kiss and the anxiety was building inside me as I mulled over how to respond.

OLIVER

Hey you. Can I come over so we can talk?

LUNA

Sure. I just got out of bed, so come over in an hour?

OLIVER

I'll be there.

I COULDN'T HELP BUT OVERTHINK WHAT CLOTHING I WAS supposed to wear. Things weren't supposed to be like this between us. As I stared at my closet, I let out an exasperated sigh and closed my eyes. It was just Oliver. A kiss meant nothing. I was going to play it cool and act normal around him. I wasn't bringing any of it up unless he brought it up first.

Grabbing my phone again, I typed out the entire night to Giana, explaining every moment. I ended it by telling her he was coming over and she quickly FaceTimed me, even though I was still in my damn pajamas.

Did he say what he was coming over for? She quickly signed to me.

I shook my head. *He wants to come over and talk.*

He's going to confess his love for you, Luna. Oh my gosh.

I stared at her, feeling like a bundle of anxiety. *I'm hanging up now.*

Wait. It will all be okay. Just remember, deep breaths. It will be fine. But make sure you tell me what I'm missing then.

I nodded back to her and quickly ended the call. I loved my other best friend deeply, but right now, I needed to be with my own thoughts. And I needed to figure out what I was going to wear for the day.

After settling on a pair of jean shorts and a tank top, I slipped into the bathroom and pulled my long hair up into a high ponytail before washing my face and brushing my teeth. Part of me was regretting telling him to come over in an hour.

I couldn't shake the bad feeling and the suspense was potentially going to kill me before my medical condition did.

After the longest hour of my life, I headed out onto the front porch to wait for Oliver. Tank found his usual position, lying on the floor beside my feet. Oliver was barely a minute past an hour as he walked from his front yard and through the gate into mine. Tank hopped up and greeted him as he reached the steps.

"Hey, you slobbery fool." Oliver laughed, patting Tank on the head as he pushed past him. His green eyes met mine and he smiled softly before sitting down on the swing next to me. "Hey, slobbery fool number two."

"Hey!" I knocked my shoulder against his, a nervous laugh instantly escaping me as I realized I shouldn't have touched him. "I'm not slobbery."

"Maybe not like your dog," he said with a smirk and a shrug. "But I've seen the drool marks on your pillows."

Heat crept up my neck and across my cheeks. "You're officially not allowed in my room anymore."

Oliver raised an eyebrow at me with mischief dancing in his eyes. "Are you sure about that?"

My stomach did a somersault and the nonexistent butterflies fluttered inside. A lump lodged in my throat and it felt like I was potentially going to choke to death on it. Yet again, Oliver stole the air from my lungs with just his words.

"What did you want to talk about?" I questioned him, forcing the conversation to shift.

Please don't say our kiss.

"I come with bad news," he told me as he leaned back against the swing and propped his hands behind his head. "I forgot about my family's planned vacation. I tried to get out of it but my mom won't let me, especially since this will probably be my last year going with them."

"Why is that bad news?" I questioned him, feeling a rush of relief that he didn't bring up last night. "You guys always go on a family vacation every summer."

Oliver turned his head to look over at me. "Because this summer was supposed to be about us and checking off your list."

"Are you going for the rest of the summer?"

"Jesus, no." Oliver laughed, and in that moment I realized that was my most favorite sound ever. "Just for a week, but we're leaving tomorrow. I completely forgot about it, and I feel like I'm leaving you behind."

Now it was my turn to laugh. "You're not leaving me

behind, Ollie. We will have plenty of time to check off the rest of my list."

Except for the two most private ones I would never share with him.

To fall in love and to lose my virginity.

His expression became unreadable and he stared directly into my soul. "I feel like I should apologize for kissing you last night, but I'm not sorry for it at all."

Oh shit.

My heart crawled into my throat. This was the conversation I did not want to have and leave it to Oliver to just spring it upon me without any warning.

"We don't have to talk about last night, Oliver," I told him, my voice quiet. I didn't know what else to say. I didn't regret it at all, but it couldn't happen again.

"Shit..." Pain washed through his eyes. "Maybe I should apologize. I thought you wanted it and now I feel like an asshole for overstepping my boundaries."

"You didn't. I did want it," I told him in a rush, my voice urgent which made me feel embarrassed. "I'm glad it happened. I wanted it to happen for so long, but it can't happen again."

Oliver's eyebrows pulled together. "Why not?"

I inhaled deeply, closing my eyes briefly before opening them up to meet his gaze. "Because we can't be anything more than friends, Oliver. I don't want to ruin our friendship and I could never forgive myself for breaking your heart if you fell in love with me."

"How can you be so sure you would break my heart?"

I struggled to swallow past the lump lodged in my throat. "I'm dying, Oliver."

"We all are," he retorted, his eyes burning holes through mine.

"But I'm going to die before you." I paused for a moment, attempting to collect myself as my emotions began to overwhelm me. "It's bad enough that one day you'll have to bury your best friend. The last thing I want is for you to bury the person you're in love with too."

Oliver stared back at me, his eyes desperately searching mine. "Luna..."

I abruptly rose to my feet, the swing shifting slightly. Tank jumped up beside me. "I'm sorry, Ollie. I need to go back inside. Have a great time on vacation and I'll see you when you get back."

Without giving him the opportunity to respond, I made my escape back into the house and shut the door behind me and my mammoth-sized dog. Pressing my back against the door, I closed my eyes and took a few moments to collect myself and catch my breath.

I hated shutting him out, but I panicked. The situation was messy and I let fear drive my actions. Instead of really having a conversation with Oliver, I shut it down before he had the chance to say anything else. He would be leaving tomorrow for their family vacation, and I deeply regretted what I just did.

And when I turned back around and looked through the window in the door, Oliver was gone.

Chapter Fourteen
LIFE IS SHORT AND SHIT

Time seemed to slow down while Oliver was away. He had been gone four days and somehow it felt like four years. I didn't know what to do with myself with him gone and I'm fairly certain Tank was getting tired of all the walks I was forcing him to go on. He was the only one I really had to keep my mind occupied right now.

Sitting out on the back patio, I bent down and picked up Tank's ball. I called his name and held it up to show him. He lifted his head and stared at me for a moment before laying it back down. I swear I heard him sigh as he directed his gaze away from me.

Who would have ever thought a dog would get tired of playing fetch?

A sigh escaped me as I settled back into my seat. Vivi texted me two days ago and wanted to get together, but I just couldn't bring myself to do it. We were already nearing the middle of summer and she had just now reached out to me.

I knew the friendships I had were fleeting. That's how it was in high school. Throw in a complex medical condition and you really get to see who your true friends are. I'm not saying she never cared about me, because she did, but our lives didn't exactly fit together.

I politely declined her invitation and told her that we would get together another day, but made no further plans. I had even been partially ignoring Giana, which was unlike me. Part of me wanted to sulk in my misery and regret for walking away from Oliver. The other part of me just wanted to be alone in solitude to try and process it.

Either way, I was beginning to feel like I was going crazy, and I just wanted my best friend to come home.

"Hey, sweetie," my mother said as she came outside and sat down at the patio table with me. "What are you doing out here?"

I glanced over at her and shrugged. "I don't know. I was playing fetch with Tank, but I'm pretty sure he's sick of me."

My mother laughed softly and I watched her face transform to one of concern. "Is everything okay? You've been really quiet and withdrawn the past few days."

I stared back at her for a moment, every damn thought of Oliver rushing to the forefront of my mind. He might be my best friend, but my mother was my true confidant. There were things I couldn't go to him about but I could talk to her and ask for her advice.

It felt foreign, talking about Oliver from a different perspective than I had before, but I needed someone's advice. I could have talked to Vivi about it, but for some reason, I felt like my mother would be the only one who would truly understand.

"Oliver kissed me the other night."

Her eyes widened slightly but it was almost as if it were forced. That's when I realized she already knew. She was pretending to be surprised because I didn't know this wasn't news to her.

"You already knew that," I declared, tilting my head to the side.

My mother nodded with a look of guilt on her face. "I happened to glance out the window the night you guys were set up on the side of the house and I saw it." She paused for a moment to take a sip of her bottle of water. "I only saw him go in for the kiss and then I walked away from the window, I promise."

"I don't care if you saw it," I told her, defeat heavy in my voice. "I just don't know what to do about it now. He brought it up when he came over the next morning and I shut him down and walked away."

"What made you react that way?"

A lump lodged in my throat and my heart constricted. "I'm afraid he's going to want more from me and I can't give him that."

"Did he tell you he wanted more?"

"No." I shook my head at her. "But when I told him it couldn't happen again, he didn't seem pleased. He wanted to know why and he left me no choice. I told him I don't want to break his heart one day."

My mother gave me an inquisitive look as she set her water bottle down on the table. "I've watched the two of you grow up together, Luna. I know you have feelings for Oliver and I know he has them for you as well. I know you well enough that you would never intentionally break his heart."

"Not intentionally, but it's inevitable."

Frustration began to build within me because my mother just wasn't getting it.

"What happens when he falls in love with me and then I die? Then he's left with a Luna shaped hole in his chest." I stopped, inhaling as deeply as my lungs would let me before I let out a shaky exhale. "I'm going to die before him, Mom, and I don't know what will happen to him after that. I don't want to break him. I can't."

My mother gave me a sad smile and her eyes shimmered under a ray of sunlight that showcased the tears she was desperately trying to hold back. "I think it's a little too late for that, sunshine." Her shoulders sagged as she sighed. "That boy is hopelessly in love with you already."

My phone vibrated from where it was sitting on the table and my heart skipped a beat as I picked it up and saw his name on the screen. I couldn't stop the grin from lifting the corners of my lips.

OLIVER

Luna. Please don't shut me out. I need you to talk to me.

As I read over his words, my heart clenched and my throat constricted. I struggled to breathe as my body reacted in the most visceral way to his plea. Neither of us had reached out to the other, but just in the way he sent the message, I knew he had been feeling similarly to how I had been feeling.

"Is that him?"

I looked up at my mother, my smile faltering a little. "It is."

"Can I give you some advice before I leave you alone to talk to him?"

I nodded, locking my phone screen to give her my undivided attention. My mother always had the best advice and I trusted her with everything. I mean, if we were being one hundred percent real, I wouldn't have been alive without this woman constantly advocating for me and demanding nothing less than the best.

"Don't let your fear dictate your future and how you live your life. Remember, we get to choose how we live it and I want you to live, Luna." She slowly rose to her feet, her eyes still on mine. "Choose to live it to the fullest, with no regrets. Death is inevitable for all of us, but don't take the choice of loving you away from Oliver. He knows what loving you means, sunshine. And he's willing to risk it all for you."

My phone vibrated again, and I smiled at my mother as her words sunk in. "Thank you, Mom," I told her. "You give the best advice."

"Always remember that," she said with a wink before she disappeared back inside the house.

I unlocked my phone and opened Oliver's message.

OLIVER

Luna, I'm going crazy here. If I don't hear from you in the next five minutes, I'm finding a way back home.

My heart swelled as I read his message three times over. Oliver Hart was unlike anyone else I had ever met in my life and I never wanted to let him go. My mother was right. I wasn't the one who got to make the choice for Ollie. The choice would always be his.

Tapping on his name, I pressed the small phone icon and held it up to my ear as it started to ring. It only rang once before I heard Oliver's voice on the other end.

"Please tell me this is real life and not a butt dial."

A soft laugh escaped me. "I'm not sure if it's that simple to butt dial from a smartphone."

"Oh, thank God, it's real." He let out an exasperated sigh of relief. "The silence between us was literally killing me, Luna. Can we agree to never do that again?"

"Yes," I agreed immediately. There was no hesitation. "I'm really sorry, Ollie. I overreacted, I think. I don't know, really. I just didn't know how to process it all. Sometimes stuff feels really overwhelming for me."

"I know, Luna." I could hear his smile in his voice. "I know you well enough to know that. I didn't mean to overwhelm you. If you don't want anything to change between us, I will respect whatever you want."

I mulled over his words for a moment. "I don't know, Oliver. I feel like this is a conversation we should have in person.

"So, that means you do want to see me again?" His voice was hopeful and it hurt my heart.

"Of course, you idiot." I laughed softly even though my throat felt like it was collapsing in on itself.

"I was afraid I was going to lose you forever."

"You'll never lose me." The lie felt bitter on my tongue.

We both knew that one day he would, but it wouldn't be by either of our choosing.

"Good," he said and I heard that damn smile again. "I miss you, Luna."

"You'll be home soon," I tried to remind him as I

pulled at the frayed hem of my jean shorts. "We can get back to our summer plans as soon as you're back."

Oliver sighed. "Soon isn't good enough. No one here is as interesting as you and my parents are getting pretty pissed with how much I've been sulking."

I laughed again, shaking my head even though he couldn't see me. "Please stop sulking and enjoy yourself. I haven't been doing anything since you've been gone."

"I don't know if that makes me feel better or worse," he said quietly. He fell silent for a moment. "I know you said you want to have this conversation in person, but I'm just going to throw this out now, because, you know, life is short and shit."

Don't we both know that?

"I'm not going to give you space, but I'll give you all the time you need to figure things out. I didn't kiss you just because it was in the moment. I meant it when I said I always wanted to be your first. You mean a lot to me, Luna, and as more than just a friend. If you only want to be friends, I am completely fine with that. As long as I get to be a part of your life, I'll be whatever you want me to be."

His words felt like a blow to my chest, but it wasn't painful. It was more powerful than anything. The way he said it with such conviction and without fear. He didn't care how I would possibly respond to his admission. He just wanted me to know the truth and whatever I decided to do with that was up to me.

"Thank you, Oliver," I told him, my voice soft and filled with honesty. "This is unfamiliar territory for me, but you're the only person I would ever want to explore it with. I think it's better if we don't rush into anything right now, but I want you to know my feelings for you are deeper than just being friends. You are so much more to me."

"Tell you what. Nothing changes between us until you're ready for it to." He paused for a moment before beginning again. "However much time you need, I will give it to you. However slowly you want to go, you set the pace, Luna Truly."

I could hear someone talking to Oliver in the background and he let out a sigh.

"I'm sorry, Luna. My parents are forcing me to go with them right now." He fell silent. "I could just ditch them and hitchhike my way back."

"Oliver Atticus Hart," I heard his mother scold him in the background. I couldn't hear anything she said after that as her voice became muffled, and I laughed out loud.

"Go have fun with your family and call me later," I told him, feeling a sense of peace. I was thankful we finally had a real conversation addressing the elephant in the room.

Oliver sighed. "Fine, but I won't have as much fun as I would be having with you."

"You're ridiculous, Ollie."

He laughed softly through the phone. "Maybe, but you love me anyway. Talk to you later, Looney Tune."

He didn't give me a chance to respond before he ended the call. Not that I would have known what to say to him. He spoke nothing but the truth.

And it was the truth I was still afraid to admit to him.

Chapter Fifteen
NOSTALGIC NIGHTS

"Are you ready for our next adventure?" Oliver questioned me as he loaded my things into his car. He had just returned from vacation with his family yesterday and came over first thing this morning. I started to wonder if he had anything in store for us or not.

"Always." I smiled at him as Tank climbed into the backseat and I took my place in the passenger's seat. "Although, I'm curious as to what happens when we run out of things to do. There are only a few more left on my list."

And two that you don't know about…

Oliver smiled back at me as he dropped into his seat and turned on the engine of his car. "You don't have to worry about that, Luna. Your list isn't written in stone, is it? We can always add more or change things. Speaking of changing… I don't think you need to go on that blind date anymore."

I tilted my head to the side, staring at him for a moment as he avoided my gaze and focused on the road while pulling the car out of my driveway. "Why not? I've never been on a blind date before and I think it would be something fun to do."

Oliver's jaw clenched, and I watched a shadow pass over his expression. His grip tightened around the steering wheel, his knuckles turning stark white as he continued to stare at the road.

"What's wrong, Ollie?" I questioned him, my voice tender and slightly hesitant.

He pulled the car up to a red light and turned to look at me. A fire burned deeply in his eyes and a shiver ran down my spine. "I don't want you going on a date with anyone else."

"It's not like it means anything. I just want to experience it one time."

"What happens if you like the guy?" There was a sense of panic in his tone and it struck me. Oliver didn't want me developing feelings for anyone else. My mind drifted to our conversation from the other night and how he said he would wait for me to be ready for him.

"It wouldn't change anything between us," I assured him, unsure of why I was still arguing at this point. A part of me liked this jealous side of Oliver because it was something I had never seen before. In a way, it made me feel like I was a prized possession he didn't want to share with anyone. It made me feel weirdly special.

"Look, Luna," he said as he looked back to the road when the light turned green. There was a gentleness in his tone, yet a heaviness lingered in his words. "It's your list. Whatever you want, I will make it happen. I don't like it, but I'm not going to deny you anything you want."

His words warmed my heart, even if it pained him to

say. Oliver had always been the one to make sure everyone else was good and their needs were met. He knew it was something on my bucket list and since I was making a big deal about it, he was folding. All he ever wanted was for me to be happy.

What he didn't know was nothing else in this universe made me quite as happy as he did.

We both shifted into a slightly uncomfortable silence after that. I had a feeling of where Oliver was driving us and when he pulled onto the gravel drive, I knew I was right. Other cars were already lining the field and off in the distance, you could see the carnival rides and games.

"For the record, I would have much rather gone to an amusement park, but I know how much you love the fair."

Every summer, they set up the fair for one week. It's just a chaotic mess of games and mazes and rides. All of the stands have the greasiest food you could ever ask for. Everything is fried and you're lucky if you make it out without a clogged artery.

There's something nostalgic about it. The smells, the sounds-every piece of it reaches out and tickles your senses. It was enough to make you feel like a kid again. It brought you back to a place where the world around you wasn't so complicated. Back to when the only thing you had to worry about was being a kid.

My childhood wasn't that simple, but that didn't diminish the nostalgia that came along with going to the fair.

"You know how unsafe these rides are, right?" Oliver asked me as he put the car in park and killed the engine. He turned to look at me with a sense of worry in his eyes.

"How did our parents let us ride these things without thinking of what could go wrong?"

I stared at him for a moment, my eyes widening. "You know it's on my bucket list because I've never gotten to ride any of these rides before. You're not making me feel any safer doing it." I paused for a moment, a nervous chuckle escaping me. "I mean, I can think of other horrible ways to go out, so I guess if I die on a sketchy carnival ride, it wouldn't be that terrible."

Oliver's lips parted and he reached out to me, taking my hand in his as his eyes desperately searched mine. "I promise I will always keep you safe, Luna. I wouldn't be taking you on the Ferris wheel if I thought it would put you in danger."

He paused for a moment, and my stomach did somersaults as the butterflies fluttered. His palm was warm against mine and I suddenly didn't care about the fair. I wanted to stay right here and hold hands with him all night.

"I will always protect you," he murmured as he lifted his other hand to caress the side of my face. His thumb was soft as he gently stroked my cheek. His eyes dropped down to my lips and I watched in awe as his tongue slipped out to wet his own. "You are the most important person in my life. You are always safe with me."

The silence settled around us and it felt like the oxygen was quickly dissipating from the small space in Oliver's car. His eyes were still on my lips and he was shifting his weight, moving closer to me as he continued to gently stroke the side of my face. He was inching closer and my heart felt like it was about to beat out of my chest.

He's going to kiss me again…

"Luna," he murmured, his voice soft. There was a shift between us and I just knew it was going to happen again. And despite the conversation we had, I wasn't so sure I was going to stop him.

Everything around us ceased to exist. In the distance, I could hear Tank panting and shifting in the backseat. The sound of the blood rushing through my veins was drowning out every sound. Suddenly, a pounding sound came from the window behind Oliver. I yelped, jumping in my seat as he abruptly pulled away from me and turned around.

"What the fuck?" Oliver muttered, the frustration heavy in his tone. I looked past him and saw Dylan peering in with a huge grin. An exasperated sigh escaped Oliver and he pushed his door open. "What do you want?"

Dylan leaned forward, his eyes bouncing back and forth between Oliver and I. "Was I interrupting something?"

"Not at all," I said quicker than I probably should have. I didn't miss the way Oliver's body went rigid for a moment. He didn't turn back to look at me before he exited the car. My heart was in my stomach and I hated the way I felt. I hated the way I made Oliver feel.

It wasn't my intention but the words came out anyway.

I got out of the car and went to the back to let Tank out. Holding onto his leash, I moved out of the way as he jumped out.

"Do you want me to bring everything or just your emergency bag?" Oliver questioned me from where he was standing at the trunk. We always brought my back up ventilator and suction machine just in case. I didn't see myself needing either of them and they were in the car if something were to happen.

I shook my head at him as I stepped closer. "I think I should be okay."

Oliver nodded and closed the trunk before putting the backpack on. I had recently transferred most of my supplies into a backpack. It made it a lot easier to carry while being out and it just seemed a little more practical.

And then I realized it was more of a pain to carry around on your shoulder. I guess a part of me wanted to appear a little more normal, like I had an oversized purse instead of a backpack. There were a lot of times in my life where I just wanted to fit in with everyone else. It took a long time for me to accept it, especially during my early teenage years, but I eventually came to terms with it.

I wasn't like anyone else and that was okay.

It was okay to be me, exactly the way I was. I didn't feel the need to try and fit in anymore. It was an exhausting thing to do and it felt like a weight had been lifted when I stopped caring.

"Luna, are you coming?" Dylan questioned me from where he stood in the center aisle between the cars. Oliver was watching me carefully, his head tilted slightly with a touch of concern in his eyes.

A nervous laugh escaped me. "Yep."

Dylan turned around and began to walk toward the fair. Oliver was waiting for me and turned with me as I walked past him. I expected him to fall into step beside me but he didn't. Instead, his hand darted out, wrapping around my wrist as he pulled me back toward him.

I abruptly stopped and turned back to look at him, my

eyes wide with surprise. Oliver stared back at me for a moment, his expression unreadable. He closed the distance between us, his hand sliding down to intertwine our fingers, his warm palm pressing flush against mine.

He dropped his gaze down to our clasped hands before his eyes met mine once again. "That's better," he murmured as the corners of his lips lifted slightly. "Shall we?"

The butterflies danced in my stomach to Oliver's melody. "We shall."

Chapter Sixteen
LUNA TRULY CALLS THE SHOTS

We ended up meeting up with some of the other guys from the football team and their girlfriends. Oliver looked less than amused which was an interesting thing to see. He was usually the laid back, go with the flow kind of guy. Instead, he just seemed as if he was irritated. And every time he tried to veer off in a different direction, someone called him back to the group.

After all the guys decided on a plan for the night, Oliver and I fell in step behind everyone, his hand still holding mine. I hung back, watching as everyone got in line for the ticket booth to get their tickets for the rides. Oliver and I walked up last, but I wasn't paying attention as he got our tickets.

Instead, my eyes surveyed the area, watching everyone as they moved about in their own little worlds. The different couples, the groups of friends. Everyone looked so happy, without a single worry troubling their minds.

"What do you say we ditch these guys?" Oliver questioned me, his breath warm against my ear as he leaned close and whispered to me. "I wasn't planning on hanging out with them and don't really want to anyway."

"Aren't they going to notice that we're missing?" I asked him, lifting up on my tiptoes to attempt to whisper back into his ear. Oliver's palm was warm as he gently grabbed ahold of my waist to help me. He ducked his head down and there wasn't much distance between us.

His smell invaded my senses, clouding my thoughts.

Oliver shrugged before he pulled back to look down at me. "I couldn't care less. I didn't come here to hang out with them. I came here to be with you."

His words sent a spark through my nervous system, but I attempted to focus on my breathing and forget he said it that way. It was hard with his warm hand still on my waist.

We lingered behind the rest of the group, watching as more distance grew between us all and the crowd around us got thicker. Oliver looked back to me, mischief dancing in his eyes as a smirk pulled on his lips. He pulled his hand from my waist and quickly grabbed mine, threading our fingers together.

"Now's our chance!" He tugged my hand as he darted through the crowd in the opposite direction of his friends. "Come on, Luna!"

Oliver broke out into a jog, pulling me along with him. He didn't move too quickly and kept it more at a pace I was able to keep up with. Laughter escaped the two of us as we bobbed and weaved through the other people until we were far enough away from Dylan and the rest of the group.

As we reached the edge of one of the rows of food

trucks, we stopped to catch our breath. I pulled my hand away from Oliver's as I bent my knees slightly and planted my palms against them. Oliver leaned back against the side of one of the trucks right next to me.

"Are you good?" he questioned me. He was barely out of breath, which wasn't surprising, given how athletic he was and being a star football player.

I glanced up at him, forcing a smile and a nod even though my heart was pounding erratically and my lungs burned with every breath. "Never been better."

Concern laced itself in Oliver's beautiful eyes and he inched closer to me. "Take your time and catch your breath. I shouldn't have done that."

I stared at Oliver, an overwhelming sense of anger washing over me. It was coupled with the frustration of knowing he was right and I couldn't stop the words before they slipped from my lips. "Stop treating me like I'm going to break, Oliver," I told him with such desperation, I could feel it in my bones. "You've never treated me like that before and I'd appreciate it if you'd stop treating me like that now."

He recoiled as if I had struck him. "Luna," he started, his voice soft as he took a step away from me. I could instantly feel the distance between us and I regretted speaking a single word. "That's not my intention at all. You've always been my main concern and you always will be."

"Just please stop acting like we can't do things because of my medical condition." I stood upright, squaring my shoulders even though they wanted to sag in defeat. "I don't need the constant reminder that my body can't keep up like everyone else's. Please, just let me be the one to judge what I can and can't handle."

"Of course," he agreed as he nodded. "You know your boundaries and I'm sorry for overstepping."

I instantly felt out of line for the way I reacted. This time, it was me who closed the distance between us, reaching out for my best friend. "Don't apologize, Ollie. I just don't want you to keep letting me hold us back from doing things."

"Noted and stored in my brain for later," he said with his infamous smirk. "Luna Truly calls the shots."

Laughter bubbled from my lips and I rolled my eyes in exaggeration at him. "You know what I mean."

"I do," he concurred with a wink. "Now that that is out of the way, can we proceed with our night?"

"That sounds like the perfect plan."

Oliver slid his hand back into mine, effectively rendering me breathless again as we moved away from the food trucks and began walking back through the crowds of people. He led me past the different rides, only stopping once we reached the Ferris wheel.

Standing beside him, I tilted my head up to look at the massive wheel. It was slowly moving with people laughing from their bucket seats on the ride. It was made of steel, painted white and decorated in different colored lights. In a way, it reminded me of a Christmas tree. Pop music from a local radio station played in the background but I couldn't hear it over the sound of my heart pounding.

Oliver looked at me, raising an eyebrow, but he didn't dare question me. He was respecting my boundaries and letting me lead.

"I can do this," I murmured to myself as we stepped in line. "Everything will be okay."

"Are you giving yourself a pep talk right now?"

I looked over at Ollie, my lips pursed. "So what if I am?"

He stared at me for a moment, a ghost of a smile playing on his lips. "Listen to me, Luna. You are a fucking bad ass. I have watched you overcome so much in life, and this Ferris wheel is nothing compared to the things you've already done. I'll be right by your side, assuring you the entire time that you can do this."

A nervous chuckle slipped from my lips and the line began to move. We walked closer to the gate. "You're right. It's kind of silly for me to be terrified of heights and dying on this rickety thing when I've had my body try to kill me multiple times."

"You're not dying today, Luna," Oliver assured me as he handed our tickets to the girl sitting by the gate. "And if you do, at least we'll die together."

My eyes widened. "How touching."

Oliver laughed softly. "I wouldn't be mad at it," he admitted with a shrug. His voice trailed off and there was a thickness growing in the air between us. I didn't get a chance to question him on it as he led me up the steps to the Ferris wheel. We reached the ride and the guy who was helping everyone took one look at us and shook his head.

"I'm sorry, but you can't take your dog on with you," he told me, a frown pulling her lips downward. "I'm afraid the three of you would exceed the weight limit and I don't think we're allowed to let animals on the ride."

I looked at Tank and then at Ollie. "I guess we can't ride it."

Oliver's jaw clenched and he shoved his hand into his pocket before pulling out his wallet. "Twenty bucks to keep the dog with you and make sure nothing happens to him," he said to the guy as he held out a twenty-dollar bill.

He shrugged and took the money from him. "Sure, as long as he's cool."

"He'll sit here and wait without a leash if Luna tells him," Oliver told him as he squeezed my hand. "But if anything happens to him, things aren't going to end well for you."

The guy tilted his head to the side as he raised an eyebrow. "Is that a threat?"

Oliver smiled. "It's a promise."

"Sit and stay," I told Tank as I handed over his leash to the guy who was working the ride. Tank listened and watched the two of us as we left him with the stranger. It didn't completely sit right with me, but I trusted Oliver and that was all that mattered.

Leaving Tank behind, we climbed into the car that was supposed to keep us safe for the duration of the ride. It rocked back and forth as we got situated in our seats, and I was already holding onto the lap bar in front of us for dear life. The ride creaked as it began to lift us into the air in a circle.

Oliver leaned back, wrapping his arm around the tops of my shoulders as he pulled me closer. "It's okay, Luna," he murmured against my ear. "Everything will be fine."

"What about Tank?" I asked him, using my dog as a

diversion from the thought of how easily things could go badly on this ride.

Oliver shifted as he attempted to look out over the edge. The bucket rocked, and I let out a small yelp.

"Do not move, Ollie!" I practically yelled at him. My hand darted out and I gripped his shirt as I tried to pull him back down into the seat.

Oliver laughed and shook his head as he settled back against me. "Tank is fine, still in the same spot we left him."

He didn't bother to comment on my minor freak out and instead just sat there beside me like the rock he had always been in my life. The ride was less than pleasant and as we reached the top of the wheel, my stomach was in knots of anxiety.

"We need to get down, Oliver."

He turned his head to look at me. "We can't do that, Luna," he reminded me, his voice gentle as he lightly stroked the top of my arm with his fingertips. "The ride will be over soon."

My eyes desperately searched his as the anxiety intensified inside. The ride paused and we were suspended at the top. "I need you to distract me, Ollie. If I keep thinking about this, I swear my mind is going to combust from the anxiety right—"

His lips crashed into mine, abruptly silencing me from the anxiety attack threatening to suck me into its dark depths. He caught me off guard and at first I wasn't sure how to respond. Oliver lifted his hand to cup the side of my face and lightly stroked my cheek with the pad of his thumb.

His lips were soft and he tasted like cotton candy as he

traced the seam of my lips with his tongue. Instinctively, I parted them and he slipped into my mouth, his tongue sliding across mine. He was surprising me with his actions but it was just the distraction I needed.

I focused on the way Oliver felt, and he was surrounding me, consuming me, overwhelming my senses. I moved my tongue with his as they tangled in their own dance. My breathing picked up and my heart was racing in my chest. I mimicked Oliver's movements until it felt like I actually knew what I was doing.

He kissed me back with a reverent need, but there was no urgency. He was careful and gentle, soft and attentive. He kissed me in a way that made me feel like I could melt into a puddle at his feet. I didn't know where things between Oliver and I were actually going. All I knew was there would one day be an end to it all and I was dreading that day more than anything.

Oliver slowly pulled away, our lips breaking apart as we came up for air. My lungs sang a joyous song as I took a deep breath, filling them with as much oxygen as I could get in in one breath. Oliver's lips were red and parted, and his eyes bounced back and forth between mine.

"Look, Luna," he murmured, his thumb softly stroking the side of my face. "The ride is over. We made it back to the ground."

I stared back at my best friend, feeling confused as hell, but I forced a smile onto my lips as we both rose from our seats. Oliver got out first and helped me off the Ferris wheel. It felt good to have my feet back on the ground, even though my heart was still soaring through the clouds.

And it wouldn't be long before it all came crashing down.

Chapter Seventeen
UNBLIND DATES

fter our kiss on the Ferris wheel, things grew a little awkward between Oliver and I, and I couldn't quite put it into words. Maybe awkward wasn't the proper way to describe it. Things hadn't exactly changed between us, but I felt the shift. I was more nervous around him than I ever had been. Every intimate moment between us had come as a surprise, I wasn't sure what to expect from him anymore.

And the last thing I wanted to do was have a conversation with him about it. Ignorance was bliss and in this case, I liked not knowing Oliver's true feelings. He could be toying with me and that would be okay. As long as I wouldn't have to humiliate myself by asking him if he liked me.

We weren't really kids anymore. Talk about an awkward conversation and one that wasn't warranted. I knew in my heart and soul Oliver would never toy with my feelings or do anything malicious like that.

But I also knew I had to be realistic about it.

There could never be a future for Oliver and I. I was already living on borrowed time. It was a miracle I lived this long. We both knew it, and I knew Oliver deserved more than I would ever be able to give him. He deserved a real future with someone, not just living one moment to the next until the light eventually fizzled out.

This place wasn't meant for me. I was stamped with an expiration date and my time was running out.

My phone vibrated on my desk next to me and I put my pen down. I stared down at the page in my notebook in front of me. It felt strange writing my own story, but in a way it was therapeutic. My parents had me in therapy when I was younger, but this seemed to work better for me. I didn't need another person trying to sift through the thoughts in my head.

Putting them on paper made it feel as though none of this were actually happening to me. None of it was real. If I was able to write a story about it, it could make this all feel like it was fiction. Almost as if I were living someone else's life and I was just standing on the outside, watching it all happen.

OLIVER

Are you ready to check off another one from your list tonight?

We talked about it when he dropped me off last night. He walked me to my door after the fair and his eyes kept dropping down to my lips. His body language felt off. He clutched my hand like it was his lifeline as he inched closer.

And just when I thought he was going to kiss me, he shifted an inch to the right and kissed my cheek before he opened the front door for me. It confused me, but I tried not to focus on it. Instead, I let the mystery of tonight cloud my thoughts.

LUNA

I suppose so. What time should I be ready?

Of course, he didn't tell me which one he planned for us today, but he made it clear we would be going somewhere. He told me to wear something nice, which didn't really give me any clue of what was going on.

OLIVER

I'll pick you up in my car around five. Remember to wear something nice, the place is a little fancier than the diner.

I tilted my head to the side, rereading his message over and over again.

LUNA

So, we're going out to eat somewhere...?

I racked my brain, trying to figure out what it would be. He mentioned the diner which made me think of food. I thought if we were going to crash a wedding, he would have told me to wear something super nice. Not just that it's fancier than the diner. Although, I wasn't sure and Oliver played a cryptic game.

OLIVER

I'm not ruining any surprises, Luna. Just make sure you're ready.

Through text, it was always hard to tell someone's tone. The way Oliver's texts were coming across felt like they were tense. Like there was something off about him. It didn't make sense in my brain.

LUNA

What's wrong?

Life was too short for me to be living from one miscommunication to another. While I might not be one to ask him about his feelings about me, it didn't mean I was going to let other things go. Oliver knew this, so there was no reason for him to be surprised with my forwardness.

OLIVER

Nothing. Just a little tired, so I'm sorry if it seemed like something else.

I reread his message a few times. His response seemed like he was just trying to pacify me. Instead of saying anything back, I let it go, knowing I would have my chance to question him later. Setting my phone down, I picked my pen back up and dove back into my story, letting it distract my mind from the boy next door.

OLIVER WAS ALREADY STANDING INSIDE THE FOYER WITH MY bags when I began my descent down the stairs. I pulled my hair back into a French twist and pulled a few hairs down to frame my face. My white dress clung to my torso and flowed around my waist, stopping just above my knees. It was a dress I didn't wear very often because it wasn't one I always felt comfortable in.

With the plunging neckline, it was impossible to conceal the central line dressing on my chest. Having my hair pulled back gave full access to my trach and made it visible for everyone to see it. I didn't tend to hide from the public, but I was usually a little more reserved and not as revealing.

When I stood in front of my closet trying to pick a dress, my fingers landed on this one. I pulled it out and held it up, my eyes scanning the material. Something inside me was blossoming. Oliver might make me more nervous than he ever had, but there was something empowering, knowing that I was having a similar effect on him.

He made me feel feminine, he made me feel human.

And it was time I grew more comfortable in the skin I was fitted with.

The smile on my face left as I reached the bottom of the stairs and my gaze collided with Oliver's. I expected a different response from him, one similar to the way he looked at me when he brought me the world or when we went to prom.

Instead, there was a storm brewing in his eyes. He stared at me, his gaze sweeping over me from head to toe. Inside the storm, there was a fire burning. His jaw clenched and his body was rigid and tense.

My head tilted to the side. "Is there something wrong? Should I change?"

Oliver's nostrils flared and he tore his gaze from mine. An exasperated sigh escaped him as he ran a frustrated hand through his wavy hair. "Nothing is wrong, Luna. We have to go if we want to be there on time."

His voice was hoarse and he avoided my gaze as he

grabbed my bags from where they were sitting in the foyer. Without another word or a glance in my direction, he disappeared through the front door, leaving me behind with nothing but confusion plaguing my mind.

I called out to my mother to let her know I'd be back later, and clipped Tank's leash to his collar. Leading him along beside me, I headed out through the front door and pulled it shut behind me. In typical gentlemanly Oliver fashion, he was standing by my door, holding it open. The back door was left open for Tank, too.

A smile touched my lips, but it didn't reach my eyes. Oliver was still refusing to look at me and his jaw was clenched so tightly, I was afraid his teeth might break. As I reached the back of the car, Tank climbed in and I shut the door before walking to my seat.

"We don't have to do whatever this is, Ollie," I told him, my voice soft as I hesitated to climb into his car.

This time, his eyes met mine and he looked at me with pain laced in his irises. "I promised you we would check off your list. We're doing it, whether I like it or not."

His words played over in my head as I climbed into the car and he shut the door behind me. Oliver was silent the entire drive into town and when we pulled into the parking lot of one of the fancier steak houses, it suddenly clicked in my mind.

He wasn't taking me anywhere to be with him. He was bringing me here for the blind date I said I wanted to go on.

Oliver killed the engine, but he move. His knuckles were stark white as he clutched the steering wheel and stared straight ahead through the windshield.

"Your date is waiting inside for you." He paused, his

throat bobbing as he swallowed roughly. "Tell the hostess you're with the Hart party of two. She'll take you to him."

My throat grew thick with emotion and suddenly all of this felt wrong. "You're not coming in?"

Oliver slowly turned his head to the side to look at me, his eyes slicing to mine. "You don't need me, Luna. I'll be out here if you do."

He was wrong.

So goddamn wrong.

I needed Oliver Hart more than I ever needed anyone in my life. He was my anchor, my lifeline, and I couldn't help but feel like the rope that tethered us together was beginning to fray.

"Go, Luna," Oliver practically whispered. His expression morphed into something resembling deep, guttural pain. "You're going to be late."

I swallowed hard over the lump lodged in my throat and nodded. I was the one who wanted to do this, and Oliver was simply helping me. Pulling the handle of the door, I pushed it open and let myself out. I grabbed my smaller bag from the backseat and took Tank with me as we left Oliver in the car.

When I walked inside and told the hostess exactly what Oliver had instructed, she smiled brightly and led me to the table. There was a guy sitting at a table and he rose to his feet when he saw me. His eyes were bright blue, his nose perfectly straight and his jawline was sharp. When he smiled and flashed his white teeth, dimples grew in his cheeks.

"You must be Luna," he said as he greeted me, holding his hand out to shake mine. "Oliver told me a lot about you. I'm Lucas."

My eyebrows furrowed. "How do you know Oliver?"

"We played football together in a rec league during the summer last year," he admitted with a smile as he walked over and pulled my chair out for me. He paused and his eyes widened as he took in Tank's appearance. "That's a big ass dog."

A soft laugh fell from my lips and I sat down, motioning for Tank to lay down as Lucas pushed my chair in. "He's harmless."

I watched Lucas as he walked around to the other side of the table and took his seat. There was nothing threatening or intimidating about the guy. Under his gaze that was free of any judgment, I suddenly felt self-conscious.

I wish I had brought a sweater to cover up. I wanted to pull my hair free and let it cover part of the stupid tube sticking out of my neck.

"Tell me about yourself, Luna. I was actually surprised to hear from Oliver since we hadn't seen each other since last summer but when he told me he wanted to set me up on a blind date, I couldn't resist."

I shrugged, smiling nervously. "There's not much to tell. Oliver and I have been checking things off my bucket list before he leaves for college in the fall."

Lucas' face fell momentarily and there wasn't a part of me that didn't doubt it was from the mention of my bucket list. "Are you going to college or staying home?"

"I'm actually just going to go to the local community college," I told him, my voice unsteady. "It makes more sense for me to stay home and be closer to my doctors and everything."

Lucas nodded and smiled, but I couldn't help but feel like there was an awkwardness between us. I mean, he was a complete stranger, but he was finding out the truth about my life. I knew this blind date wouldn't go any further than this table at the restaurant and I was completely okay with it.

Lucas looked past me, his eyebrows tugging together as he tilted his head to the side. "Oliver," he said with confusion. "What's up, man?"

My heart skipped a beat in my chest and my breath caught in my throat as I turned around to look where Lucas' gaze was landing. Oliver was less than a foot behind me with that intense storm in his eyes.

"I'm sorry, bro, but this date is over."

"What do you mean?" Lucas asked him. He fell silent for a moment as Oliver moved toward the side of the table and a knowing look passed across Lucas' expression. He directed his eyes back to me as he fought back a smile. "It was really nice meeting you, Luna."

I watched as confusion and excitement danced in my veins as Lucas rose to his feet. Words stuck in my throat and I couldn't get anything out as I stupidly nodded at him and watched him disappear from my sight.

Oliver sat down in Lucas' seat.

"What are you doing?" I questioned him, my voice low and slightly harsh. "You can't just come in and crash my date."

"The hell I can't." He chuckled as he scooted in his chair and picked up the menu. "I set the date up and I decided that it was over."

A frustrated sigh escaped me. "Well, now we can't cross it off my list."

Oliver stared at me, his gaze thoughtful as his eyes slowly searched mine. Something about the way he was looking at me had my stomach doing flips and it suddenly felt like someone turned the heat on in the restaurant.

I watched him as he picked up the cloth napkin and rose to his feet. Oliver walked over to me, stepping behind me. He lifted the napkin to my face and placed it over my eyes before he tied a knot in it around the back of my head.

His hands landed on my shoulders and his breath was warm against my ear as he leaned forward. "You wanted a blind date, so that's what I'm giving you. You can't see with the napkin covering your eyes so you're practically blind. And I'm your date now."

I fought the urge to pull the fabric away from my face and instead I rode the euphoric feeling of excitement. Using my other senses, I felt Oliver's hands lift from my shoulders and I listened to him walk back to the other side of the table.

"Did Lucas text you and say he needed you to come end the date?" I asked Oliver as I began to second guess it all. Instinctively, I reached up to touch my throat. "I knew I shouldn't have worn this dress."

"Luna, stop it," Oliver practically growled. His hand wrapped around mine, pulling it back to the table and he held it while he stroked the skin on the back of my hand with his thumb. "You look absolutely stunning. Lucas didn't say anything to me. I was the one who couldn't stand it anymore. I couldn't stand the thought of knowing someone else was in here occupying your time. I'm selfish, Luna Truly. I don't want to share you with the rest of the world. I want you all to myself."

My breath caught in my throat as the air between us grew thick with emotion. His words swirled around in my mind and I couldn't let them go. They were permanently imprinted into my soul and there was nothing that could ever erase them.

Pulling my hand away from Oliver's I reached behind my head and undid the knot in the napkin. I removed the fabric from my face and Oliver's eyes searched mine as I neatly folded it before placing it on the table beside me.

"Why did you take it off?" Oliver questioned me as he leaned forward and rested his arms on the table. "What about your blind date?"

A smile lifted the corners of my lips and I stared back at the boy I loved with my entire heart. "Blind dates are overrated. I prefer unblind dates instead."

Oliver smiled back at me as he lifted his glass of water in the air. "To unblind dates."

I clinked my glass against his and an ease settled in my bones. I wanted a blind date to see what it was about, but I never needed any of that. Everything I ever needed was sitting right across from me, and I didn't want to share him with the rest of the world either.

He wanted me all to himself.

And I would gladly give him every piece of me, including my very last breath.

Chapter Eighteen
NOTHING BUT LOVE

"I can't believe we're really doing this," I said to Ollie in a hushed voice as he helped me out of the car. He was dressed like he belonged, wearing a black suit with a gray dress shirt underneath. His tie was a darker shade of gray that matched the chiffon dress I was wearing. "Who's wedding is this again?"

Oliver looked down at me with a smirk and shrugged. "Some girl my mom works with at the hospital. I overheard my mother talking about the wedding to my father and how they wouldn't be able to attend. I managed to grab the invitation to send back before my mom threw it in the trash."

"What if she told her she wasn't able to make it to the wedding, though? What if there isn't actually a place for us?"

Oliver paused outside the door of the church and turned his body to face me. He lifted his hands to cup the sides of my face and stared down into my eyes with those sage green irises of his. "It will all work out, Luna. I sent in the reservation card, so we should be good to go."

Nervousness danced in my stomach and I smiled up at him. "I can't believe we're actually doing this. I've always wanted to see someone get married before and here we are."

Ollie brought his lips down to my forehead where they lingered after he pressed his soft mouth to my skin. He pulled away as a small group of people scooted past us. "Shall we, Mrs. Hart?"

My eyes widened and hearing the words sent a warmth through me. My heart beat erratically in my chest. I nodded at him as I attempted to ignore the visceral feeling. He was calling me by his last name as if we were playing the part, as if his mother and father were attending the wedding.

It meant nothing more.

As much as I loved the way it sounded, I would die with the last name I was born with. Marriage wasn't on my bingo card and Oliver would find a nice girl one day to make Mrs. Oliver Hart.

The church was crowded inside. Most of the pews were already occupied and we managed to slide into seats toward the back of the building. It was decorated with delicate lilac and white flowers while an orchestra played a soft melody. There was something beautiful about it and excitement buzzed in the air as the groom stood at the end of the aisle waiting for his bride.

"What are their names?" I asked Oliver in a hushed voice as I leaned over and spoke into his ear.

Ollie chuckled quietly. "Stephen and Alexandra."

"Do we call them Steve and Alex?"

Ollie shrugged as he leaned back in his seat and wrapped his arm around my shoulders while he pulled me flush against his body. "We'll figure that out after we listen to some other people talk about them. See how they address them and we'll go from there."

"You do know when she sees we're not your parents, she'll probably kick us out."

"It's her wedding day. I'm sure she doesn't give a shit who is really here," Oliver replied in a hushed voice just as the orchestra switched into "Canon in D" by Pachelbel. "Shh, it's starting."

I smiled at Oliver, and turned in my seat with his arm still wrapped around me as we watched the bridal party begin their walk down the aisle. Each walked with poise and precision; it was truly a beautiful ceremony. I watched in awe as they all lined up down at the end with the groom.

And then it was time for the bride.

She looked beautiful in her flowing white gown. Her hair was in loose curls, half up and half down as it hung down the center of her back. I remembered her from one of the picnics the Harts had before. She was in her late twenties, so she wasn't exactly close friends with Oliver's mom, but I had seen her before.

Everyone in the church rose to their feet, and I watched the groom's face transform as his bride walked down the aisle toward him. There was a moment of shock, of pure bliss and then it looked as if he was desperately trying to hold back the tears threatening to spring from his eyes.

His face shone brightly and he lit up more than I had ever seen someone before. It was a magical moment and something I had never experienced. You could feel their love radiating over the crowd, situating itself under your skin. Oliver held me tighter as we took our seats.

I listened intently, although it was difficult to make out all the words they were saying from how far back we were sitting. None of that really mattered. Just watching the way their bodies were speaking to one another was more than enough. The entire building was overflowing with joy and love and I was reveling in it all, soaking up every last drop I could catch.

When it was time for the two of them to exchange vows, their voices got even quieter. There was an intimacy that came with giving yourself fully to another person. Vows were sacred, and sometimes the words spoken were only meant for the two souls aligned to absorb.

I wiped tears from my eyes as I was overcome with emotion and watched as the bride did the same as her groom spoke special words just for her.

Oliver rubbed my arm and I looked up at him, my eyes still filled with tears. His expression was soft, his touch gentle and he reached up to catch my tears with the pad of his thumb. Neither of us spoke any words, but we didn't need to. We were at someone else's wedding, yet it felt like no one around us existed.

The only thing that mattered was Oliver and the way he was looking at me.

His face was bright, full of wonderment and nothing less than adoring. He stared at me like I was the sun shining brightly in his sky and it really settled in my soul.

It was the same way the groom stared at his bride as she walked down the aisle toward him.

With nothing but love...

Everyone around us began to clap while some were

hooting and hollering, cheering for the couple as they kissed in front of everyone at the altar. Oliver and I both rose to our feet and clapped along with the rest of the crowd as the newlyweds walked down the aisle and through the front doors of the church.

Oliver and I hung back for a few moments as we waited for some of the other guests to clear out. We filed along with the others as we went through the front door. From what Ollie had told me, the reception was being held at a different location that wasn't far from here.

We walked back out to his car, both of us floating on a cloud from the euphoric moment of watching a couple unite. It was a short drive to the reception hall and when we walked inside, it took my breath away. It was even more breathtaking than the church had been and was decorated with the same delicate flowers.

"This place is absolutely amazing," I told Oliver as we walked over to the table with the list of guests and seating chart. Ollie simply looked at me and winked as he slid his hand into mine. He scanned the list and pointed at the number fourteen for the table we were seated at.

"Did you recognize any of the other names on the list?" I asked him in a hushed voice as he led me over to the table. There was only one other couple sitting there when we reached our destination and they didn't notice us at first.

Oliver shook his head. "I'm fairly certain I don't know a single person here."

He smiled at me, and I laughed lightly as he pulled out my chair for me to sit down. We had decided to leave all my medical equipment in the car and it was truly as if we were two completely different people. I also left Tank at home which felt very strange, but there was a part of me that was thoroughly enjoying all of this.

It was like none of my medical conditions mattered. Like I didn't have an expiration date I was living past. It was as if I was just like every other person in the room, here to celebrate the happy couple without any other worries in this moment.

The night flew by and much to my surprise, no one noticed us. We sat at the table with the other guests where we watched the bridal party make their entrance and start the typical wedding reception routine, including the first dance. I had never been to one before but I watched my fair share of *Four Weddings* on TLC. TV sucked in the middle of the day and I spent many days laid up just watching whatever was on at the time.

We were served our meals, and I was grateful that Oliver had selected the fish for me. It was all divine and such a magical evening and experience. As people made their way to the dance floor, I found myself sitting there as a heaviness weighed on my chest.

The bride was in the center, holding up a glass of champagne as she danced around. All of her friends and family surrounded her, dancing around her as they cele-brated this moment. Her husband stepped toward her, taking her hand in his as they danced together.

A deep sadness rooted itself in my bones as reality reared her ugly face.

This was a moment I would never experience firsthand...

I would only ever be on the outside looking in.

Oliver's palm was soft against the exposed skin on my back. He slid his hand across to my shoulder and his breath was warm against my neck as he leaned forward to speak to me.

"Dance with me, Luna."

I slowly turned around to face him, the tears burning my eyes as I rapidly attempted to blink them away. The sadness was overwhelming and the way Oliver was looking at me sent me over the edge. Without a word, I abruptly rose to my feet and jogged out of the room until I was running through the front doors and out onto the sidewalk.

My chest was tight and my throat constricted as I stopped on the sidewalk and bent over. I inhaled deeply, attempting to suck in any molecule of oxygen I could get, but it didn't help with the suffocating feeling that was consuming me. All of it was too much.

"Luna." Oliver's voice came from behind me, but I didn't lift my head. I didn't look in his direction. Instead, I closed my eyes tighter and wished I could just vanish into thin air. I didn't want him to see me like this, on the verge of a mental breakdown, struggling to breathe.

Oliver had seen me in worse condition, but this time was different.

Tonight brought a reality check I wasn't expecting, and it hit like a ton of bricks to my chest.

"Luna," he said again, this time his voice was closer and I could feel his presence consuming me. Any oxygen left in the air surrounding me was extinguished by him. He wrapped his hands around the tops of my arms and dropped to his knees in front of me. "What's going on, love?"

It took every ounce of strength to lift my head and look at Oliver, but I did it. And one look at my face was all he needed to know I was struggling. His throat bobbed and he rose to his feet as I stood up straight. "It's too much, Ollie. It's all too fucking much."

"I'll take you to the car or go get your bags. You'll be okay, I'm here."

"I don't need my damn bags, Oliver," I snapped at him, although my voice was hoarse and thick with emotion. It was barely audible with the way I was struggling to breathe.

His eyes searched mine with such desperation, it was heartbreaking. "What's too much, Luna? Tell me what you need, what can I do?"

"Life is too much, and there's nothing anyone can do about it." My voice cracked around my words and I finally broke, shattering into a million pieces in front of Oliver. "I'll never have that in there," I told him as I pointed toward the venue. "I'll never have any of it."

Oliver pulled me to him, wrapping his arms around me as he held me close. I buried my face in his chest and let my emotions pull me deep within the depths. The waves of sadness and longing crashed around me and the saltiness of my tears mirrored the ocean.

Wrapping my arms around his waist, I fisted the back of his suit jacket in my hands. Tears soaked his shirt and sobs tore through my body with such reverence. I spent many years trying to suppress these feelings. I didn't want to burden anyone with my emotions when I was already a burden on every life I touched.

Yet I couldn't hold it in any longer. It was as if witnessing this wedding made me realize just how fleeting my life really was. All of the times I laid in the hospital, with doctors and my family convinced it was finally time, didn't come close to how this moment made me feel.

It made me feel extremely hopeless and just fucking heartbroken.

"Luna, love," Oliver murmured into my hair as he held me close. He slowly stroked my back with his hand and I just wanted to melt into him. "It's all going to be okay."

"I'm drowning, Oliver," I cried against him, my sobs subsiding as I was slowly regaining control over my emotions. "I can't breathe and I feel like I'm sinking."

He wrapped his arms tighter around me as he rested his head against mine. "Let me be your life vest. Hold onto me and I'll never let you sink."

It was like a weight lifted off my chest. The sadness still lingered. It was festering in my soul, entangling itself in the fibers of my being, but it wasn't foreign. It became a part of me, it just wasn't a part I revealed to the rest of the world. Hearing his words, his voice, him holding me close —it felt like I could actually breathe again.

Embarrassment began to creep in as I felt myself coming back down from the strange high of my borderline mental breakdown. I shouldn't have let my emotions get the better of me like that.

"I'm so sorry for that, Ollie," I murmured against his chest and cringed as I realized just how soaked the material was from my tears. "I don't know what came over me, but I just couldn't hold it in any longer."

Oliver pulled his head back, just far enough to look at me while he kept his arms around me. "Don't do that, Luna. Don't ever minimize your feelings or your emotions. They're more valid than anything else." He paused for a moment, his eyes bouncing back and forth between mine. "I meant what I said. I promise you I'll never let you sink."

"You won't be able to hold me up forever," I whispered, not fully trusting my voice. "One day, you're going to have to let me go…"

"I'll never let you go. Where you go, I go, love. It's that simple."

I tilted my head to the side, tears filling my eyes again. "Where I'm going, you can't come with me."

"Well, if you get there before me, then promise me you'll wait for me to get there too."

"I promise," I whispered, smiling up at him through my tears.

Oliver smiled back at me, his face dipping down as he gently pressed his lips to mine. He stole the air from my lungs before breathing life back into me. As he pulled away, a mischievous smirk pulled on his lips. "What about that dance?"

My eyebrows pulled together and I looked around us. We were still standing on the sidewalk in the darkness of the night as the reception continued inside the building behind me. Cars were driving up and down the street behind Oliver with their lights shining through the dark.

"Out here?"

Oliver nodded, his eyes shining brightly at me.

"But there's no music."

He reached for my hands and lifted them up to his neck. Instinctively, I wrapped my arms around the back of his neck and he slid his down to my waist. With our bodies pressed against one another, I rested my head against his chest and listened to the steady sound of his heart beating as he buried his face in my hair.

"Just close your eyes and listen, Luna. The music is all around us and inside of us. You just have to open your heart and let your soul feel it."

Oliver began to sway back and forth, moving me along with him. I fell in step with his rhythm and together we danced to the music of our own souls. The seed had been planted many years ago and now he was rooted in my soul as the love blossomed between us.

I never knew home could be a person until he burrowed himself deep within my fragile heart.

Oliver Hart was my home.

Chapter Nineteen
HOT CHOCOLATE IN JULY

The night of the wedding, Oliver didn't give me any false hope that I would one day experience getting married myself. And I was eternally grateful for that. Given the fact I already outlived what the doctors expected, anything was realistically possible. But it was the false hope that was worse than anything.

It was better to expect the worst, to be prepared for every worst case scenario and to always hope things would work out differently. I was a firm believer in the universe giving back what you put out into it, but I think its powers could only work so far. Anything beyond that would be a damn miracle and those weren't exactly handed out like candy on Halloween night.

Maybe life would keep me around long enough to get married, but then again, there was the thought of who I would even want that with. There was one person who I could see myself spending the rest of my life with but I would never put him in that position.

Come to think of it, I didn't think I would want to put

anyone in that position, whoever they might be. It would just be a selfish move on my part. My incessant need to want to be able to do normal things in life would just cause someone the most devastating heartbreak.

Who would want to marry someone, knowing one day soon they would lose their spouse? I couldn't go into an arrangement like that knowing I would leave someone as a widower.

"You're quiet today," Oliver mused out loud as we sat in our treehouse in his backyard. He texted me earlier and asked if I wanted to hangout, but my mind was preoccupied and still thinking about the wedding from the weekend. "Penny for your thoughts?"

I looked over at him and tilted my head. "Does anyone actually carry pennies anymore?"

Oliver stared at me for a moment. "You know, that's a valid question. Cash and change are almost obsolete at this point."

"Exactly... So how are you going to pay for my thoughts without a penny?"

"I could cash app you or something?" Oliver replied with a smirk and a shrug. He always had some remark to come back at me with and never failed to amuse me.

I smiled back at him and shook my head. "Nice try."

The last thing I wanted was to divulge my thoughts to him after that night. It was the first time I broke down in front of him like that and I wasn't about to explain what I was thinking about again. It was borderline embarrassing and I'd rather forget it happened. I knew he genuinely cared and I knew I had been a little distant, and I was sure it was confusing him.

However, that didn't mean I wanted to talk to him about my thoughts on marriage.

Lord, how much more embarrassing would that be than my minor mental breakdown?

"So, I was thinking... I don't really have anything planned for us today, but how would you feel about going ice skating?" Oliver asked me, almost shyly.

We both grew up in Vermont. He was athletic and had ice skated numerous times. He used to play ice hockey but didn't go any further than playing recreationally since football was his true love. Me, on the other hand—I had never been on the ice once in my life.

"It's the middle of the summer..." I reminded him, my eyebrows pulling together. "Do any of the rinks even have anything going on?"

Oliver nodded. "Regal Rink has a public skate this afternoon. I don't know how busy it gets, but I figured it was something we could check off at least." Oliver paused for a moment as he cocked an eyebrow at me. "For the record, you were the one who added ice skating to your summer bucket list."

"Maybe I should take it off the list then," I told him, attempting to play it off as if his logic with it being summer was the sole reason.

I was actually terrified to put on a pair of skates. What would happen if I fell? I'm not saying I was going to die or anything, but I could seriously injure myself.

Oliver shook his head at me as he rose to his feet. "Nope. You put it on the list and we're doing it. Plus, you live in a hockey town and have never been ice skating before. It's a little weird if you ask me."

I climbed to my feet and inched closer to him, playfully

challenging him. "Excuse me? I'm sorry I'm not in the habit of breaking any of my bones. I think I get poked and prodded enough by the doctors."

"Calm down, killer." Ollie laughed at me. "You're not going to break a bone and you wanted it on your list. I'm just here to serve you, my queen."

I laughed at Ollie and the ease between us. My mind momentarily drifted back to the wedding when he held me close and we danced out on the street. He'll never know how much that meant to me and the way he constantly made me feel.

"You're doing it again, Luna."

His voice brought me back to reality, and I glanced over at him. He had moved over to where the doorway was to leave the treehouse and I hadn't even noticed because I was too in my head. He watched me carefully.

I winced and gave him an apologetic smile as I walked over to him. "Sorry. I'm just a little distracted today."

"I can tell," he murmured to me as he held open the door for me to pass by him. "I would give anything to see inside that beautiful mind."

I laughed lightly, half choking on my breath as I walked down the steps in front of him. "Trust me, it's a mess in there."

"What a beautiful mess it must be, though," he mused out loud and my heart skipped a beat.

Neither of us spoke another word as we walked through his backyard and around the side of the house. Tank was lying by the tree still and hadn't noticed that we were out of the treehouse. Oliver whistled to him and he came running.

"I don't know if we can take him to the rink. I mean,

I'm sure we can, but I don't know how he would go on the ice."

I glanced down at my dog. "Sorry, bud. You're going to have to hang out at the house until I get back."

It was almost as if Tank could understand the words I was speaking with the way he gave me those puppy dog eyes even though he wasn't exactly small anymore. He followed me through the gate connecting the Harts backyard and ours. I took Tank into the house and left him with a treat before grabbing my bags and heading out the front door.

Oliver was already waiting on the front porch and took the bags from me without a single word. Gentleman Oliver. He was predictable and part of me appreciated that. There were so many variables in my life, but knowing I could count on him and knowing what to expect with him helped ease my anxiety immensely.

I followed him out to his car and we hopped in before making our way to the ice rink. Oliver turned the music up loud enough that I didn't feel like we had to have a conversation. Not that I didn't want to talk to him, but he knew I was in my own little world and he was respecting it. I couldn't ask for any more than that and the sentiment was enough to warm my soul.

Which was a stark contrast to how damn cold the ice rink was when we stepped inside.

"I feel extremely unprepared," I admitted to Ollie as I wrapped my arms around my body. Given it was summer, I didn't think to put on anything other than a t-shirt. I already had a pair of leggings on and thankfully wore socks and sneakers.

I failed to think about anything else I may have needed.

"And it's a good thing I came prepared." Ollie winked at me as he motioned down to an extra bag I hadn't noticed he brought. He set it down on a bench and reached inside. He pulled out one of his hoodies and handed it to me, along with a pair of gloves.

I watched him as he put on his own sweatshirt and I pulled the one he gave me over my head. Instinctively, I closed my eyes and inhaled deeply, breathing in his scent that still lingered in the fabric. As I opened my eyes, I met Oliver's gaze and a fire was burning in his irises as he carefully watched me.

Heat crept up my neck before spreading across my cheeks.

"One last thing," Oliver murmured as he reached back into the bag and stepped into my space. He lifted his hands above my head, pulling a beanie down over it. His hands were soft and warm against my skin as they lingered on the sides of my face, slowly trailing down my neck before he grabbed the hood and pulled it over my head. "Perfect."

Oliver left me by the bench and went over to get me a pair of rental skates. He had his own pair and left them sitting in the bag on the bench. When he returned, he helped me get mine on and tied them for me before tying his own.

"Are you ready to do this?" he asked, holding his hand out for me.

I nodded and slowly slid my palm against his as he helped me onto my feet. My ankles wobbled and it felt extremely unnatural standing on a set of blades. There had been many times in my life I felt unsteady on my feet but none of them were remotely comparable to how this felt.

"I guess I'm as ready as I'll ever be," I told him as I attempted to bury the nervous feelings circulating through me. There was no way I was going to be able to do this across a sheet of ice, considering the fact I could barely even walk in these things.

Oliver smiled at me, giving me a knowing look that said he knew I was more nervous than I should be. When we went on the Ferris wheel, that freaked me out because of the height. This was a whole different type of fear.

He stepped out onto the ice first and then turned to help me. My right foot slid in the opposite direction as soon as it touched the slippery surface. It was the weirdest feeling. The lack of control over your body even as you try to tell it how to move. It was something I experienced time and time again and in a way, it was almost triggering.

My heart pounded erratically in my chest and I sucked in a breath as my breathing grew shallow. Oliver was patient and waited quietly as I mustered up the courage to put my other foot on the ice.

"See, it's not that bad," Oliver said softly as he turned to face me and held both of my hands. He started to skate backward and his movements were effortless. He was pulling me along with him, moving slowly, but I bent my knees and held on for dear life.

I was certain I would be falling on my ass at one point today.

"Don't go so fast," I muttered at him, my voice shifting into more of a panicked tone. His gaze met mine and he abruptly stopped, causing me to run into him.

My feet slipped and were moving out from under my

body. As I began to fall, Oliver put his arms around me, lifting me up before I had the chance to hit the ice.

"I got you, Luna love," he murmured as he steadied me on my feet. "I won't let you fall."

His words were comforting and there wasn't a part of me that didn't believe him. If Oliver had the power to, he would keep me as safe as possible. But things didn't always work out that way, and I couldn't help but be a little skeptical as to whether or not he would be able to catch me every single time.

I got my feet underneath me again, and Oliver moved both of us over to the edge of the rink, where I was able to hold onto the boards. Putting my right hand on the side, I held onto his hand with my left and attempted to move my feet of my own accord. Other skaters moved past us like it was nothing, and I lifted my head and watched them in awe as they moved around the rink with such ease.

It was beautiful, watching the way some of them skated. There were a few kids who were younger than us skating around like they lived on skates. You could easily pick out the hockey kids from the ones who just did it for fun. And then you had the ones who were clearly figure skaters with how they moved. They moved almost as if a melody flowed through their veins.

It was beautiful, and I suddenly felt envious as I shuffled my own feet across the ice, moving as slow as a sloth.

"You're doing great, Luna," Oliver encouraged me as he slowly skated beside me. I couldn't help but feel like I was slowing him down in a sense, but he didn't bother to complain.

That was Oliver and his gentle soul.

"I wish I could skate like that."

Oliver followed my gaze as we watched one of the girls' skate past, shifting her weight from foot to foot in the most elegant movement. "You do know that most people who skate like that have been skating since they were kids, right? They're the ones who are always here, always on the ice."

"Sometimes I just feel like there's nothing I have that is mine, you know? Like, you play football, people have different hobbies and activities. Different things they are good at… I don't know if I have a single skill or attribute to be honest. Hell, I'm not even good at breathing, which is the most basic thing someone could do."

Oliver cut me off, his skates sliding across the ice as he stopped in front of me and blocked my way. "What are you talking about, Luna? You are good at a lot of things. The violin. Drawing. Writing. You don't give yourself enough credit." He stopped for a second. "Where the hell is all this coming from? Something has been off with you. Am I ruining your summer by doing your list with you?"

The sadness in his words hit my chest harder than I expected. His eyes searched mine in a panic, but there was a hesitancy. He never wanted to be the one who pushed too hard. Always forever gentle.

"Not at all," I told him with a sigh. "I just—I don't know what my problem is."

"You know, you're always the sunshine on the cloudiest of days. You don't have to be, though." He reached up to adjust my beanie, his hands lingering as he smiled down at me. "Honestly, I like this other side of you. It isn't one we get to see very often and it means a lot to me."

"What do you mean? *I* don't like this side of me. I want

to be the sunshine person who just smiles and keeps on moving through life. Instead, I keep overthinking everything and these damn emotions are really starting to get to me."

Oliver stared at me, tilting his head to the side as he absentmindedly played with the strings of my hood. "Sometimes, I used to wonder if you were actually human."

His words caught me off guard, and I looked at him in shock. "Because I had a machine that breathes for me?"

Ollie rolled his eyes and let out an exasperated sigh. "No, Luna. I don't give a shit about any of your medical stuff." He stopped, his eyes widening and a wave of regret passed through his irises. "That sounded worse than what I meant. What I mean is I don't see any of that and I haven't since we were kids. You're Luna Truly, the best person I know. Fuck the rest."

I get lost in his eyes momentarily as his words penetrate my soul.

"No one is happy every moment of their life. We're supposed to feel a myriad of emotions and it's okay to let yourself feel them." Oliver slides his hands under my hood and cups the sides of my face. "It almost seemed unhuman, but now you're showing me this side instead. I'm glad you feel comfortable enough around me."

"I don't know what I feel around you anymore," I mumbled more to myself, but the words were never supposed to leave my internal thoughts. As soon as they left my mouth, I could feel the shock in my expression.

Oliver chuckled. "I'm going to let that go for now, but just know we're having a conversation later. You don't get to drop a bomb like that and not expect me to ask questions."

"I didn't mean to say that…"

Oliver simply smiled. "I know, but you did. And now you have no choice but to let me inside that beautiful mind of yours."

He gently pressed his lips to my forehead before moving away from me. The cold air quickly replaced his warmth and my teeth chattered from the ice beneath my feet. Oliver must have felt it and glanced over at me and nodded. Instead of pressuring me to keep skating, he led me off the ice and into the snack bar room where we got some hot chocolate in the middle of July.

Some things in life just didn't make sense and this was one of them.

Instead of questioning it, you just went with it.

You let yourself live.

Chapter Twenty
YOU ARE LIMITLESS AND ENDLESS, LUNA TRULY

"A re you sure you guys don't want a tent?" my mother questioned me as she came down from our attic with two sleeping bags. "We have so much camping equipment we only ever used that one time we went. Do you remember how much of a disaster that was?"

Her words instantly took me back in time, and I smiled at her as I nodded and we both drifted down memory lane together. "We didn't even sleep in the tent. We ended up at a hotel instead."

When I was around ten, my family decided to take a camping trip because it was something we'd never gotten to do. My parents went out and bought everything you could possibly think of to take along, yet it didn't work out like anyone expected. My brothers and Tank were the main causes of the havoc that ensued.

One of my brothers ended up getting covered in poison ivy and was uncomfortable which prompted to getting a hotel room so he could take a bath. Tank found a dead squirrel and decided to bring that into our tent. And then Eli was the one who almost caught all of our things on fire.

"What a night that was," my mother said as nostalgia floated through the space between us. "Thank God we never decided to do that again. I don't think any of us are really camping people."

"No." I laughed along with her. "I don't think any of us are."

"If you want to use a tent, we did save one from that trip. Thankfully, Tank only brought the dead animal into ours so we still have the boys' tent."

I shook my head as I grabbed some blankets and we headed down the stairs together. "That kind of defeats the purpose. I want to sleep under the stars and if I'm in a tent, then I won't be able to do that."

"That makes perfect sense," my mother concurred as we set the things down on the dining room table. "I'm really glad Oliver is doing all of this with you."

"Me too." I smiled at her, feeling the happiness creep in. A lump lodged in my throat as I glanced out back and saw Oliver out there talking with my father.

"What's wrong, sunshine?" my mother questioned me, her voice filled with concern, yet it was soft and gentle. "You've been happy this summer, but there's been a shift in you. Not that I don't like it. You've been wearing your heart and your emotions on your sleeve more, instead of harboring it all inside. I'm glad you're finally settling in and getting your voice."

"I don't know what to do about Oliver," I admitted, my voice hushed. My mother was the only one who I really confided in when it came to things that hopefully wouldn't burden her. I'd been more vocal about my feelings and I know it's been bothering her. "Everything with him is starting to hurt my head. It's making me feel like I'm going crazy."

My mother smiled at me. "Love will do that to you, Luna. When you fall in love with someone, you feel everything with such an intensity. That's what's really been going on, isn't it? This shift with you… it's because of your feelings for him."

I stared at her and nodded, not wanting to admit it out loud. She was right. I was in love with Oliver Hart and it was messing with my emotions more than anything else ever had. "I don't know what to do."

"Have you considered telling him?"

My nostrils flared as I inhaled deeply. "I can't. I can't let him know the truth."

My mother's eyebrows pulled together and she tilted her head at me as she gave me a questioning look. "Why not? What's so bad about him knowing the truth?"

"Because… as much as I want him to feel the same way about me, he can't." I paused for a moment, swallowing back the emotion that grew thick in my throat. "He deserves someone who can give him everything. All I will ever give him is a broken heart."

Sadness filled my mother's eyes and her expression softened as she closed the space between us. "That's not true, Luna. You give that boy more than you will ever realize and as much as you hate it, what he feels isn't within your control. You don't get to decide for him."

"I still can't tell him."

My mother nodded. "Just consider it, okay? You don't have to tell him today or tomorrow, but don't toss out the idea completely."

"I won't," I tell her, although in the back of my mind, I know I won't ever tell him.

The back door opened and my father strolled inside. It had since grown dark outside and I could see the lights Oliver set up for us out there. "I'm going to retire to bed, but you have fun, Looney Tune," my father said as he pressed his lips to the top of my head.

Oliver came inside and winked at me as he grabbed the stuff from the dining room table and carried it outside. He had already taken my ventilator and other equipment outside and had it set up for when it was time to go to sleep.

My mother followed me over to the door as I watched Oliver continue to set things up. Tank kept grabbing the opposite corner of the sleeping bag and gave a tug on it every time Oliver tried to shake it out to make it straight.

"Enjoy your time with him, sunshine," my mother said as she pulled me in for a warm hug and mimicked my father, kissing the top of my head. "And think about telling him how you really feel."

My arm pressed against my chest and I felt a twinge of pain by the central line threaded under my skin. As my mother released me, the pressure relieved itself and I felt the sensation dissipating into more of an annoying ache.

Stepping away from my mother, I walked through the back door and out into the yard where Oliver was waiting. He sat down on one of the sleeping bags and motioned for me to join him. As I sat down beside him, Tank pushed his way between the two of us and flopped down onto the mounds of blankets and sleeping bags.

It was kind of cute. Oliver set up a bunch of blankets on the ground to take away from how uncomfortable it was before laying two sleeping bags side by side. I loved how there was never any pressure or expectations from him. He really just followed whatever I wanted to do and never made a move without making sure I was okay with it.

But in the back of my mind, I knew he was an eighteen-year-old guy who'd had sex before. He'd kissed other girls. He was experienced in ways I wasn't. There was a weird expectation from me that he should be trying to make a different kind of move on me. That's what guys did when they liked a girl, right?

Oliver may have kissed me a few times now, but he never tried to take it any further than that.

Perhaps he didn't have feelings for me like I did for him.

"So, I know we're supposed to be out in nature and everything, but I did bring my laptop in case you want to watch a movie or something," Oliver told me sheepishly as he lifted his laptop case from beside him. "I've never done this before, so I don't know what people really do outside like this."

I glanced around, taking in the few lights Oliver had set up. My parents were kind enough to turn off all the outdoor lights, and I'm assuming Oliver's parents knew too because there wasn't a single light coming from his house.

"I don't really know. I think we're just supposed to lay here and stare at the stars. You know, think about the universe and stuff."

Oliver smiled at my stupid explanation. My brain felt like it was stumbling over itself and I just let it go. Neither of us got underneath our sleeping bags as we both laid down. Ollie waited until I was comfortable before turning off the small battery powered lights he had.

Tank shifted between us and my eyes adjusted to the lack of light. Even though we were in the suburbs, you were still able to see so many stars in the sky. It was a clear night with not a single cloud in sight. I'd stargazed before, but never like this. Never with such intent where it really made it possible to feel like you were staring at a million shimmering lights.

"There's so many stars," Oliver mused out loud. "We just have to stay up until two o'clock, right?"

I didn't look over at Oliver, but I nodded anyway. "That's when it's supposed to be the best time to view the meteor shower tonight," I told him. "The peak times are between two and four."

"We can do that," he declared as he lifted his phone to look at it. "Only three more hours."

It worked out perfectly. Ollie knew I loved meteorology and he actually did his research before picking tonight as the night for us to sleep under the stars. He looked up everything he could find about meteor showers and when he saw there was going to be one tonight, it sealed the deal on our little adventure.

Tank moved again and a small sound of air passed from him. My eyes widened and I glanced over at Oliver who looked horrified, considering the fact Tank's rear end was pointed in both of our directions.

"Oh, hell no!"

"Tank!"

He lifted his lazy head and turned back to look at us, not knowing what the fuss was about. The smell was putrid and I started pushing him away as Oliver gagged. I couldn't stop the laughter as it bubbled out of me, tears springing to my eyes as I attempted to move the two hundred pounds of stink between us.

Oliver started laughing along with me and tried to help me, even though the smell was clearly bothering him.

"What the hell do you feed this beast? Dead animals?!"

I laughed even harder, snorting as I flopped onto my back and gave up trying to move my dog. Oliver finally got him to move and he sighed, blowing out hot air as he rose to his feet and moved off the blankets. Tank almost looked ashamed of himself as he made his way onto our back deck and laid down where he could still see me.

Tears streamed down my cheeks and my stomach and face hurt from laughing so hard. "I am so sorry." I laughed, rolling over to look at Ollie. "He tends to do that from time to time."

"I get it." Ollie laughed along with me as he rolled to face me. "He's a gross dog, but goddamn. That smell could raise someone from their grave."

The smell dissipated and our laughter began to subside. "I really am sorry. I didn't expect him to do that."

"I don't think that's something anyone could ever be prepared for." Ollie chuckled. His gaze scanned my face and he reached out to me, absentmindedly brushing away the tears from my face. "I like these. These are the good kind of tears."

"You're peculiar, Oliver Hart." I smiled at him as he continued to collect the moisture with the pads of his thumbs.

"Mmm," he murmured as he lifted his sage eyes to mine. "And why is that, love?"

"You're the only person I know who likes tears."

"They glisten on your skin. Your eyes shimmer with them. I don't like your sad tears, but your happy ones are one of my favorite things." He slid his hand underneath the side of my face pressed to the pillow and he scooted closer to me, closing the distance between us. "You wanna know a secret, Luna Truly?"

My breath caught in my throat and excitement simultaneously filled me. I nodded as he looked down at my lips and back to my eyes.

"You're my most favorite thing ever."

My stomach did a somersault and the butterflies in my stomach fluttered rapidly. Oliver lifted his other hand to the opposite side of my face as he stared at me. It felt as if my heart was going to beat out of my chest. The annoying pain around my central line vanished and all I could focus on was the heat that was burning from his green eyes.

"I really want to kiss you right now, Luna."

My tongue darted out to wet my lips. This was the perfect moment to put space between us and take a step back. Instead, I decided to take a step forward, into the unknown. "Well, what are you waiting for?"

A smirk pulled on Oliver's lips as he moved closer, his face dipping down to mine. My eyelids fluttered shut and I felt the warmth of his lips as he pressed them to mine. He was gentle and tender in his movements. His thumb stroked the side of my face as he slid his other hand down my body until he was wrapping his arm around my lower back and pulling me flush against him.

He was warm, and I pressed my hands against his firm chest. I could feel his muscles and athletic body beneath his t-shirt. Oliver slid his tongue into my mouth and it danced with my own. Curiosity got the better of me and I let my hands begin to explore the planes of his body and I slowly slid them down his torso and across his sculpted abdomen.

Oliver groaned into my mouth and the air left my lungs in a rush when I felt something hard pressed against the top of my thigh. It was something I'd never felt before, but I wasn't naive. I knew the male anatomy and what happened when someone got turned on.

Oliver had a boner right now and it was throbbing against my leg.

An unfamiliar sound escaped me and Ollie's mouth moved with reverent need against mine. Something shifted between us and while he was still tender, there was more urgency with his movements. He shifted his hips slightly, pressing his erection harder against me.

My hands were still wandering and I didn't realize how low they were going until my fingertips were brushing the waistband of his pants.

Ollie abruptly pulled back and we were both out of breath. My chest rose and fell in rapid succession and he sucked in a shallow breath.

"Fuck, Luna," he murmured, resting his forehead against mine. "You have no idea what you do to me… well, maybe you do now."

A choked laugh forced its way out of my mouth. I opened my eyes briefly and studied Oliver's mouth as we gave ourselves the opportunity to get our breathing under control. The way we kissed was foreign to me, yet it felt so familiar.

He felt familiar because he was where I belonged.

"I don't want you to think we stopped because I don't want you," Oliver murmured as he kept his forehead to mine, his arm still wrapped around my waist. "I want you more than anything, but I will never ask that of you if you don't want it."

I swallowed roughly over the lump lodged in my throat. "What if I told you I do want it?"

Oliver abruptly pulled away from me, his eyes searching mine. "What did you mean by what you said when we were ice skating—that you don't know what you feel around me anymore?"

Shit.

This was the conversation I had been avoiding. I was thankful he hadn't brought it up before now and there was a part of me hoping maybe he'd forgotten. *Silly, Luna. Oliver never forgets.*

"I don't know," I whispered, and looked past him as I attempted to brush it off. "I didn't mean anything by it."

"Bullshit, Luna," he growled, his eyes focusing in on mine as they burned holes through my irises. "You look past me when you're lying. Tell me the truth."

I directed my gaze back to his. "I can't do that."

"Why the hell not?" he questioned me, his voice firm, yet still gentle.

"Because I will only hurt you in the end."

His eyes softened and he tightened his grip around me. "Luna, Luna, Luna. You could break me into a million fucking pieces and I wouldn't care."

"I would," I admitted as my eyes bounced back and forth between his. "Who would pick up the pieces?"

"Fuck the pieces. I wouldn't even want them if it wasn't you putting them back in place."

"Ollie…" I started as my voice trailed off. I let out the breath I didn't realize I was holding. "I can't give you what you deserve. I can't give you more than the moment happening between us and you know that."

He shook his head at me and his frown cut deep. "I don't accept that, Luna. You have more than this single moment and you know that. That's not what it is. You're scared, and I don't know why. What are you so afraid of?"

"You!" I practically shouted at him as I pushed away from him and sat up in a rush.

Oliver didn't miss a beat and sat up with me, instantly entering my personal space as he positioned himself front of me. "Why are you afraid of me?"

"Because you make me want what I can't have."

He tilted his head to the side, his eyebrows pulling together in confusion. "What's that?"

"A future."

I watched his expression transform and he closed the little amount of space between us, pulling me into his lap. Oliver held my face in his hands, and I instinctively wrapped my arms around his waist as the tears blurred my vision.

"Luna, love," he murmured, and I closed my eyes as he caught my tears with his thumbs again. "A future isn't guaranteed for any of us. Don't limit yourself in life because you think the stars are unreachable for you. You are limitless and endless, Luna Truly. Whether it's in this life or the ones that come after, you continue on for an eternity."

My tears slowed and I let his words seep into every fiber of my being until I felt like it was something I could possibly believe.

"Luna, look at me," he said softly.

My eyelids fluttered open and I could see clearly as I stared back at my best friend—my true soulmate in life.

"I know you're confused about your feelings for me and you don't want to hurt me, so I'm not going to push you. There is one thing I want you to know, though." He paused for a moment as his eyes shined brightly back at me through the darkness. "One day, you're going to fall for me and I promise you I will catch you when you do."

Chapter Twenty-One
LIFE WAITS FOR NO ONE

Twenty-two shooting stars while he held me close.
Twenty-two wishes before we both drifted to sleep.
And every single one was about him.

"What are you always writing in that little journal of yours?"

Oliver's voice broke through my thoughts, and I quickly closed the cover before turning around in my desk chair to look at him. I knew I looked guilty and could feel it written all over my face as my eyes widened when he stepped deeper into my bedroom.

It was my own personal story, yet everyone just assumed it was a journal. A diary. Something I wrote my thoughts down in. And it wasn't necessarily wrong. All of my personal thoughts did go onto the pages, but it wasn't just my thoughts.

It was all of the things I would never be able to tell anyone. It was my soul and I bled all over every single page I touched.

A part of me felt embarrassed, like I had been caught since I was writing about Oliver and sleeping under the stars with him. That was just last night and I couldn't wait to write it all down. I wanted to capture every last memory with Oliver.

If it were all written down, if I wrote it like a story, it wouldn't have to have an ending. It could go on forever and ever.

"It's nothing," I told him sheepishly, and shrugged as he sat down on my bed across from me. "What are you doing here?"

Oliver helped me clean up our stuff in the backyard a few hours ago before he went home to get showered and do who knows what. I didn't ask him and he didn't offer up the information. But seeing him in my bedroom right now had my heart doing things that made me think my cardiologist would recommend I stay away from him.

"I wanted to talk to you about the last thing on your list. You wanted to go see the ocean and I may or may not have been attempting to concoct a plan." He paused for a moment as he leaned forward and propped his elbows on his knees. "I need to know it's something you really want to do before I make the arrangements."

I raised an eyebrow at him. "What are you up to, Ollie?"

"I want to take you to see the ocean, but I think we should make a little trip out of it. It would already be like a mini road trip since we have to drive a few hours, but I think we should make a weekend out of it."

"A weekend?" I questioned him as I lifted my hand and itched at my central line dressing. I needed to ask my mom if she was able to change it because it was starting to irritate my skin. "I don't know if my parents would be okay with that. And don't you leave for football camp soon?"

Oliver was supposed to be leaving in two weeks to head off to college early for camp. He would be back for the last week of summer before leaving for the school year. It was something I was trying to avoid thinking about. I wasn't ready for him to go.

"Don't worry about your parents," he said as he waved his hand at me dismissively. "You let me handle them. I want to know it's something you would be okay with—that it's something you want to do."

"Absolutely."

There was no hesitation, no thinking, no second guessing. Ollie wanted me to live life and experience it all, and I was not about to pass on an opportunity like this. Our family had never taken a trip to the beach before and I couldn't think of anyone else I would rather do this with.

"Really?" Oliver questioned me, the excitement written across his expression. He sat up straighter, his eyes bright and his smile wide. "You really would want to do it?"

"Why wouldn't I? If we take all of my stuff along, and it's not like we're venturing into the jungle. I'm sure there's a hospital close enough, just in case."

He stared at me and I mean really stared at me. "You would be okay with leaving all of this with me? Going for an entire weekend?"

I nodded, smiling back at him, although it was suddenly feeling quite hot in my bedroom from the heat in his gaze. "As long as we get a hotel and don't sleep in a tent. That is one thing I'm never doing again."

"You got it. Hotel for sure." Oliver hopped up to his

feet and the excitement radiated off of him as he jogged toward me and abruptly pressed his lips to mine. "I gotta finish planning. I gotta talk to your parents. We're making this happen, Luna. I don't give a shit what anyone says. I'm getting my girl to the ocean."

He effectively stole the oxygen from the room as he left as quickly as he came, almost as if he were a whirlwind. Those two little words were lingering in the back of my mind and I couldn't get them to go away long after he left.

My girl.

Surely he didn't mean it.

It had to have been an accident, one I'm sure he didn't even realize he made.

But what if he did mean it?

I STARED AT MY MOTHER IN PARTIAL DISBELIEF.

"What do you mean I can't go?"

She looked back and forth between Oliver and I. "I don't think it's a good idea, sunshine. Your health has been stable enough. I'm sure your doctors would be fine with it, but I'm not sure I'm okay with it."

Oliver rolled his lip between his teeth, but he remained silent for a moment.

"Why aren't you okay with it?" I questioned her, my voice demanding an answer.

My mother looked directly at me. "What if something happens to you and you're so far away? Your medical team is here."

"I can't believe this," I told her as I abruptly pushed my chair back. My knees felt wobbly underneath me and my chair clattered onto the floor as it tipped backward. This was all out of character with me, but I was done suppressing things. I was tired of just being so agreeable. For once, I wanted to be the one making my own decisions. "You don't want me to go because you're not going. You won't be there to control everything that happens. I hate to break it to you, Mom, but everything that happens to me is out of your control."

"Luna," my mother said as she rose to her feet.

"Erin," my father said as he grabbed her arm and held her in place. "Leave her be. Come with me."

My body was shaking with anger as I exited the room and stormed out the front door. I left Tank behind, too blinded by my own emotions to even care. I walked down the steps and headed toward the front gate.

"Luna! Wait up!" Ollie called out after me. I heard his footsteps behind me as he jogged after me, so I slowed down to wait for him. "Where are you going?"

I shrugged as I reached for the handle of the gate and fumbled with it. It was old and needed to be fixed. It tended to get stuck a lot and you had to shimmy it open. "Anywhere but here. I can't believe her."

"I can," Oliver retorted as he gently moved me out of the way. He took the handle of the gate and pushed his hip into it while lifting the latch. It instantly unlocked and he held it open for me to walk through. "She's afraid of what might happen if she isn't with you."

"I can take care of myself," I informed him as I began walking down the sidewalk. I had no destination in mind, no idea of where I was going. I just had to get out of that house before I freaked out.

"No one said you can't."

My footsteps were heavier and I was walking with such determination. I could feel the anger running through my veins and I didn't know how to extinguish it. "I've been away from her before and nothing happened then."

"You've never been that far from her for very long, Luna," Oliver reminded me.

I stopped abruptly and whipped my head around to glare at him. "Whose side are you on here? All of this was your idea and you don't even seem like you care about it."

"I'm on your side, Luna. I'm always on your side. I'm trying to look at it objectively and trying to understand where she is coming from." He paused for a moment, tilting his head to the side as he assessed me. "Give her some time to come around to it."

"I get it, but she has to let me live my life. She can't keep me on a leash like this just because she's afraid of what might happen."

"If something happened to you and she wasn't there to help you, she would never forgive herself. You know your mother better than anyone else, Luna. Please just try and understand where she's coming from." Oliver reached out and slid his hand into mine. "I told you to let me worry about them so let me try and talk to her without you… like I had originally planned."

I winced at Oliver's words and gave him an apologetic smile. "Yeah, sorry about that. We were all together so it seemed like the perfect time to say something."

Oliver smiled back at me, chuckling softly as he shook his

head. "Don't apologize, Luna. You were excited about the whole thing and you weren't expecting her to be reluctant like that." Ollie slowly turned both of us back in the direction that we came from. "Let's head back into your house and we can watch a movie or something as a distraction."

"What if she doesn't change her mind?" I asked him quietly as we walked back toward my house.

"Don't worry about the what if's, love. We'll figure it all out."

We both fell silent and walked hand in hand until Oliver had to shimmy our gate open again. Tank was waiting just on the other side and greeted us with his tail wagging and he hopped up and down with excitement. As we walked up to the house, I was surprised when I found my mother sitting on the porch.

Oliver's footsteps fell short and he stopped at the bottom of the stairs. I stopped with him and glanced over to see what he was doing.

"I think I heard my mom calling for me to come help her with something," Oliver lied with a wink. He leaned forward, his lips brushing against my cheek. "Text me later and let me know how things go."

"You're really going to leave me to deal with this by myself right now?"

Oliver nodded. "Just try and put yourself in her shoes, okay?"

"I'll try."

Oliver gave me one last smile before he looked over at my mother. "Goodnight, Mrs. Truly."

"Goodnight, Ollie," my mother replied to him with a small smile and a wave. I watched Oliver as he headed through the yard and slipped through the gate that led into his own backyard.

I inhaled deeply then let out the breath, and made my way up the steps to my mom. She moved over on the swinging bench she was sitting on and patted it for me to sit down next to her.

"I want you to know I love you very much, Luna. No decision I make is ever made with the intent to upset you. You are my world and it has been my job for the past eighteen years to protect you and to keep you safe."

"I know, Mom," I agreed with her, my voice soft as I tried to give her some grace. "I'm sorry for the way I overreacted earlier. It was extremely childish and immature of me. I didn't think about how all of this would affect you."

She looked over at me and gave me a small smile. "The thought of you being hours away for a few days makes me nervous, but after talking to your father, I think it's time I take a step back. You're old enough to make your own decisions, and I don't want to be the one who holds you back."

Her words took me by surprise and my eyes widened as I looked at her. "Does this mean I can go?"

She smiled at me, although it didn't quite reach her eyes, she still shared the same excitement I could feel building inside. "Yes, sunshine. You're an adult now and you can make your own decisions. Go and live your life, have fun, and make memories with that sweet boy."

"Thank you, Mom, thank you so much!" I said as I threw my arms around her and hugged her tightly. She hugged me back, her arms lingering a little longer, almost as if she didn't want to let me go.

I hated knowing she might struggle with this change,

but at the same time, I knew it was necessary. It wasn't like I was moving out but it was time I got to do things how I wanted to.

"Go tell Ollie," my mother told me as she released me and patted my knee. "I know he's been working hard to plan everything perfectly, so I think he'll want to know immediately."

"Yes, of course." I nodded, smiling at her as I hopped to my feet. "I love you, Mom. Not just because you said yes, but because you're the strongest, most amazing person I know. I'm so grateful to have you as my mother and I wouldn't want anyone other than you."

My mother's throat bobbed as she swallowed hard and her eyes grew moist as she nodded. "I love you too, sunshine."

She waved me to go inside, and I smiled at her once more before I went in with Tank hot on my heels. The house was quiet and my feet didn't stop moving until I made it to my bedroom and was shutting the door behind me. I dropped down onto my bed and grabbed my phone and went straight to Oliver's name.

LUNA

You're never going to believe it...

I stared at the screen, a smile pulling on my lips as he immediately responded.

OLIVER

She said yes?!

LUNA

YES!!!!

I could barely contain my excitement. Oliver and I were really going to get to do this.

OLIVER

Hell yeah!! Planning it now, Looney Tune. Start packing your bags, because we're doing the damn thing.

The butterflies fluttered in my stomach and my heart pounded erratically. I couldn't remember the last time I was this excited about something. Tank sat on the floor by my feet with his head tilted to the side with a questioning look.

"We're going to go on a road trip and to the beach, Tank," I explained to him like he had any idea what I was saying. "I don't even know what I'm supposed to pack. What do people take to the beach?"

He stuck out his tongue and panted as his tail began to thump against the floor.

"Of course you wouldn't know." I laughed to myself before picking up my phone again as it vibrated.

OLIVER

I'm serious, Luna. We're going this weekend, if you're free…

"Oh my god, Tank, he wants to go this weekend." I stared at my dog in disbelief. "That's like two days away. How the hell am I supposed to be prepared by then?"

OLIVER

Luna…

"What do I say?" I asked Tank, like he had the answers to the universe. "Do I tell him yes? Yeah, I think I do."

LUNA

I'm free. You want to go this soon?"

OLIVER

Life waits for no one, my love. If you aren't living it, it will live on without you.

I smiled at my phone.

LUNA

Let's do it.

Chapter Twenty-Two
WHERE THE OCEAN MEETS THE SKY

As I sat in the front seat of Oliver's car, it almost felt as if I was living in a dream world. We had it packed full of my stuff and his, along with Tank in the backseat. There wasn't much room for him to move around, but he seemed content as his head hung out the window, his tongue flapping in the wind.

Oliver booked an oceanfront room for us from Friday until Sunday. We were able to check in at three in the afternoon, so we left a little before noon, just in case we needed to stop for food or anything.

I looked at the GPS on the screen in his car, noting that we were only about twenty-five minutes away. The entire ride ranged from the music being turned up loud and us being silent, to us talking about anything and everything that crossed our minds.

I made a mental note that I really enjoyed road trips with Oliver.

As I adjusted in my seat, I unbuckled my seat belt and

there was a loud ding in the car. I quickly buckled it again and gave Oliver an apologetic smile.

"Are you good?" Ollie asked with a touch of concern in his tone. "We can stop if you're uncomfortable and get out and stretch our legs.

I shook my head at him, appreciating his worry. "I'm fine. I've never been in a car for this long and as comfortable as your seats are, they do get a little uncomfortable after a while."

"Tell me about it." Oliver chuckled as he switched lanes and headed toward the nearest exit. "Let's take a quick stretch break."

"We really don't need to," I told him as I turned to face him. "We're almost there. I can wait another twenty minutes."

He assessed me with his eyes and was able to see how adamant I was about the issue. It may have seemed futile to him, but it was important to me. It was something I wanted to prove to myself I could handle. Sitting in a car shouldn't feel like a difficult thing, but when your body isn't used to it, it's easy for your muscles to feel weak.

I wasn't going to let anything stop me this weekend.

This weekend was about not letting life pass me by.

"Fine, but if I think you look uncomfortable again, I'm pulling over."

I looked away from Oliver, feeling the heat creep up my neck and spread across my face. I kept my gaze out the window as I waited for my face to cool down. I liked when he got protective and apparently my body did as well.

As we fell back into silence, Oliver granted me some grace and turned the music back up as he switched lanes again and continued heading east. It wasn't long before we were turning off the highway and heading down Main Street toward where we were staying.

Leaning forward, I turned down the music and put my window down the entire way looking at the little beach shops as we drove past them. I had only ever seen places like this in movies and read about them in books. It was my first time seeing it in person and I loved the quaintness of it all.

People wandered up and down the streets, some carrying bags from the stores, others carrying ice cream. Everyone was dressed in their summer outfits, some in bathing suits with cover-ups on.

"Penny for your thoughts?" Ollie questioned me, drawing my attention away from my people watching.

I looked over at him and smiled. "Didn't we already talk about pennies?"

Oliver chuckled and shrugged. "How about dinner then? I'll buy you dinner in exchange for your thoughts."

"Absolutely not. You already paid for our hotel, I have money for everything else."

Oliver raised an eyebrow at me. "This is a fight you won't win, Luna love. I'm covering everything this weekend and it's not up for debate."

I raised an eyebrow, half mocking and half challenging him. He could try all he wanted, but there was no way he was paying for everything for me while we were here. The least I could do was buy my own food. He had already paid in advance for everything he possibly could—just to avoid the conflict, I'm sure.

"I'll give you my thoughts, but they're free. I was just watching everyone walking up and down the streets. Do you ever think about how everyone else has their own thoughts and is living their own life, and we have no idea what is going on inside it?"

Oliver glanced at me from the corner of his eye. "I mean, I've thought about it before, but not often. It's kind of weird if you think about it."

"Isn't it?" I agreed with him as we pulled into the hotel parking lot. "Like every stranger you pass is in the middle of living their own life that might not align with the things happening in your life."

"Do you think about it a lot?" he questioned me, with his voice tentative. There was a gentleness and it was free of any judgment, yet it made me feel a little strange, like not everyone else thinks like I do.

I shrugged. "Sometimes."

"There's nothing wrong with it, it just makes sense now."

My eyebrows pulled together as I watched him park the car. "What makes sense?"

"The little scenarios and stories you create about people."

I instantly blushed under his gaze as he killed the engine and rolled up the windows. There were times we went people watching and had this fun little thing we did. We would study the people and try to figure out their life, creating little stories for them as we went along.

"You do it too."

Oliver smiled at me as he chuckled softly. "I know I do. It's fun and I like that better than thinking about them having their own lives outside of our imagination. At least in the stories, we can give them happy endings."

"Well, not everyone gets a happy ending."

Oliver was silent as he studied me for a moment. "But we do."

I didn't want to bring the harshness of reality to his attention, so I simply nodded and smiled in an easy agreement. Oliver let out a sigh, his shoulders slumping slightly before he climbed out of the car. I followed suit and was standing along the side of it as he reached me.

"I'm going to go get us checked in and grab one of those luggage carts."

I nodded, and watched him walk away without another word. Tank bounded out of the car when I opened the door for him and I grabbed his leash before leading him over to the grass area that had a sign for dogs. He did his business and I let him sniff around while I waited for Ollie.

There was a soft breeze carrying the smell of salt across my skin. I inhaled deeply, closing my eyes as I savored the smell. I had never smelled the ocean before and it was a scent I wanted imprinted in my mind.

Somewhere I could drift off to when my present wasn't somewhere I wanted to be.

I walked back over to the car, meeting Oliver as he came across the parking lot with one of the luggage carts. He stopped with it by the trunk and popped it open before he began to put things on it. I held Tank's leash in one hand as I grabbed a bag from the backseat and brought it over to the cart.

"Luna, I'll get it all," Oliver told me as he closed the trunk and turned to face me. "Just take it easy and let me, okay?"

Part of me wanted to argue with him and help. After all, it was the least I could do. With all the planning Oliver did, it felt like I was just being a burden by having him take care of me, but it was what he wanted to do.

And if there was one thing I learned in life, it was to choose my battles wisely.

This was a battle I would always lose with Oliver Hart.

I stood by while he loaded the rest of our things onto the cart and then I followed him inside the hotel. We got a few sideways glances, mainly directed at Tank. He confused people with how big he was and his teddy bear personality. He literally would not hurt a flea.

We took the elevator up to the sixth floor and Oliver led the way down the hall until we reached our room. 637. Oliver held the key up to the door and it clicked as a small light next to the pad turned green. He reached forward and opened it for me, letting Tank and I walk in before he came in with our stuff.

Letting go of Tank's leash, I walked around the room, inspecting it in awe. There was a massive bathroom in the small hallway that was by the entrance. I peeked my head inside, staring at the huge shower and the soaking tub inside. Two things I never had the opportunity to enjoy, but I knew what I was going to do while we were here.

Absentmindedly, I scratched at my chest and ignored the annoying throbbing feeling as I walked deeper into the room. Oliver was standing there and he turned around to face me with a shocked look on his face. It was a huge room with a small sitting area, a big TV hanging on the wall and one giant king-size bed on the other side.

"I asked for two queens. I don't know why there's only one bed."

I stared at him for a moment and then it registered in my mind. We would be sharing a bed. It's not like we hadn't done it already. We slept outside in each other's arms, but were never confined to our own private space like a hotel room.

"It's okay, Ollie," I told him with a shrug. "It's not a big deal."

He didn't look convinced. "I figured you would have wanted your own bed, so I asked for two queens. I didn't want you to feel any pressure or think I had ulterior motives for this trip."

His words took me by surprise and stung a bit. There were times I almost wished he had ulterior motives. Then maybe things between us would seem a little more normal than they actually are. "If you want two beds, that's fine with me or I can always sleep on the couch."

Oliver looked offended. "Absolutely not. You are not sleeping on the couch and I never said I wanted two beds. I'm just trying to be respectful and keep you in mind, Luna."

"So, you don't want your own bed?" I asked him, feeling the hit of dopamine in my brain as warmth sizzled up my spine.

"No," he said without any hesitation. Just a simple, pure fact. "I don't."

I could feel the color of my skin changing with the heat that crept upward and this time I didn't hide it. Instead, I smiled at him and walked toward our balcony. Pushing open the glass doors, the smell of salt entered my nostrils, and I inhaled deeply while taking a step outside.

It was truly beautiful. We had a perfect view of the beach and the ocean. It stretched out to the horizon, past where our eyes could see. It was a captivating sight and I couldn't take my eyes away from it. The wonderment of what could possibly be out there.

As I stared out at the horizon, I found myself wanting to experience it.

I wanted to go to where the ocean met the sky.

Oliver walked out to where I was standing and stopped beside me. He was silent for a moment as we both stared out into the abyss. A smile touched my lips and my heart swelled with emotion.

"The view is absolutely breathtaking," I murmured as I ran my hand along the railing at the edge of the balcony. I lifted my gaze and looked over at Oliver and found him staring directly at me.

"The most beautiful thing I've ever seen."

The air left my lungs in a rush and my heart skipped a beat. Damn Oliver and his ability to steal the oxygen from the air around us. I shifted nervously on my feet under his gaze, yet he didn't bother to look away. He just continued to stare at me with the most adoring look in his eyes.

"Now that we're here, is there anything in particular you wanted to do?" he asked me.

I mulled over his words as a smile crept onto my face.

"Everything."

Chapter Twenty-Three
A RITE OF PASSAGE

fter we got settled into our room, it wasn't long before the afternoon shifted into the evening. We found a seafood restaurant not far from our hotel and the food was absolutely divine. Not only were we checking things off my bucket list, but there was another list I stored mentally. A list of firsts. And anything we did here would most likely be a first for me.

Oliver held my hand as we walked down the boardwalk. I had Tank's leash in my hand and he had been acting strange all day. He wasn't one who typically whined but he'd stare at me and make a low rumble in his throat before nudging me. He acted like this before, but this time I was quick to ignore his behavior.

If I had any say in what happened, I refused to ruin this trip.

The boardwalk was crowded and there were so many other people walking around. I usually didn't like crowds but something about this was different. It was almost as if we could be whoever we twanted to be, surrounded by complete strangers. We just fit into the madness and it felt good.

We walked past shops and restaurants and as we reached the end, there were carnival type games with people calling us over. Oliver pulled me along, walking straight up to one of the men standing nearby. There was a wall lined with darts behind him and he looked back and forth between the two of us.

"The two of you want to try and win a prize tonight? Behind each balloon, it will say what type of prize you get." He paused and swept his hand around in an effort to show what we could win.

Ollie let go of my hand and reached into his back pocket to pull out his wallet. He looked at me and winked with a smile on his face.

"What are you doing?" I questioned him with my voice low.

He handed the man a ten-dollar bill and took the darts from him before looking back at me. "Winning you a prize, love."

He stepped up to the countertop of the stand and began to throw the darts at the wall. I watched the way his muscles rippled in his arm. He drew back, lifting his hand to the side of his head as he focused on his target and then threw it forward, almost like he was throwing a football.

I loved watching Ollie in action. He was extremely athletic and the way his body moved—his form and muscles. I'm sure a lot of other people enjoyed watching him as much as I did.

He didn't miss a single balloon, popping each one that he aimed for. The man looked as surprised as I felt and clapped his hands before checking the wall. He turned back around after collecting his darts and looked at Oliver.

"You won one of the giant prizes," he said as he pointed above to where the massive stuffed animals were hanging. "Which one would you like?"

Oliver turned to look at me. "Pick one, Luna."

I tilted my head to the side. "But you won it, you should pick."

"I won it for you. It's a rite of passage when you're on the boardwalk with your girl." He smiled down at me and winked again. "Which one will it be, love?"

Lifting my head, I looked up at the various stuffed animals until my gaze landed upon a tan colored sloth. I pointed to it, the corners of my lips lifting toward the sky. "That one."

The man got it down and handed it to me. It was soft and plush and more than half my size. I tried to wrap my arms around it, laughing as it covered my face and I couldn't see anything. Oliver lifted it from me and threw it over his shoulder before slipping his hand back into mine.

We continued our walk down the boardwalk, hand in hand, Oliver with a stuffed sloth over his shoulder, and Tank trotting along beside us. I'm sure to the outside world, we looked comical, but to me, we looked perfect. Oliver was giving me the best days I could have ever asked for.

And it killed me to know one day this would all come to a screeching halt.

Later that night, we were both tucked away in the king-size bed in our hotel room. Tank had found a spot on the floor to call his own and he was peacefully snoring away. He was still being weird and was on the floor right beside me. If I would have let him in the bed, he would be crammed between Oliver and I.

The tubing was already connected to the line in my chest, delivering the nutrients I wasn't getting from the food I ate or the food that went through my feeding tube. My skin around it was warm and burned, but I tried my best to ignore the sensation. I never did have my mom change the dressing, but it would have to wait until we got home now.

Moonlight shone through the glass doors of the balcony, illuminating Oliver's face as we both laid on our sides, facing one another. Oliver cracked the doors before we got into bed, allowing the salty breeze to drift through our room. It was a smell I don't think I could ever replicate or put into words.

The sounds of the waves lapping against the shore sounded in the distance. As we laid together in the dark, I tried to focus on that sound instead of the sound of my breathing. I needed to hook myself up to my ventilator before I drifted off to sleep, but I didn't want to break this moment. I didn't want to interrupt the softness of the silence between us.

There was something comforting about it. The way Oliver gently stroked the side of my face, pushing my hair back behind my ear as his eyes stared directly into my soul. He saw past what everyone else saw on the outside. Oliver Hart was the only one who saw the real me and I was certain no one else on the planet could ever see me the way he did.

"I hope you had a good first day," he said softly as his fingertips lingered on my skin. "It went by so fast."

My breathing was growing more shallow with every breath. My body was fatigued from the trip and the long day. We did a lot of walking and it was really taking a toll on my body.

"I did." I smiled at him, inhaling the scent of him and the ocean. "I'm ready to see what tomorrow brings."

Oliver's eyes lingered a moment longer before he moved away from me. I immediately felt his absence and shivered from the chill in the air as he climbed out of bed. I rolled onto my back, watching him with confusion as he walked around the bottom of the bed.

He stopped by my equipment and the loud beep from my ventilator sounded through the room as he turned it on. I watched him carefully as he went through the proper steps, making sure everything was connected and the humidifier was working properly. Usually when I went away, we just used a dry vent system if I needed it, so I had a humidification device in the tubing circuit of my ventilator.

Since we were staying two nights in a row, my mother insisted the actual humidifier came with us, which turned it into a wet circuit. The air from the ventilator went through the humidifier first, which warmed the air and added moisture to it before it went to the tubing connected to my trach tube.

It was just another thing most people didn't realize the importance of because they didn't have to worry about their mucus turning into a rock if there wasn't moisture added into the air they were breathing. When you breathe through your mouth or nose, the air is naturally humidified and warmed from your body.

When the air went directly into your throat through a tube, there was nothing there to do it naturally. That's why I needed the heater or if I wasn't on the vent and my trach wasn't capped, I needed to have my HME.

All bodies produce mucus, whether you are sick or not. If I didn't have the proper equipment, my mucus could literally kill me by blocking my airway.

Thank God for modern medicine.

There was no way I would have survived this long without it.

The whooshing sound of the ventilator continued as it filled up the artificial lung that was connected to it. It was more like a balloon that would inflate as a breath was delivered and then deflate when it was time to exhale. It kept the circuit sterile and it stopped the annoying alarms from going off.

Oliver held his hand out to me, and I took the cap from the end of my trach and handed it to him. He placed it in the same case I kept my speaking valve in and put it in the side pocket of my ventilator bag. After following the necessary steps, he disconnected the artificial lung from my vent tubing and connected it to my trach.

"Better?" he questioned me as he climbed back into bed, his voice soft as he ran his fingertips across my arm.

I looked at him and nodded, relief flooding me as the ventilator helped to assist my breathing. "How did you know?"

"I know you, Luna Truly." Oliver gave me a small smile. "I can pick up on your physical cues. The way your breathing changes when you're growing tired. Small and simple, yet detrimental things. I know you like the back of my hand, love. What I don't know is what goes on in that beautiful mind of yours." He paused and tapped his fingertip against my temple. "I'm still holding onto hope that one day you'll let me see inside." He dragged his finger down the side of my face, down my neck, across my chest, stopping when he reached my heart. "And one day, you'll fully let me in here."

I stared at Oliver as I got lost in the depths of his green eyes. He always found a way to surprise me with his words, yet I found myself wondering how he couldn't possibly know the truth. I hadn't verbally told him how I felt, but it had to be obvious to him at this point.

"Such a fool," I murmured, feeling my breathing growing deeper as my eyelids grew heavier. My body felt like it was weighed down and I was sinking deeper into the bed as my body teetered on the edge of sleep.

"Why's that?" he questioned me as he wrapped his arms around my body and pulled me flush against his chest.

I nestled myself against him, feeling the weight of sleep pulling me deeper. My eyelids fluttered shut and I inhaled the smell of Oliver one last time.

"You're already in there."

Chapter Twenty-Four
TAKE WHAT YOU WANT

The sand felt strange under my feet and it was a feeling I wasn't particularly fond of. Oliver insisted we take our flip-flops off as soon as we reached it but now I was wishing I still had them on. It felt crusty and scratched the bottoms of my feet as we walked out toward the ocean.

The sun hadn't crested the horizon yet. There were a few people out here already waiting for the sunrise. Oliver made sure to have an alarm set so we could get out before the sky started to change colors. It was a deep, dark blue, but it was continuing to grow lighter with each passing second.

"I don't think I'm a fan of the sand," I admitted as we stepped onto wetter sand which felt even weirder. With the dry sand, there was a little bit of softness to it. Now, it just felt wet and cold and uncomfortable.

Oliver raised an eyebrow at me. "Not many people are."

"So, everyone just comes here for the ocean and doesn't worry about the fact the sand sucks?"

A soft chuckle escaped him and he led me directly to the water. It was cold against my toes, but there was a calming effect. It was soothing, the sounds, the smells. Feeling it on my skin. It was much more desirable than the feeling of the sand.

"You have to take the good with the bad. The sand serves its purpose, even if we don't like it. Everything has a place and a purpose. If you want to appreciate the good, you have to accept the undesirable parts that come along with it."

I stared at the side of Ollie's face, my eyes traveling along his sharp jawline. His nose was perfectly straight and when he stood still like this, it was almost as if he were like a sculpted statue. The only thing moving was his firm chest, rising and falling with every breath. His hair danced as the breeze tousled the waves on top of his head.

"You're missing the view," he told me as he continued to stare out at the ocean, watching the sky as it transformed from the sun just beneath the horizon.

I didn't tear my eyes away from him. "Quite the opposite."

Oliver tilted his head to the side as he looked over at me. He gave me a knowing look, a fire blazing deep in his irises. Screw the ocean and the sunrise. None of that mattered. The only thing that mattered was the person standing in front of me. Oliver Hart was my entire world and he didn't have the slightest clue.

The corners of his lips lifted upwards and he reached out for me, pulling me closer to him. He positioned himself behind me, wrapping his arms around the top half of my torso before resting his chin on my shoulder. His lips were soft against the side of my neck as he pressed them to my skin.

"I promise you, you don't want to miss this."

I would have easily taken his word for it, but instead, I followed along. I didn't know when I would have the opportunity to experience something like this again. I reveled in his arms, allowing his warmth to seep into my soul as I rested the back of my head against him. He straightened his back, resting his head on the top of mine as we watched the sky transform before our eyes.

The blue slowly changed into different hues of pink and orange. It was the most fascinating thing I ever watched and I was captivated by the beauty of it. The morning was quiet, the breeze salty and the ocean calm. There wasn't a single thing wrong with this moment and it was one I would be saving in my brain for the rest of my life.

As quickly as it started, the sun popped up along the horizon and lifted higher into the sky with each passing second. It was amazing how fast the sky changed colors. And then it was over. The sun was in the sky where it belonged and the colors dissipated to a golden glow as it was slowly resuming to its blue color.

Oliver didn't let me go. He held me in his arms as we soaked in the atmosphere and the scene in front of us. The other sunrise watchers had since disappeared from the beach, yet we remained unmoving. My eyelids fell shut and I breathed in deeply, savoring the scent of the ocean as I lifted my hands to hold onto Ollie's forearms.

"Did you want to go get some breakfast?" he questioned me, his voice soft and silky as it floated across my eardrums.

"I do, just not yet," I told him as we both stayed, unmoving. "Just a little bit longer."

Oliver buried his face in my hair and I could feel him smile. "You tell me when, love. I have no problem spending the rest of my life right here, just like this."

A soft laugh escaped me, and I turned to face him in his arms. "You know we can't do that, Ollie. As nice as that sounds, you still have a life you need to live. Did you forget about college and football?"

His arms slid down my body, resting around my waist as I lifted my arms to link them around the back of his neck. Oliver's eyes bounced back and forth between mine, in a slow deliberate search. What he was searching for—I would eventually find out.

"That's not life, Luna," he said softly as his gaze shifted down to my lips before resting on my eyes again. "That's all just a part of it. This is all that has ever really mattered and all that really will. Don't forget, you have a life you need to live too, but if you want to stay like this, I'm not opposed."

This time, it was me who's gaze shifted back and forth between his eyes and his lips. Oliver had been the one who always initiated everything and each time was with my consent. I didn't want to strip that from him, but I also wanted to be the one to make a move.

Oliver's throat bobbed as he swallowed roughly and I focused on his lips as I wet my own with my tongue. "What are you thinking about, love?"

"That I want to kiss you."

The corners of his lips twitched and his grip tightened

around me. "I'm yours for the taking, Luna. Take what you want."

Lifting up on my toes, I pressed my lips to Ollie's as my eyelids fluttered shut. My stomach was doing flips and my heart was pounding against my ribcage. I was tired of sitting on the sidelines and not being the one to act. Oliver told me to take what I wanted and that was exactly what I was doing.

His lips were soft against mine, his mouth accepting. He didn't try to take control. Instead, he handed the reins to me and let me kiss him the way I wanted. There was a tenderness between us, yet a burning fire of curiosity. I was exploring parts of myself with him, while still exploring him. Kissing him came easily and it was something I would never grow tired of.

My heart was racing around in my chest and it felt like it was going to beat right out of me. A shiver pulled up my spine but I brushed it away. Nothing was going to ruin this moment between us. I was living life and anything that threatened to derail that could fuck off.

Oliver kissed me back as both of our tongues danced with one another. At one point, he lifted his hands to cup the sides of my face and he pressed his hips against me until we were flush against one another. The ocean rocked back and forth across my ankles and my feet grew cold, but none of that mattered.

All that mattered was him.

"YOU'RE GOING TO BURN," I TOLD OLIVER AS I SAT UNDER the shade of our umbrella and put another layer of sunscreen on. "Your face always gets red when you're in the sun for a long time."

Oliver looked over at me from the towel he was sitting on. His body was wet from the ocean, beads of water rolling across the planes of his naked torso. Lifting a hand, he pushed his damp hair away from his forehead.

"I'll be fine, Luna. I put sunscreen on earlier. I don't need multiple layers like you do. You're the one we need to make sure doesn't burn with your fair skin."

He wasn't wrong. I never asked anyone if it was part of my disease process, but I assumed it was. I was anemic as it was, and the lack of oxygen in my bloodstream made me look pale in comparison to a properly oxygenated person. Perhaps it was just my skin tone, though. My father had fair skin, although he didn't look ghostly like I did.

"Did you want to go back to the room soon?" Oliver questioned me with a hint of concern in his voice. "You look more pale than you normally do and that's saying something."

I shook my head at him. "It's because of the sun. I always look more like a vampire in the sunlight."

"At least you don't sparkle," Oliver said with a wink.

"Did you really just make a *Twilight* reference?" I asked, raising a suspicious eyebrow at him.

Ollie smiled sheepishly at me and shrugged. "Maybe…"

I couldn't stop the laughter that bubbled out of me. Giana and I went through the whole *Twilight* franchise kick when we were younger, and I made Oliver watch every single movie with me. According to him, he didn't really enjoy it, but I digress.

"I knew you actually liked it even though you told everyone you didn't!"

He chuckled along and then grew serious as he held his finger to his lips. "Shh. If you tell a single soul, I'll deny it."

I rolled my eyes at Oliver. "Who else could I possibly tell? You're the only one I'm close to that I talk to about everything."

The corners of his lips twitched. "Good. Let's keep it that way."

I stared at him for a moment, but he pulled his sunglasses over his eyes, shielding them from my wandering gaze. Oliver began to pack up our things and I followed suit, helping him. We left Tank back in the room since it was pretty hot outside.

As we made our way across the hot sand and back to the hotel, fatigue really began to set in and I was grateful that we were going back to our room. We stepped onto the elevator and I yawned as I pressed the button for our floor. I could feel a nap in my near future and was really looking forward to it.

The doors started to slide open and I adjusted the strap of the bag on my shoulder before I went to walk out. Oliver reached out and grabbed my arm, pulling me back. "Where are you going? This isn't our floor."

I looked up at the number on the small screen above the elevator door. "Floor three. That's not our floor?"

Oliver's eyebrows pulled together. "No… we're on the sixth floor."

I tilted my head to the side. "Are you sure?"

He fell silent as he stared at me for a moment. He reached into his pocket and pulled out the small envelope that had our keys in it. On the front it said our room number and sure enough, it was on the sixth floor.

"Hmm," I said before letting out another yawn. "I must have just confused the numbers."

Oliver didn't say anything. Instead, he slid his hand down to hold mine again and pressed the correct number on the panel in the elevator. The doors closed and we rode up to our floor. Oliver took the bag I was holding, and I didn't object to it for once. My body needed to rest and I was beginning to feel lightheaded.

As we stepped into the room, a shiver rippled down my spine and Tank greeted us at the door. I walked over and grabbed his leash and Oliver set all of our things on the small couch in the room.

"What are you doing?"

I looked up at him, the room spinning slightly as I stood back upright. "Taking him out to go to the bathroom." I paused for a moment as I rubbed my hands over my arms. "Can we turn the air conditioning off or something? It's freezing in here."

Oliver gave me another look of confusion. "I'll mess with the thermostat and make it warmer." He took the leash from me. "I got Tank. You get comfortable, okay?"

Another yawn escaped me and I nodded as I rubbed my eyes. "Okay," I agreed.

I waited until Oliver and Tank left the room before I stripped out of my bathing suit and put on a pair of shorts and an oversized t-shirt. I climbed into bed and hooked myself up to my ventilator. My eyelids were so heavy as I settled against the pillows.

I didn't always need it if I took a nap, but with how fatigued I felt, I knew it was probably for the best. Just as I was about to drift off to sleep, I heard Oliver and Tank come back into the room. Tank met me on my side of the bed and rubbed his wet nose against the side of my face as he whimpered.

"Hey," I mumbled as I pet him on the top of the head. "I promise we'll take you out later."

"Luna," Oliver said, his voice tender as he slipped under the covers with me. "We don't have to do anything later. I feel like we're overdoing it and I don't want to exhaust you too much."

I shook my head at him in protest. "You're not. I know what I can and can't handle. I'll let you know if it gets to be too much."

Oliver pursed his lips and I could see the disbelief written in his expression, but he kept quiet. Instead, he settled on the plush mattress with me, pulling me against him as he held me until I couldn't stay awake any longer. I let the sleep pull me under as I slid into a dream world with Oliver, where none of our problems existed.

Into a world where we actually had a future...

Too bad it was just a dream.

Chapter Twenty-Five
WILDFIRE KISSES

As I rolled over in bed, I found the other side empty and cold. I slid my hand across the sheet as I peeled open my eyes and realized Oliver wasn't there with me. Panic welled inside me and I sat up in a rush, my head swimming with the sudden movement. It was dark in the room with nothing but the soft glow of the TV illuminating parts of it.

I disconnected my vent and powered it off.

"Ollie?" I called out as I leaned over and flicked on the light. Tank lifted his head from where he was lying on the floor beside my bed. "Where is he, boy?" I murmured to my pony-sized dog like he would actually know.

As I climbed out of bed, I heard the click on the lock to our door. I froze in place, my heart hammering away in my chest. The door was pushed open and I glanced around looking for something I could use as a weapon. I spotted an oxygen tank on the floor and I quickly grabbed it, raising it above my head.

The door closed and footsteps came down the small

hallway. Oliver appeared in the entryway of the room carrying a plastic bag that had containers inside. He paused, raising an eyebrow as he cocked his head to the side.

"What are you doing?"

Heat instantly flooded my cheeks, and I abruptly lowered the oxygen tank. I set it back where it originally was and cleared my throat. "I was, um—I was working out?"

I wanted to palm my forehead for the stupid response.

"Since when do you work out?" Oliver asked with a hint of amusement in his tone. "You were going to knock me out with that, weren't you?"

My eyes widened. "Not you. The intruder or whoever was coming in who might not have been you."

"You always find a way to surprise me, Luna." Ollie chuckled and continued his walk through the room. He dropped down onto the couch and set the bag of food on the table. "Are you hungry?"

I glanced over at the clock, noting it was already seven o'clock in the evening. I slept for a solid five hours. The guilt instantly set in and I grimaced. My stomach, however, growled at the thought of food.

"I am so sorry. I didn't mean to nap that long. My body must have been more tired than I thought."

Oliver patted the couch beside him, and Tank perked up as he looked over at him. "Not you, Tank," he mumbled, shaking his head before he looked up at me. "Come eat, Luna. I can hear your stomach from here and you need something to give you energy."

My footsteps were heavy with guilt as I walked over and dropped down onto the cushion beside him. Our bare knees brushed against one another and warmth spread like wildfire through my body. "I ruined the entire day."

Oliver handed me one of the containers with a grin. "The day isn't over yet."

A smile spread across my lips as I looked inside and found shrimp tacos with rice and beans. I looked over at Ollie. "My favorite."

He winked at me. "I told you, I know you, Luna Truly."

We both began to eat as we watched some unfamiliar movie on TV. I took a few bites of my tacos and rice before I felt as if I couldn't eat anymore. Even though my stomach had been growling, I didn't have much of an appetite. It was probably from the sun earlier in the day and I'm sure I didn't hydrate properly.

"Is something wrong with it?" Ollie asked as he set his container down.

I shook my head at him. "I'm just full. I'll put it in the mini fridge and save it for later, though."

He gave me a quizzical look but didn't press the issue. Oliver always watched me like a hawk but he didn't push unless he felt like he needed to. I was thankful in the moment that he didn't because if he did I would have to lie to him. We were already heading home tomorrow, so I would worry about things then.

"What do you want to do tonight?" I asked him after putting my food in the fridge. "I don't know what there really is to do so I wasn't sure if you had anything in mind that you wanted to do."

"I do have one idea," he said with a mischievous smirk playing on his lips. "We didn't get a chance to go swimming in the pool or the hot tub."

"Is it still open?" I asked as I looked back over at the clock, noting it was now eight o'clock.

Oliver shrugged. "I say we get our bathing suits on and go check it out. If you're up to it, of course," he added quietly.

"Of course I am," I told him, not sure if I really did feel up to it or not. If it was something Ollie wanted to do, we were going to do it. If I could help it, I wasn't going to be holding him back anymore.

He hopped up like a little kid getting ready to run down the stairs on Christmas morning. "Do you want the bathroom to change or out here?"

"It doesn't matter to me," I told him as I slowly rose to my feet. Oliver gave me a look that said he needed me to make the decision. "I'll take the bathroom."

He nodded, and I grabbed my bathing suit and ducked into the other room, pulling the door shut behind me. As I slipped out of my clothes and into my suit, I found myself looking in the mirror. Underneath it all, I looked sickly. Thin, bones protruding. I didn't have much fat or muscle in places most people would.

I had a pretty face, but that's all I'd ever be. My body didn't compare. My breasts were smaller than most girls my age. Hell, I rarely ever got a period and if I did, it was short lived. I could thank my disease process for that one.

My friends claimed they were jealous I didn't have to deal with it, but they didn't look at the bigger picture. I would never be able to have kids and they would. Being a mother was something I never considered because I was told from a young age it would never happen. That was something I was jealous of.

I would have gladly had a period if it meant that some part of my life would physically be normal.

There was a soft knock on the other side of the door.

"Are you okay in there?" Oliver asked me.

I swallowed back my emotions and fixed my smile in place before heading out of the bathroom. I paused just by the door, grabbing one of the robes to cover my body before I finally went out. Oliver was already standing there, holding both of our towels and wearing just his swimming trunks. My mouth went dry as my gaze traveled across his perfectly chiseled torso and followed the V that disappeared beneath his waistband.

Ollie cleared his throat, and I blushed deeply as I looked back up at him. "Shall we?"

I nodded, and followed along with him. Maybe I would get lucky and drown in the pool so I wouldn't have to keep dealing with this humiliation of getting caught every time I was checking out my best friend.

We took the elevator down to the first floor. There was an indoor pool on the top floor, but it was probably locked this late in the evening. Instead, we went out to the outdoor one, in hopes that no one would see us. The outdoor lights lit a path leading out to the beach so if you walked to the furthest corner of the pool, it was almost as if it were tucked away in the dark.

No one would ever see us over here.

Oliver set our towels down on the ground, tucking them under one of the chairs to try and hide them. He turned to face me as he held his hands out. I glanced down at his palms and back up to his face with a quizzical look.

"Your robe," he murmured with a slow smile.

If he could see me in the dark, he would most definitely see how bright red my cheeks were at that moment. I pulled on the tie around my waist but I pulled the wrong way. Instead of untying it, I simply made a huge knot.

"Shit," I mumbled under my breath as I tried to untie it in the darkness of the night. I couldn't see it well enough and my fingers felt numb. The soft breeze that drifted from the ocean kept pushing my hair into my face.

Oliver took a step toward me and closed the distance between us. "Let me."

My heart crawled into my throat and I dropped my hands away as he began to work at the knot. I must have pulled it tighter than I thought because it took him a minute to separate the straps. He finally got it untied and released them as the front of the robe fell open, exposing me in my bikini.

Oliver inhaled sharply and he didn't bother being discreet as his eyes traveled across my body. It wasn't his first time seeing me in a bikini but this was different. The moment was intimate as we stood in front of each other under the moonlight.

He took another step toward me until the fronts of our bodies were almost touching. His fingertips were warm as he slid them across my shoulders, pushing the robe down my arms as he removed it for me. I stood frozen in place— barely breathing—as he dropped the white fabric to the floor and reached up to tuck a stray hair behind my ear.

A shiver rippled down my spine and I wasn't sure if it was from the chill in my bones or from the way Oliver was looking at me right now. His eyes were hooded and the flames flickered in his irises. He dropped his hand away from my face and slid it into mine before he led me toward the pool.

The water was warm around my ankles as we slowly eased in. I had been swimming before, but it was something I always had to be careful doing. If I were to get water into my trach, it could cause some serious problems because the fluid would go directly into my lungs.

Since it was just the two of us and Oliver knew, he moved with precision through the water, careful to not create too many ripples. He moved his hand from mine and dove into the water. I watched as he disappeared beneath the surface and the water lapped against my stomach. His movements were smooth enough that he barely created any waves.

I inched closer to the edge of the pool where there was a ledge to sit on. The water felt like silk against my skin. I was careful to keep my chest above the water so it didn't get my central line wet. It was already irritated and I was trying to make it a habit to not look at it any time I was near a mirror. Although, it was getting harder to ignore the pain and the way it was heating my skin around it.

Oliver's head popped up and he lazily swam back toward me. He didn't stop moving until his hands reached my knees. My heart picked up the pace and he moved his hands onto the ledge of the seat, caging me in. Water dripped from his wavy hair and landed on his forehead and cheeks.

"You don't want to swim?" he questioned me with his eyebrows pulled together.

I looked at him for a moment as the truth weighed heavily on my shoulders. It was right there on the tip of my tongue. I could tell him what was going on, but then the entire trip would be ruined. As much as I didn't want to lie to Oliver, I wasn't ready for any of this to be over yet.

"I like watching you." I smiled at him.

His gaze lingered on mine and the corners of his lips twitched. "Oh yeah?"

I nodded. I knew how to swim, but being able to do it was a completely different story. And swimming under-water was never an option for me. Watching Oliver was mesmerizing, the way his body slid through the water with nothing holding him back.

Oliver moved closer to me as he lifted his chest from the pool. His thighs brushed against mine and my legs instinctively parted as he gripped the concrete on either side of my head. He was surrounding me completely, and my heart pounded erratically in my chest as his eyes drifted from my lips and back up to my eyes.

"I like watching you too, Luna," he breathed as his gaze dropped back down to my mouth. His tongue slipped from his mouth as he wet his own lips. "Can't seem to keep my fucking eyes off of you."

Folding my lips in between my teeth, I swallowed hard over the lump that was lodged in my throat. My heart had a mind of its own and if I weren't so caught up in the moment, I'd be concerned for my health and whether or not it was going to burst inside my chest. My breathing was shallow and the water between us shifted.

Warmth spread through my body and I wanted to clench my thighs together, but I couldn't. Oliver situated himself between my legs, yet the only parts of us touching were our thighs. It felt like he was completely consuming me but I wasn't overwhelmed.

I wanted more.

"I like you watching me," I murmured as a ragged breath escaped me. My hands were shaky and nervous as I lifted them to wrap my arms around his back. Even though I was nervous, I felt more confident touching him. There was power in being the first one to make a move and having it be reciprocated.

I watched the fire burn brighter in his eyes.

"Is that so?" he questioned me with a glimmer of mischief passing through his sage irises. "I could watch you all day, love. You're the one thing in life I will never grow tired of. I'm addicted to you, Luna Truly. You run rampant through my veins, and my whole fucking my system. And I can't seem to get enough of it."

I applied pressure with my hands, urging him closer to me. His hips collided with mine and I could feel how hard he was as he pressed against my center. It was only our bathing suits separating us. The intimacy between us was growing with an intensity and I didn't want it to stop.

Oliver's jaw clenched and he pressed into me harder. His erection brushed against the most sensitive part of my body and a whimper escaped me. My eyes widened and Oliver's grew hazy with need.

"Fuck it," he breathed as he slid his hands through my hair to cup the back of my head before his lips crashed into mine. He was gentle, but there was an urgency with every movement. Oliver pressed me against the side of the pool and the water lapped around our bodies as he kissed me like he was starving for the oxygen in my lungs.

His fire spread through my body like wildfire.

And I wanted to burn in him.

Chapter Twenty-Six
YOU

Oliver's lips bruised mine as he kissed me fervently and I never wanted him to stop. My lungs were constricting, screaming in protest from the lack of oxygen. My head was spinning, floating through the clouds. I was lightheaded as hell, but none of it mattered.

All that mattered was this moment between us.

Because time was fleeting.

And I knew this was something I would never get back.

He was the one to break away first. His hand was still around the back of my head and he rested his forehead against mine as we both struggled to catch our breaths. Oliver's erection was still pressed against me and I decided to make a risky move. I wrapped my legs around his waist and held him against me.

"What are you doing, Luna love?" He let out a ragged breath, his voice hoarse and strained.

"Taking what I want."

He pulled back slightly, his eyes desperately searching mine. "What do you want?"

I stared back at him. "You."

"You already got me, love."

I shook my head at him. "I want all of you."

A shadow passed through Oliver's expression and a look of torment washed over his eyes. "Are you sure you know what you're asking of me?"

"Yes, Oliver. I want you to be my first. You're the only one I've ever wanted and I don't want it to be with anyone else."

In that moment, I swear his eyes glowed back at me. The look on his face was indescribable. He didn't look like he was in pain but it was almost as if there were a million different emotions washing over him at once. I watched as his throat bobbed and his face dipped back to mine as our mouths melted together.

His kiss was tender, his touch gentle. His cock was throbbing against me and I shifted my hips, feeling it brush against my clit again. Oliver moaned into my mouth and his fingers dug into the back of my head. The concrete edge of the pool was digging into my spine, but I ignored it. The warmth that spread through my body was over-powering and washing away any pain that I was feeling.

"I need you, Luna," Oliver murmured against my lips as he released the back of my head. He ran his fingers down the side of my neck and across my collarbone. "Not here, though. I want you in our bed where no one can interrupt us."

A soft laugh escaped me as Oliver moved away from me and held his hand out for me to take. "Yeah, that would be a little embarrassing."

"And infuriating," he added as he led me out of the pool. "I don't want anyone else to see you but me. I don't need to go to jail this summer."

I tilted my head to the side, staring at him with my eyes wide as he released my hand and grabbed the robe. He lifted it up and wrapped it around my body before he wrapped a towel around his lower half.

"Why would you go to jail?"

Oliver looked at me with the most serious of looks as he took my hand in his again. "Because you're mine, Luna. I don't share what's mine, not even with someone else's eyes."

My breath caught in my throat, and I let him lead me away from the pool and back into the hotel. The marble floor was cold under my bare feet as we walked past the front desk. No one was there and Oliver let out a chuckle as I started to pick up the pace, hoping we wouldn't get caught.

As we reached the elevator, he pressed the button and abruptly spun me around to face him. He slid his hands under my butt and lifted me into the air in one fluid movement. I let out a yelp as I felt my body suspended in the air and wrapped my legs around his waist. Oliver adjusted me in his arms as he stepped onto the elevator and I linked my hands behind his neck.

He pressed me against the wall in the elevator and kissed me until we reached our floor. The elevator dinged as the doors slid open and we broke apart. We were both breathless but Oliver seemed unaffected as he carried me straight to our room. He fumbled with the key and I played with the hair at the nape of his neck as he unlocked the door and let us in.

Tank greeted us at the door, but Oliver simply pushed past him. "Go lay down," I instructed him. The last thing I needed was my damn dog interrupting any of this or killing the mood. Who knew if I would ever get this chance again. Tank sighed and went and laid down on the couch, distancing himself from us.

I pushed him from my thoughts and Oliver carried me straight to our bed. As he gently laid me back on the bed, the mattress dipped underneath both of our weight. He climbed on with me and my robe fell open, laying out on the bed around me. Oliver's mouth dropped down to mine and he nipped at my bottom lip.

"Are you sure you want this?" he whispered against my mouth before his tongue slid against mine.

I pushed him back, our gazes colliding as I nodded. "I've always been sure of you."

Oliver claimed my lips with his once more as his hands began to explore my body. They traveled down my chest, careful to not touch my central line. He moved over my breasts that were covered by my bikini top. He trailed his fingertips along the naked flesh of my stomach and warmth spread through me. Every single nerve ending in my body was tingling.

His hands brushed underneath my breasts before he moved them under my bathing suit. My heart raced and I moaned into his mouth as he cupped my breast and brushed his thumb across my nipple. Oliver pushed his hips against me and I could feel his erection through his bathing suit and towel.

He lifted his face from mine and he planted one hand on the bed beside my head as he continued to trace circles around my nipple with his fingers on his other hand. "Do you trust me?" he asked, his voice soft and tender.

I swallowed hard and nodded. "With my life."

Oliver smiled down at me. He dropped his face down to the crook of my neck and pressed his lips to my skin. He began to move down my body, tasting and touching his way until he reached my breasts again. He slid his hands behind my back and gently lifted me up with him. He was situated between my legs and my stomach did a somersault as he undid the straps to my bikini, simultaneously freeing me from it and the robe.

He moved off the bed as he removed my bikini bottoms and threw them onto the floor along with his bathing suit. He stood at the edge of the bed, his gaze raking over me as his jaw clenched and his throat bobbed while he swallowed hard. "Fuck, Luna," he breathed, his chest rising as he inhaled deeply. "You're breathtaking."

With the way he was looking at me, I believed him. He made me feel like I was the most beautiful thing he had ever seen. He warmed my soul with his words and his gaze. He gently pushed me back against the bed and followed along with me until he was hovering over me. His bright eyes searched mine.

"Can I tell you a secret, love?"

My tongue darted out to lick my lips as I slowly nodded. "You can tell me anything."

"I'm not as experienced as I've led you to believe." He paused for a moment as he brushed the hair from my face. "I've been with other girls before and have done stuff with them, but whenever it came to actually having sex, I couldn't go through with it."

My eyes widened and I stared at him in shock. There

was no way. Oliver dated a few girls while we were in high school and the girls always bragged about him. Why would they lie about it? Unless they wanted to feel cool just by saying it and people believed them.

"You mean you're a virgin too?" I questioned him, my voice quiet as I stared at him in disbelief.

Oliver nodded at me. "I am. I just couldn't do it. Every time I got to that point with any of them, I realized it wasn't you and it just felt wrong."

"You're lying." I laughed softly as I shook my head at him. "I heard the girls you dated in school. They all talked about how good you were."

"I asked them to do that for me." He gave me a look that was laced with guilt. "None of them were really happy with me about it and I lied to them. I made up bullshit excuses and then told them if anyone asked, to say we actually did it."

His words took me by surprise even more. My eyebrows pulled together. "Why would you want them to do that, though?"

"I don't know, Luna. Because I was young and dumb. I didn't want anyone to know I couldn't have sex with another girl because my brain only cared about my best friend. The one who I was in love with for years, but thought I would always be in the friend zone with."

The air left the room in a rush. He drained every liter of oxygen from my lungs with his words. I stared up at him with my eyes wide and I shook my head. "No, Oliver. You can't love me. You were never supposed to love me."

He narrowed his eyes and refused to move as I planted my hands against his chest. "You don't get to make that choice for me, Luna. I love you and I'm not going to hide it anymore. I fucking love *you*, Luna Truly."

"Stop it." I closed my eyes as tears began to fall from them. I shook my head. "You can't love me, Oliver. I won't let you. I won't be the reason you're left living with a broken heart after I'm gone."

Oliver stared down at me with a fire burning in his eyes. There was a mixture of emotions that felt like a knife twisting in my chest. "You have no right!" His voice grew louder and cracked around his words. "Loving you is *my* choice, Luna, not yours. Just because you're afraid doesn't mean you get to take that away from me. You have no fucking right."

"I'm only going to break your heart in the end."

"Don't you see? I don't fucking care about that. At least I'll be able to say I had the privilege of loving you and being loved by you." He paused as his expression softened. He caught my tears with his thumbs and brushed them away. "Loving you, touching you, mourning you. All of that is my choice. Not fate's, not God's, not even yours."

Oliver dropped his lips to my forehead. He was still settled between my legs and already in my goddamn heart. "I love you, Luna Truly. Whether you want to accept it or not. I fucking love you."

"I love you, Oliver," I admitted quietly, not fully trusting my voice. "I always have and I always will. I wanted to save you, to protect you from me and my fate, but you're right. I know what it feels like to have choices taken away and I won't do that to you. If you want to love me, then love me. Because I love you too."

Oliver pulled back to look at me and his eyes searched

mine. "I'm going to kiss you and I know when I start, I'm not going to be able to stop."

"I never want you to stop," I admitted as I wrapped my arms around the back of his neck and pulled his face to mine. "Kiss me, touch me, *love* me."

"Always and forever," he murmured against my lips before claiming them with his own. He was soft and gentle, tender and patient. We took our time, memorizing every inch of each other's bodies as we connected in the most intimate way possible. Oliver left his mark on my soul, and I never wanted to know what life would feel like without him.

He did exactly as he promised and he loved me all through the night.

Chapter Twenty-Seven
HE COULD LIVE WITHOUT ME

"Luna…"

His voice sounded so far away. I wanted to reach out and grab the sound and pull it closer to me, but I couldn't. He was just out of touch, a fraction too far.

"Luna, wake up…"

His voice sounded again through the darkness. There was something off with his tone. It was high pitched and laced with anxiety. Oliver only sounded like that when he was scared. I wanted to reach out and hold him in my arms.

It's okay, Ollie.

I was nestled deeply in the darkness surrounding me. It was warm and felt safe, but I wanted Oliver with me. I never wanted to let him go, yet it felt like we were two souls floating past each other, unable to meet in the middle.

"Luna, please…"

There was a heavy weight on my chest and I began to

feel like I was being dragged down. Something was weighing me down and I fought against it. It was suffocating. The heat was intensifying until it felt like my skin was going to melt away.

And like a thread pulled taut, something snapped.

My eyelids were heavy and it took every ounce of strength to lift them. They cracked open, just enough for my brain to register my surroundings. It all came back to me—the night before with Oliver and I. We were still in the hotel. He told me he loved me.

He was pacing back and forth in the room with his phone pressed against his ear. I couldn't make out what he was saying, but he looked panicked. My entire body was burning, yet there was a constant chill settling in my bones. Every limb felt like it weighed more than a horse. I was sinking into the bed and it was going to swallow me whole.

Tank was sitting right beside me with his head pressed against my arm. My eyes searched his and he whined as he nudged me. I wanted to pet him and tell him it was okay, but I couldn't muster the energy to lift my hand.

My vent alarmed and I glanced at it from the corner of my eye. My respiratory rate was higher than normal as it alternated between 32 and 36. Oliver's head whipped over and he looked between the ventilator and me.

His lips parted and a ragged sigh escaped him as he hurried over to the bed. "Oh, thank God," he breathed as he dropped to his knees beside me. "Luna, love. I called your mom and 9-1-1. Something's wrong and we need to get you to the hospital."

My stomach sank and my heart continued at its rapid pace inside my ribcage. "My central line," I practically whispered the words. It hurt to try and talk. My mouth was dry, my lips were cracked and I could taste a hint of metallic as I ran my tongue over them.

Oliver tilted his head to the side, his jaw clenched as his eyebrows pulled together. "You knew, didn't you?" He paused for a moment before moving to sit on the bed. He reached for my shirt and he pulled it down to look at my chest. His face screwed up the moment he really looked at the area. "Fuck, Luna. It's definitely infected. Why didn't you say anything?"

Tears pricked the corners of my eyes. "I didn't want to ruin the trip," I admitted, although my voice was barely audible and only every other word sounded somewhat clear.

"Oh, Luna love," he breathed with a pained look in his eyes. "That wouldn't have been possible. We're going to get you to the hospital and get it handled, okay?"

My chin wobbled and I nodded as the tears fell down the sides of my face. Oliver was fighting back his own emotions, trying to be strong. I wanted to tell him it would be okay, that he didn't need to be strong. This was the end —I could feel it in my soul.

We all knew that one day my life would come to a halt and it would be earlier than everyone else's. There was a loud pounding sound on the door to the hotel room. Tank started barking and Oliver quickly pressed his lips to my forehead before rushing away.

I had a good life and I honestly wouldn't have wanted to live it any other way. Oliver Hart told me he loved me. The one boy who I tried so hard to keep at arm's length, even though he already burrowed himself in my heart. He made everything perfect. I got the chance to be loved by him.

I didn't want to leave him, I didn't want to leave him with a hole in his chest, but he would get past it. As I watched the way he moved around the room, he took control while explaining everything to the EMTs and paramedics that arrived.

A smile pulled on the corners of my lips. Oliver was the strongest person I knew, and I knew in my heart he would be okay in the end.

He could live without me.

The paramedic was trying to talk to me, but my head was swimming and it sounded like waves were crashing in my ears. I watched her lips move before I looked back at Oliver. The weight was getting heavier and my body was growing weaker. I was fighting so hard just to keep my eyes open and I couldn't do it anymore. I needed a break. I needed to rest.

Tears spilled from my eyes and Oliver met my gaze.

"I love you," I mouthed to him as my body failed to create any sound. His eyes widened and he shook his head at me. I smiled at him once more. The beautiful boy who held my heart in his hands. My eyes fell shut as the darkness began to suck me back under.

"She's coding!" I heard an unfamiliar voice yell in the distance.

And then as if someone turned off the TV—darkness completely consumed me and everything went silent.

Chapter Twenty-Eight
ALWAYS AND FOREVER

I rolled over in bed, lifting my arms above my head as I stretched my spine. The tingling feeling from a good stretch spread through my body and I smiled to myself. As I peeled my eyes open, I slowly let them adjust to the bright sun shining through my window. My plush bed was empty and my bedroom was quiet.

As I sat up, I surveyed the area. The walls were painted white with modern decor hanging on the walls. On the right wall in the room, the one with the most windows, I noticed one of our pictures was lopsided. A frown tugged my lips downward. I made it a point to make sure everything was level when we hung them up. There was no reason why it should be hanging crooked.

It gave me a strange feeling—one I couldn't quite put my finger on, but I was easily distracted when I heard commotion coming down the hallway. The small footsteps instantly made my heart swell and I sat back against the headboard of our bed.

Suddenly, the bedroom door was flung open and our

three little ones came rushing into the room. Owen, who was six, had a plate full of pancakes and a huge grin on his face as he walked over to my side of the bed. Lila, who was three, thankfully wasn't carrying anything. She flung herself at the bed, her little feet kicking as she propelled herself upward. She let out a string of giggles, and I opened my arms for her to climb into them.

And Milo, who was seven—the oldest of our three—came in last, carrying a mug of coffee and a glass of orange juice. His sage green eyes met mine and his smile matched his brother's as he set them down on my nightstand.

"Happy Birthday, Mom!" the three of them all exclaimed at the same time before piling onto our king-size bed with me. They practically tackled me and we were all laughing as everyone was fighting to get their space near me.

They situated themselves on the bed and my gaze collided with Oliver's as he leaned against the doorway to our room. His dark hair was a tousled mess and his hands were in the front pockets of his plaid pajama pants. He looked just as delicious as he did when we first fell in love, many years ago.

"Happy Birthday, love," Oliver said to me with a look of admiration as he walked over to all of us. "The kids wanted to surprise you with breakfast in bed."

I looked between all three of our little ones. "And what a surprise this was," I told them with a huge smile.

"You better eat your pancakes, Mommy," Lila said in her most serious voice. "You don't want them to get cold."

The laughter escaped me, and Oliver shook his head as he laughed along. "She has a point."

"Okay, okay." I put my hands up in submission. "I was just enjoying my morning snuggles, but you guys win."

Owen slid off the bed and grabbed the plate before handing it to me. Oliver directed his attention to the three kids. "Why don't the three of you go finish your pancakes and we'll be down in a little bit."

"Okay, Daddy," Lila agreed without an ounce of hesitation. She was the true definition of a daddy's girl. She may have both of our dark hair, but she had my blue eyes. The boys had their father's green eyes and looked like exact replicas of him.

I watched the three of them disappear from the room as I took a bite of my pancakes. The clock on Oliver's nightstand caught my eye as the numbers were flashing. "Did the power go off last night?" I questioned him as I glanced at my clock and saw the same flashing numbers. 6:37, but there wasn't an AM or PM with the time.

Oliver's eyebrows pulled together and he shook his head. "Not that I know of."

"Hmm," I mumbled over a bite of my breakfast. "That's strange."

"What do you want to do for your day today?" Oliver questioned me, mischief dancing in his eyes as he moved closer to me. He pressed his lips to mine, our flesh sticking from the syrup on my pancakes. "Mmm," he murmured as he pulled away. "You taste good, Luna love."

"Don't you dare start something you know we can't finish," I told him as I caught that familiar look in his eyes. You would think we were newlyweds with the way we couldn't get enough of each other. "The kids could come back up here any minute."

"I'll give them as much screen time as they want if it means I get to make you feel good."

"Oliver Hart," I scolded him, laughing as I smacked his hand away. "You can wait until later."

He let out an exasperated sigh, but he agreed. "Fine… but tonight you're mine."

"Always and forever," I reminded him as I leaned forward and quickly kissed him. "Do we have any plans for the day, other than Milo's hockey game this afternoon?"

Oliver shook his head. "Not that you know of, at least," he said with a wink.

"You're impossible."

Ollie smiled at me before he climbed off the bed. "But you love me anyway."

"I CAN'T GET THIS DAMN TIME TO CHANGE ON HERE," I complained to Oliver as I fiddled with the clock on the stove. I had changed the time on it and the microwave three different times now. Each time I changed it, it reset back to 6:37.

Oliver glanced over at me from the foyer where he was helping Lila to get her shoes on. The boys were out in the driveway playing ball hockey while they were waiting for us to go to Milo's game. We had a low key morning, which I was glad for.

Our lives were so busy and we were constantly on the go. All I wanted for my birthday was to spend the day with my family and relax a little bit. They graciously gave me what I asked for, but there was something that just didn't feel right with the day. Something was off.

"I don't know what to tell you, love," he said with a shrug. "I'll try them later or we can call someone to come look at them if we can't get them fixed by Monday."

I nodded and let out a breath of frustration. We were blessed that my career as a photographer took off and was more than enough to support our family. It bought us the house we lived in and gave us the freedom to do so much in life.

Oliver quit his job as a financial advisor and helped me, along with coaching hockey and football. Football was his true passion, though. He didn't play beyond college, but it was something that always stuck with him. And having two boys was perfect to cater to the athlete in him.

"I'm going to go make sure the boys are ready to go and we'll meet you in the car?" Oliver said, half questioning me, half declaring it.

"Absolutely." I smiled at him and watched him disappear toward the front door with Lila in tow. I glanced back at the clock again and glared at it. It was working its way under my skin and grating my nerves.

I tried to ignore it as I grabbed my purse from the counter. Stopping in the foyer, I pulled on my boots and just as I was grabbing my coat, there was a loud crash from the family room. The sound startled me and I inhaled sharply, momentarily feeling like I couldn't breathe. My heart pounded erratically in my chest and I struggled to catch my breath as I went to investigate.

We had a large clock hanging on the wall in the family room. It was black—a manual clock with Roman numerals. Somehow, it had fallen to the floor and the glass on the face was shattered.

"You've got to be kidding me."

It was still ticking but as I neared closer, I noticed the time on it. I swear the oxygen completely vanished from the room. 6:37.

"Luna, are you coming?" Oliver called from the front door.

I didn't answer him. I couldn't speak. It felt like my lungs were hardening and I couldn't breathe. He came bounding into the room as I was about to hyperventilate. "What's going on? Are you okay?"

"The clock," I choked out as I pointed to it.

"It's okay, love," he murmured, stroking my back. "The clock can be fixed. Just breathe."

I whipped my head to look at him. "I don't care about the clock! Look at the time on it!"

Oliver glanced over and shrugged. "Go get in the car, and I'll get this mess cleaned up and we can go. We don't want to be late for Milo's game."

I wanted to argue with him, but I didn't have the energy. The day was beginning to drain me and I needed to put on a happy face for him and the kids. Maybe it was all in my head and there wasn't anything going on with the clocks. All I knew for sure was I felt unsettled and I was ready for this day to be over.

As I stepped outside, dark clouds were growing in the distance. The tree in the front yard swayed as the wind picked up a little. There was an ominous feeling that just intensified the feeling I already had building inside.

A storm was brewing. Something was coming.

But what, exactly?

"I am so proud of you, buddy!" I told Milo as we all piled back into the car after his game. He played so well, scoring two goals with two assists. He was getting better and better with each season. Even though this was just a summer league, it still counted in all of our eyes.

Milo smiled at me from the backseat. "Thanks, Mom."

Oliver looked over at me as he climbed into the car. "We're taking you to your favorite restaurant for dinner tonight," he said with a smile.

"Zoey's On Main?" I asked him, feeling my stomach flutter with excitement. "You know how much I love their French toast."

"Which is exactly why we're going there," he said with a wink as he pulled the car out of the parking spot. "Look at you eating breakfast twice today."

I smiled back at my husband. "You know how to treat a girl."

He reached over and grabbed my hand, pulling it over to his mouth before pressing his lips to my skin. "My girl."

The kids giggled from the backseat, breaking up the moment between Oliver and I. As we drove farther down the street, I glanced in my mirror, catching sight of the ice rink. My breath caught in my throat and I strained my eyes as I tried to make sense of what I was seeing.

It looked like it was fading into thin air, lifting straight from the ground.

"Something wrong?" Oliver questioned me quietly.

I looked over at him, unable to speak before I glanced back into the mirror. We were already far enough away that the property was out of sight completely. I glanced back at my husband as I forced myself to gain some composure. "Everything's fine."

My eyes had to be playing tricks on me. That's the only thing that would make any sense. Thunder rumbled in the distance, and a shiver slid up my spine. I ignored it and tried to focus on the kids in the back as everyone fell into a conversation about our beach trip coming up.

I found myself drifting, unable to stay engaged in the conversation. It was like I was an outsider watching the four of them interact. I felt completely detached, almost like this wasn't where I belonged. I quickly shoved the thoughts away and plastered a smile on my face, forcing myself to engage.

Dinner passed by in a blur. I ordered the French toast I absolutely loved, yet I found myself with no appetite. My stomach felt off, just like the rest of me. Oliver didn't question my silence on the ride home as I told him I was tired. He backed the car into the driveway and the kids began to file out as they made their way into the house.

Oliver walked over to my door like the perfect gentleman he had always been and helped me out. "Why don't you go relax, and I'll handle the kids."

"Are you sure?" I asked him, my eyes searching his sage colored eyes as he cupped the sides of my face.

He lifted his lips to my forehead and they were soft as he gently kissed me. "Absolutely."

I followed Oliver into the house, but slipped into the sitting room while he went upstairs to bathe the kids and put them to bed. I still couldn't shake the unsettled feeling and I couldn't get comfortable as I tried to lounge on the couch. Everything just felt off and I ended up walking around the house instead.

I found myself standing in our hallway, inspecting all of our family photos. The wall was covered and strategically organized, but it was off. Pictures were missing. There were gaps in the timeline we had created. And some of the photos looked different. Almost as if none of us were real.

My throat felt thick and I tried to clear it. Again, I found myself gasping for air as my heart took off, racing in my chest. It was beginning to scare me. I would be calling the doctor first thing in the morning if this didn't get any better. The last thing I wanted to do was go to the hospital, so if I could put it off, I would.

"Luna, love," Oliver called down from the top of the stairs. "Did you want to come up and say goodnight to the kids?"

Shoving away the panicked thoughts, I sucked in a shallow breath and headed up to find him. He had a look of concern on his face, but he didn't voice it and instead stepped out of my way as I made my rounds through the kids' rooms.

I started with Lila first. The three of us sat while Oliver read a book to her. She was on a *If You Give A Mouse A Cookie* kick and we'd been reading it every night for a month straight now. After the story was over, I pulled the blankets up over her shoulders and leaned forward to give her a kiss.

"I love you, Lila love."

She smiled up at me. "I love you too, Mommy."

"Always and forever," I told her before heading to the

boys' room. They shared a room for now while we redid the other bedroom for Milo. He decided he wanted it painted a different color and wanted it decorated with hockey stuff. Oliver hired an actual artist to come in to paint a hockey player on his wall.

"Goodnight to my two favorite boys," I told them as I kissed both of their foreheads. "Thank you both for an amazing birthday. I love you, Owen and Milo."

They both smiled at me from their beds as I made my way back to the door. "Love you too, Mom," they said at the same time.

"Jinx!" Owen yelled at Milo.

"Always and forever," I repeated to them before blowing them both kisses and leaving their room. It was something Oliver and I had started with each other and it just became a habit with the kids, too.

After tucking the kids into bed, I made my way back downstairs. Oliver wasn't inside but I knew exactly where he would be. As I stepped out onto the front porch, a smile pulled on the corners of my lips as I saw him sitting on the top step, waiting for me. We had a swinging bench but the two of us preferred the steps.

Oliver wrapped his arm around the tops of my shoulders when I sat down next to him. "How was your birthday, my love?"

"It was perfect," I told him with a sigh of content. Thunder rumbled again in the distance, but I ignored it as I reveled in his closeness. "It was nice to just be able to relax, but I can't shake this feeling that something bad is going to happen."

"Nothing bad can happen here," he said matter-of-factly, like it was something I should have known.

I lifted my head away from his chest and stared at the side of his face. "What do you mean? Bad things happen all the time. Just look at those clouds," I declared as I pointed to the angry sky. "There's a nasty storm coming and we have no control over that."

Oliver looked over at me and simply smiled. He didn't argue, he didn't dispute a single word I said. He wasn't making sense and it wasn't bringing me any peace. A young couple walking down the street caught my attention.

I glanced at them in front of our house where they had paused. The boy had dark tousled hair and was wearing a football jersey from the same school district we lived in. The girl's back was turned to me and I stared at her in wonderment.

"Come on, Tank," she said with such exasperation and defeat as she heaved her body and attempted to pull on a leash. "Ollie, can you please help me with him?"

The boy laughed and adjusted the backpack straps on his shoulders before taking the leash from her hand. "Why did you have to pick out a service dog the size of a small horse?"

A dark brown head popped up and I smiled as I watched the two teenagers and the dog. The way the boy looked at the girl had my heart clenching. It was young love in its purest form, and I slid my hand into Oliver's as we both watched the two of them.

"You complain about him, but you know you love him," she told him with a soft laugh.

He stared at her and reached out to brush a hair away from her face. "I love you, Luna. Always and forever." He paused and smirked. "I just tolerate your dog."

It felt like the floor had been ripped out from under my feet. *Always and forever.* My stomach bottomed out and I let go of Oliver's hand as I rose to my feet. *Ollie and Luna.* None of it made sense. *My dog, Tank.* I glanced around the yard. I didn't have a dog.

Nothing made sense. Everything suddenly grew darker and thunder rumbled off in the distance again. My feet began to carry me in their direction. My body tingled while simultaneously feeling like there were sandbags on my chest. I couldn't breathe and I reached up to my throat but there was nothing there. The two kids on the street were now turning to look at me.

I stopped in my tracks in the middle of the walkway, halfway between the sidewalk and our front porch. She was me—a younger version—but she was different. She looked pale and fragile.

"You have to go back," Luna said to me with such a declaration in her voice.

Panic welled inside me. "Go back where?"

"He needs you," younger Ollie told me as he stared at me. "They all need you."

"Go back where?!" I yelled at the two of them with my frantic voice. My heart was pounding erratically in my chest. I couldn't breathe. This body didn't even feel like it belonged to me anymore.

"None of this is real," Luna told me with a touch of sadness in her voice.

I shook my head at her, refusing to even entertain the idea. "I'm not leaving. This is my life, with my husband and our children. I'm not giving this up."

She smiled at me. "What you have here is beautiful, but what you have in your real life is so much more beautiful."

They started to fade, vanishing into thin air like they were simply mirages. I watched in horror as they began to dissipate like clouds. "Wait!" I called out as I ran toward the fence. They were floating higher into the sky. "Don't leave! I don't understand what you're saying."

"You need to wake up, Luna. It's time."

And then they were gone.

I whipped back around to face the house expecting to see Oliver, but he was no longer sitting on the top step where I left him. Panic instantly flooded me. My stomach rolled with a wave of nausea and my heart was pounding with such ferocity inside my chest.

Where did he go?

My footsteps were rushed as I ran to the house just as the sky above split wide open. Huge droplets of rain fell in rapid succession as the thunder shook the earth and the lightning pierced through the black sky. I burst through the front door, almost pushing it off its hinges as it bounced against the wall inside the foyer.

I couldn't breathe. All of the air was abruptly sucked from my lungs and I was momentarily frozen in place as I looked inside my home. It was completely empty. All the family pictures that were hung on the walls were gone, the furniture was gone. As I rushed around the first floor, there was not a single trace of anyone living here.

The clocks in the kitchen blinked faster, the same damn numbers flashing brightly in my face.

"JUST STOP!" I screamed the words in my mind, but they didn't leave my mouth as I opened it wide. There was a crushing feeling on my chest and I held my breath since I wasn't able to pull in a single inhale.

The house around me shook, all the way down to the

foundation. Chunks of the walls fell to the floor, along with light fixtures and cabinet doors.

What the hell was happening?

I raced up the stairs, attempting to yell for Oliver and the kids, but again, the words failed to form. The steps were beginning to crumble as I reached the top. Panic was consuming me and my mind was stuck on a terrifying roller coaster I desperately wanted to get off of.

I needed some kind of an emergency brake. A lever I could pull and halt it all. I just needed a moment but everything was literally falling to shambles around me.

I checked every single room—there was nothing. No Milo. No Owen. No Lila. And no Oliver. They were all gone, as if they were figments of my imagination. My body began to sway and I reached for the doorway, holding onto the frame as I tried to steady myself.

In an instant, memories of the past flashed before my eyes. Oliver and the summer. All of my health issues. My family and friends. Except it wasn't my past… it was as if it were an entirely different world than the one I was in right now.

The walls around me started to deteriorate. What I literally had less than twenty minutes ago was suddenly gone, just like that. None of this made sense, but I knew I wasn't home. This wasn't real and it wasn't what I wanted. I wanted him, I wanted my life back.

Please just wake up, Luna.

I need you.

Suddenly, the floor fell from beneath my feet. I was free falling, spiraling down the hole the entire world was being sucked into. It was like the earth opened up the gates to a black hole. I always imagined what Alice felt like when she was falling. This was nothing like I imagined.

And then it was all gone.

My eyes sprung open and I moved them around, looking about the room even though the harsh light was painful. Something in the distance began to beep louder and at a faster rhythm. My mind was still reeling from wherever I was before this, but I found peace in knowing I was in the hospital now.

I looked across the room at the clock on the wall as everything came back into focus.

Six thirty seven.

Tears instantly sprung to my eyes as I closed them and let out a breath of relief. As I opened them again, I saw him from the corner of my eye. Using every ounce of strength, I turned my head to the side and there he was in all his broken glory.

Oliver Hart—the love of my life.

His head was hanging with his face pressed against his hands. I tried to reach for him but my arms still felt heavy. I held my breath for a moment, fighting against the ventilator in an effort to block it. Tears sprung from my eyes and his head abruptly lifted as an alarm sounded from me blocking the air trying to pass through the vent.

Our gazes collided and tears spilled down his cheeks as a smile lifted the corners of his lips. He rose to his feet and moved as close to my bed as possible.

"Luna, love." His voice cracked around my name and he slid his hand into mine. "You came back to me."

Chapter Twenty-Nine
I CAME BACK FOR YOU

I stared back at Oliver, both of us crying as he dropped to his knees beside the bed. He rested his forehead against my hand as he held onto it for dear life. It took most of my strength to lift my other hand to rest it on top of his head. His hair was soft and I slid my fingers through his waves. Even though I had just lived an entirely different life with him inside my head, I missed him.

He was my Oliver and I was never going to let him go.

I came back for him.

"I have to go get the nurse and your parents," he said softly as he lifted his head again. His eyes searched mine with desperation. There was fear in his sage colored irises. "I don't want to leave you."

"Please don't," I whispered the words as I tightened my grip on his hand. My voice was barely audible because of the ventilator, but I knew Oliver understood me when he nodded. "Press the call button."

"Good idea." He smiled as he pressed the red button

on the inside of the bedrail. One positive about having a trach was that even though I was on the ventilator, I was still able to somewhat talk. It was different from being intubated with a tube down the entirety of my trachea.

Usually, when I was connected to the ventilator, small amounts of air still managed to pass through the tube, even with the cuff inflated. It gave me the ability to talk with it like that. I'm assuming with the condition I was in, they inflated it enough so no air was escaping.

The nurse came rushing into the room less than a minute after Oliver pressed the button. She glanced at me and looked at the monitors before looking back at me with her eyes wide. "Oh my goodness, she's awake."

She smiled brightly and stepped toward the equipment beside me. I watched her grab the phone hooked on her pants and she pressed a button before putting it back in place. "I'm Leila, your nurse. I just paged Dr. Wyn and I'm going to do a quick assessment while we wait on him."

Oliver pulled his chair closer to the bed and sat down as he continued to hold my hand. We both sat in silence and I watched the nurse as she checked over all of the ventilator settings and my vital signs. Oliver's eyes were trained on me and as I caught his gaze, the look on his face made my heart skip a beat.

He was staring at me as if he couldn't believe I was real. Not quite like he was staring at a ghost, but almost like I was a figment of his imagination.

The nurse grabbed her stethoscope and began her head to toe assessment of my body. I rolled my head back to the neutral position while she poked around a bit. Oliver was watching, but I fought to look back over at him. If I saw the look in his eyes again, I was fairly certain I would have a breakdown of epic proportions… and I was already teetering on the edge.

Leila looked satisfied as she stood upright and hung her stethoscope around the back of her neck. Her lips parted, as if she were going to say something to me, just as Dr. Wyn walked in. He had been my doctor for as long as I could remember.

Which brought things into perspective for me. This was the hospital I frequented. I don't know how or when I got here. I don't remember what happened after the paramedics showed up at the hotel room. At least, nothing from real life. I remember every single piece from the life I was living outside of this world.

"There's my favorite patient, Luna," he said with a smile he usually only reserved for me. Dr. Wyn was a peculiar person. He often appeared cold and like he had a black heart. His humor was as dry as it came and he didn't typically make jokes that were in good taste.

He had a soft spot for me and it had been that way since I was a small child. He was the first doctor who was willing to take on my case and through genetic testing, he actually narrowed down what I had. He had solved the mystery of my diagnosis and was dedicated to trying to save me in whatever way he could manage.

Dr. Wyn treated me as if I was his own and it blew most of the hospital staff's mind. He didn't get invested or attached to any of the other kids he worked with. I suppose I was the exception.

"You look like you're feeling the after effects of that nice long nap you took, huh?" he said with a chuckle. My mother would have quickly scolded him, but his words always brought a smile to my face. He wasn't afraid to talk about life and death and the hard subjects. He didn't sugarcoat a single thing and I appreciated that more than anything.

I nodded. "I'm feeling it for sure."

The words didn't come out, and he tilted his head to the side. He glanced over at the nurse. "Deflate her cuff a bit so we can actually hear her."

Leila glanced at him with a worried look in her eyes. "Are you sure? She just woke up and we haven't even tried weaning her vent settings yet."

"Just do it. If she can't handle it, we'll know." He looked at me. "Are you okay with that, Luna?"

I nodded again. Dr. Wyn looked satisfied and Leila looked pissed but she obeyed his command. Just as she was taking some of the saline from the balloon, my parents stepped into the room. Being in the ICU, you were normally limited to only two people, but again… Dr. Wyn ran the unit and always allowed exceptions for us.

My mother dropped the bottle of water from her hand as she let out a loud gasp. Tears instantly flooded my father's eyes and I watched his chin wobble. My mother reached out and grabbed my father's arm before they both closed the distance between us.

Oliver backed out of the way, and Dr. Wyn stood over to the side with Leila as they all watched our reunion.

Both of my parents each took turns hugging me. When my mother wrapped her arms around me, she held me tightly as we both cried together.

"Oh, Luna," she sobbed, stroking the sides of my face as she pulled away. "I can't believe you're awake. We've waited so long to see your shining eyes again."

I stared at her as she wiped away my tears. "How long?"

"How long were you out?" She paused for a moment, collecting herself as she swallowed hard. "Three weeks, sunshine. You coded in the hotel room but they were able to bring you back. They took you to the nearest hospital but as soon as they were in touch with Dr. Wyn, we were able to get you airlifted here."

Leila peered over at my ventilator before looking at Dr. Wyn. "She seems like she's doing fine with her cuff deflated a bit."

"As I figured she would," he said matter-of-factly. "We'll switch her into assist mode tomorrow. Give her the day to recoup a little more before we really test her. Data from her assessment?"

I tuned the two of them out as I looked back to my mother who was now sitting on the edge of my bed. Oliver was close by and my father was standing behind my mother with his hands on her shoulders. "It was my central line, wasn't it?"

My mother gave me a look of disapproval. "I'm not even going to scold you now since you just woke up, but I am not happy you knew something was wrong."

I gave her a small smile. "I really wanted to go to the beach with Ollie."

"Yeah, well, that infection you had brewing almost killed you. You were in septic shock by the time you got to the hospital. You slipped into a coma and then they put you into a medically induced one so they could properly treat you. They took you off those meds once they were able to get you stable. That was a week ago" She paused, a look of sadness consuming her expression. "We've been waiting for you to wake up for a week and weren't sure you were ever going to."

The realization of her words hit me like a ton of bricks to my chest. It was a blow I could barely handle. I lost three weeks, but it was only one day that I lived a different life. How did that even translate into one another? I couldn't imagine what they were going through, waiting for me to wake up and unsure if I would

"I'm sorry."

My mother shook her head. "Don't apologize, sunshine. You're here now and that's all that matters."

Dr. Wyn rudely cleared his throat which got a laugh from my mother. "Gregory," she scolded him, giving him her motherly voice. He was practically an extension of our family and he took it in stride.

"I understand you are all having a little reunion, but we need to talk about some things." He was curt and to the point, in typical fashion. No one ever seemed to mind. "Thank you for bringing Luna up to speed."

He inched closer to the bed as Leila disappeared from the room. "Luna, your mother will scold you enough for the two of us, but as your doctor, I will also have to unfortunately scold you. When you're feeling better, of course," he added with a small smile. "You need to rest. You're going to be exhausted and fatigued. You're going to have a long recovery, but I know you. You are strong enough and will get through it. Tomorrow, we will switch your ventilator to assist mode so it is no longer breathing for you. If you tolerate that well, we'll start weaning the next day and try to have you back home as soon as possible."

"How is everything else looking for her?" my father asked.

Dr. Wyn nodded his head slowly. "We're getting back to her baseline, which is what we want to see. Now that she's awake, we just need to make sure her lungs are cooperating and then she'll be on the road to feeling back to normal."

"Thank you for everything," my mother said to him with nothing but admiration in her voice. This man had saved my life time and time again. He was the one doctor who didn't want to send me to hospice for them to just treat with palliative care.

He's another person who never gave up on me.

Dr. Wyn excused himself and slipped from the room as my parents fussed over me. I let them have their moment, because they had been waiting a long time with my life hanging in the balance. Oliver sat quietly with a smile on his face as he watched the three of us.

The image of him from my coma dream flashed into my mind. Him and I on the sidewalk with Tank. He had a football jersey on. Suddenly, it hit me like a flash of lightning. I tried to sit up, but I didn't have the strength. I whipped my head to the side to stare at him head on.

"You're not supposed to be here."

Oliver's eyebrows pulled together. A pained look mixed with the confusion in his expression. "Should I go?"

"Yes. No." I paused and closed my eyes for a moment. My body wanted to rest, but there was a part of me that was afraid to go back to sleep. I didn't want to leave this world again. I opened my eyes and met his gaze again. "What are you doing here?"

"Come on, Erin," my father said as he pulled my mother to her feet. "Let's go call Eli and Jackson and give them some time to talk."

My mother nodded and followed after them. I should have said something to them, but I couldn't tear my eyes away from Oliver's. Part of me was mad, part of me was sad, and a bigger part of me wanted to break down and cry tears of joy.

Oliver sat on the edge of the bed, caging me in as he planted his hands on either side of me. "You are the only thing that matters to me, Luna Truly. Fuck football, fuck college. You really think I would leave when you were in a coma? There's not a chance in hell."

I stared at him, my eyes filling with tears as everything came crashing down at once. "I saw it all, Ollie," I breathed as tears streamed down the sides of my face. He lifted his hands to cup my cheeks as he caught the salty liquid with the pads of his thumbs.

"What did you see, love?"

"We were married. We had a house and three kids." I paused for a moment feeling the emotion threatening to pull me under. "I didn't have any medical issues. Everything was literally perfect."

Oliver gave me a sad smile and shook his head as tears filled his own eyes. "Everything is perfect the way it is. You are perfect, Luna. It was just a dream."

"But it felt so real," I whispered, not fully trusting my voice. "I didn't want to leave. I wanted to stay in that world with you forever."

He swallowed roughly, his eyes desperately searching mine. "It wasn't real, love. This is real. You would have left me alone in this world so you could live with a different version of me in another life?"

His words felt like a blow to the chest. He was right. I knew nothing about that world except for the day I spent in it. And all it took was a moment of second guessing for it all to fall to pieces.

"No."

Oliver stared directly into my soul. "What made you come back if it were so perfect there?"

"I heard you." I paused for a moment as I slid my hand up to hold the side of his face. "I saw the real us and I knew I couldn't stay there."

Oliver's eyes shined brightly at me and they glistened with the tears that lingered in them. "I've only left your side to shower and get food. I have been begging you to come back since you left."

"I came back for you. I came back because this is the life I want… with you."

"You mean that?" he questioned me as his eyes bounced back and forth between mine.

I smiled back at the boy I loved with my entire heart. "Always and forever."

Oliver pressed his lips to mine, but he quickly pulled away. "I don't want to make it any harder for you to breathe. And we don't want to start something we can't finish," he added with a wink. "Be mine, Luna Truly. You're all I've ever wanted and the only person I could ever imagine spending my life with."

"Do you know what you're asking for, Ollie? You know life will never be easy. I'll always have restrictions. And we will never grow old together."

"I know exactly what I'm asking for." He said it with such simplicity like it was a known fact. "Will you be my girlfriend?"

"Are you sure you want to do this before you go off to college? I don't want to ruin the experience for you."

Oliver rolled his eyes so hard. "You're absolutely impossible," he said with a soft chuckle. "You don't ruin things—you only make them better. Now, answer the question, Luna."

I smiled back at him. "I've always been yours, Oliver. Since the moment we first met and you invited me to come help you dig for worms in your backyard."

He didn't stop himself as he pressed his lips back to mine. He was careful not to linger and slid his arm under the back of my neck as I rolled onto my side to face him. We laid on the hospital bed, surrounded by the beeping of monitors as we held each other and got lost in our gaze.

"I love you, Luna Truly," he murmured softly as he linked our pinkies together. "Always and forever."

I stared back at him as his love filled my soul with light.

"I love you, Oliver Hart."

Epilogue

OLIVER

TEN MONTHS LATER

I pulled my car onto the highway and smiled to myself, knowing I was finally on the home stretch. It had been a long year being away at college. I came home every weekend I was able to and any break that we had. It was a lot, but I got through it.

The six-hour drive wasn't as bad as it sounded after doing it so many times. My car hated me for all the miles and wear and tear I put on it, but that was insignificant in the grand scheme of things. There was only one thing on my mind that really mattered.

Luna Truly.

And I was finally coming home to her.

The past year wasn't an easy one with the distance between us. I wanted to wait until Luna was discharged from the hospital before leaving. I was in jeopardy of losing my scholarship and as soon as Luna found out about that, she wasn't having it. She was furious and insisted I go.

Even though I didn't want to, I listened to her and went. I missed the first week of camp and was severely disadvantaged when I got there. I had to work my ass off to prove myself as still being worthy of my scholarship. I made it through but only because I was doing it for Luna at that point.

She was my biggest cheerleader and even though she wasn't physically with me, she was still cheering me on every day. We FaceTimed and talked on the phone every chance either of us had. I hated being away from her, and after this year I realized a lot about myself.

I would tell her sometime this summer, but I forfeited my scholarship at the end of the year. I already started the process of transferring to a school much closer to home. One where I wouldn't have to be far away from Luna. When it came down to it, she was the most important thing to me. Football didn't matter. I could go to college anywhere else and still be able to play without such a huge commitment.

I didn't want to lose any more time with her than I already had lost.

The past year wasn't exactly easy for Luna either. Thankfully, since she was taking classes at the local community college, she was able to switch to taking them online for the first half of the year so she could have more time to mend at home.

It took about a month before she was able to tolerate being off the ventilator again during the day and breathing without the assistance of the machine. She lost a lot of muscle, weight, and strength while she was in the coma.

Dr. Wyn was on top of taking all of the necessary measures to get her right back to where she was before she ended up in the hospital.

By the time Halloween rolled around, Luna was finally feeling like she had completely recovered. She was the strongest person I ever met and probably would ever know. She never failed to amaze me, but I never doubted her ability to get back to her baseline.

By Christmas time, a miracle had happened and Luna didn't even need her ventilator to sleep anymore. It was almost as if her body was healing itself. And it honestly didn't surprise me when it came to Luna Truly.

She was tenacious and nothing was going to stop her or get in her way.

I glanced at the clock as I pulled off the highway. It was already after six o'clock but I would be home in less than twenty minutes. Thankfully, the days were growing longer and it was still light out. It wouldn't get dark until later in the evening. I pressed the gas pedal closer to the floor and sped down the back roads as I made my way to our town.

As I pulled onto our street, my heartbeat quickened and my stomach did a flip with anxiety. I had a lot of finals before the semester was over and I hadn't been able to get back home for a few weeks. It was a lot longer than I wanted to be away from Luna and I was just ready to see my girl.

I didn't even bother stopping at my own house and instead I pulled directly into Luna's driveway and parked my car behind her mom's. Turning the key, I killed the engine and hopped out of my car, but not before grabbing the bouquet of flowers I picked up for her.

Standing outside of her front door, I knocked lightly

and patiently waited. She knew I would be coming home sometime today but I didn't tell her when. I wanted to surprise her. Tank barked on the other side of the door, alerting whoever was inside that there was someone on the front porch.

Less than a minute passed, yet it felt like I was standing and waiting for an eternity. I just wanted to burst through the door and take her into my arms. I missed her so damn much.

The doorknob slowly turned and the door was pulled open.

There she was.

My heart and soul. She stood there for a moment, her bright blue eyes shining back at me. She looked healthier than ever before. She had gained some of the weight back and there was a little bit of color in her cheeks. I didn't care how she looked, because she always looked beautiful to me.

"Oliver," she breathed, the corners of her lips pulling upwards. Tank was trying to get through the door and he finally succeeded as he rushed at me. Luna was right behind him and I laughed as she pushed him out of the way.

I held my hands out, lifting her into the air as she wrapped her legs around my waist. Her hands were linked around the back of my neck and I spun her around as her lips claimed mine. It took me by surprise since Luna wasn't always the most forward, but she was learning.

She was learning to take what she wanted—what was hers. And I fucking loved it. I loved seeing her open up and how comfortable she was in our relationship. She pulled away, leaving both of us breathless and she hugged me fiercely.

"Luna love," I breathed against her neck before inhaling her scent. "Fuck, I've missed you."

We held onto one another for a few more moments before she tried to wiggle herself out of my arms. I tightened my grip around her and trapped her in my embrace.

Luna laughed softly. "Put me down, Ollie. I can walk."

"What did I tell you about walking, love? If I can carry you, I will do it for you." I paused for a moment as she stared down at me with those ocean eyes. "Plus, I'm not ready to let you go yet. I feel like it's been a lifetime since I last had you this close to me."

"You can't carry me around all the time." She smiled as she shook her head at me.

The corners of my lips lifted and I raised an eyebrow at her. "Watch me."

Luna laughed again as I carried her into her house. Tank followed after us and I kicked the door shut behind the three of us. He trotted through the house and I walked after him, taking Luna into the kitchen. No one else was around so I set her down on the counter, but I didn't move from between her legs.

I slid my hands through her long hair and gripped the back of her head as I brought my lips back to hers. She tasted sweet like candy and I wanted to drown in her. I didn't give a shit about what was going on in the world around us.

She was my entire world.

As I traced the seam of her lips with my tongue, she parted them and let me in. The kiss grew deeper and feverish as we both devoured one another like we were starved. It would be a lie to say I wasn't. I couldn't keep my hands off her whenever I was close to her. I literally could not get enough of her.

Luna was the one to break apart first. Her lips were swollen from our kiss and her cheeks were tinted pink. A ragged breath escaped her as she smiled at me. "Someone could walk in and see us."

"They know we're together," I said with a shrug and a smirk. Luna was a little more reserved than I was, but I would always respect her. "Do you have your list ready?"

We were going to spend another summer checking off a brand new bucket list she made. She refused to show it to me, and not knowing what was on it was killing me.

"Yep," she said with a wink. "I hope you can handle it."

I laughed softly as I held her close. "I can handle anything you throw my way, Luna Truly. I hated being away from you and missed you so damn much. You're the brightest star in the sky. You're my heart and my soul and I thank the universe every day for you. I love you."

She fell silent as she looked past me for a moment. I glanced over my shoulder to see what she was staring at. The clock on the stove read 6:37. I turned back to look at her and she smiled brightly at me.

"Six three seven," she said softly as wonderment filled her eyes and peace washed over her expression.

My eyebrows pulled together. "What does that mean?"

"I didn't understand it at first, but when I was in a coma, those three numbers were everywhere in my dream. When I woke up, they were the numbers on the clock in the room." She paused for a moment, her gaze never wavering. "It's us, Ollie. Six letters for always, three for and and seven for always."

My heart skipped a beat in my chest as I stared back at her, feeling her words sinking into in the fibers of my soul. Tears pricked the corners of my eyes as a grin spread across my lips. "Always and forever."

She nodded, smiling back at me as she illuminated my entire world.

"Always and forever."

Extended Epilogue

As I rolled over in my bed, I could feel his warmth radiating from his body. A slow smile crept onto my lips and I studied his face as I listened to his slow, deep breaths. He had a little bit of scruff growing along his sharp jawline and I kind of liked it. His dark hair hung just above his eyebrows and my eyes followed down his straight nose.

He was my Oliver. The same Oliver I had always loved, just a little older now.

There was no sound of my ventilator or machines in the background. About six months ago, Dr. Wyn granted me clearance and I no longer needed to use it when I was asleep. We were in the process of removing my trach altogether. By some miracle that modern day medicine couldn't explain, my body appeared to be healing itself.

"I can feel you watching me, Luna," Oliver murmured without opening his eyes. A smile pulled on the corners of his lips. "A penny for your thoughts?"

I laughed softly and his arm tightened around me. "We

both know you don't have enough pennies for my thoughts."

"You're right. But at least you finally let me into that pretty little head of yours."

This was our second summer together and our final days were approaching quickly. I wasn't ready for Ollie to head back to school so soon, but I knew I couldn't be greedy. He gave me as much of his time as he could and I didn't want to get in the way of his future.

He made it clear I was already a big part of it, but I didn't want to be his entire world. Oliver needed to have his own things that didn't involve me. I needed to know that he would be okay without me one day, and I tried to convince myself of that regularly.

I attempted to roll the opposite way and Oliver tightened his arm around me even more. "Where do you think you're running off to?" He slowly opened his eyes and I was lost in the green hues swimming in his irises.

I shrugged lightly. "I figured it was time to get up and start moving."

Oliver shook his head at me as he held me flush against his side. "Not today, love. We're staying right here until we absolutely have to get up."

We had gotten halfway through my bucket list before Oliver insisted we stop. He reminded me of what he said one day about making new ones. They were meant to last for five years, not for one summer. It was almost as if it gave him this false sense of assurance that if we still had things to check off on my bucket list, nothing was going to happen to me.

"Whatever you say." I smiled at him before I curled my body back into him. I rested my head on his chest and listened to the steady drum of his heart beating inside. He ran his fingers through my hair, softly stroking it before trailing down my back.

His fingertips were feather light against my skin as he absentmindedly drew patterns that didn't exist. We had become inseparable this summer, and no one objected when he became a permanent fixture in our household. His parents didn't argue when he refused to come home at night and my parents never uttered a word about him being in my bed.

We were respectful. We were still under their roof, so if anything was going on between us, we made sure we were quiet and everyone was asleep. Given the fact we were two college kids in love—it was a little ignorant to think we wouldn't be regularly having sex.

"I can't believe the summer is almost over," I murmured against his skin. I paused for a moment, inhaling his scent and savoring it. "It feels like it just started."

"It really does, doesn't it?"

I moved my hand across his chest and over his collarbone before holding onto his shoulder. Lifting myself slightly, I buried my face in his neck. "I'm not ready for you to leave."

He fell silent for a second but his fingers didn't stop moving. "What if I didn't have to?"

"What are you talking about?" I breathed against his skin.

"I'm not going back."

I lifted my head abruptly and my eyes bounced back and forth between his. "Yes, you are. You have to go back."

Oliver shook his head. "There's nothing there for me, Luna."

I stared at him in disbelief. "Are you insane? Everything is there for you. Your education, football…"

"I can get an education anywhere." He paused for a moment, his tongue darting out to wet his lips. "Football really isn't that important to me, Luna. I've realized a lot this past year about what is actually important. I can play football anywhere I go."

"What about your scholarship?"

He shook his head again. "That doesn't matter either. I forfeited my scholarship at the end of last school year. Everything was already processed for my transfer and I'm enrolled to attend Wyncote University in the fall."

I was a little shocked I was just now finding this out. Oliver had been keeping this from me for a few months now and I wasn't sure if it was actually longer than that. How long had this been his plan? A part of me was happy he was going to be going to school only a half hour away, yet another part of me was pretty pissed.

"When were you going to tell me?" I questioned him, trying to conceal the disapproval in my tone. I couldn't help but feel like he was forfeiting his future *for me*.

Oliver let out a deep sigh. "I wanted to tell you as soon as I made the decision but I knew you would try to talk me out of it." He paused again and slid his opposite hand up to cup the side of my face. "You're a force to be reckoned with, Luna Truly. I don't like being in the dog house with you. I promise, I meant to tell you sooner… I just couldn't find the right time."

I stared at him for a moment, the warmth from his

hand seeping into my soul. "Promise me you didn't do this because of me."

"Everything I do is because of you," he said matter-of-factly.

I narrowed my eyes on him. "Oliver…"

"It's the truth and it's not a bad thing. I didn't make the decision because of you in the way that you're thinking." He rubbed his thumbs over my eyebrows, attempting to smooth them out. "I made the decision because I don't want to be away from you. Last year was a test of my strength and it nearly killed me being away from you like that. I don't want to miss a single moment with you."

Falling silent, I mulled over his words. Oliver always had me in mind when it came to the things he decided to do. I never wanted him to make a choice based on how fleeting time was. I never wanted the fact that I was living on borrowed time to be the reason behind him doing or not doing something. I only wanted Oliver to make decisions based on what was best for him.

"Will you be staying with your parents?"

He let out a sigh of relief. "So, you're not mad at me?"

"No." I smiled at him and settled my head back against his chest. "I just wish you would have told me sooner or let me know you were thinking about it. You can make your own decisions and choices."

"Thank you, Luna," he murmured against my hair before pressing his lips to the top of my head. "And I'll officially be staying with my parents, but I was hoping I could unofficially live here. You know, like I have been all summer."

A soft laugh escaped me. "I don't see anything wrong

with that. Although, I think that's something you might need to talk to my parents about."

Oliver was silent for a moment and he held me tightly. "I just don't want to be away from you if I don't have to."

"And you don't."

Oliver lifted my head from his chest and he cupped the sides of my face in both of his hands. He gazed straight through my eyes and directly into my soul. It was where he had made his home. I gave him my heart a long time ago and it was something that I never wanted back.

"I was going to wait. I wanted it to be the perfect moment, but fuck it," he said as a smile pulled on the corners of his lips. "Marry me, Luna."

The air left my lungs in a rush and my eyes widened as I searched his eyes. "What?"

"I've loved you since the day I met you. You are all I ever wanted in life and all I will ever want. You're already my everything and I want you to be my wife."

Tears filled my eyes and I slowly shook my head at him. "I can't."

He narrowed his eyes on me. "Don't you dare fucking tell me no, Luna Truly. Don't you dare turn me down because you're scared."

"I can never give you a family. I could never be the wife you deserve."

"Fuck that," he growled as he slid his hands down to my waist and rolled onto his back as he pulled me on top of him. "Stop doubting yourself. I don't want a wife if it isn't you. And you're the only family I need. If we want kids someday, we can always adopt, but that doesn't even matter to me. *You* are all that matters."

"What happens if you change your mind?"

He stared at me with soft eyes. "You are the one thing I will never change my mind about."

"I just don't want you asking me this because you're in your emotions," I explained to him, still attempting to back track from his question. Only an idiot would say no to him and I was most definitely an idiot.

"If you think it's just because of my emotions, go check the front pocket of my backpack and see what you find in there."

My stomach did a somersault. "You didn't…"

He smiled at me. "I bought it months ago. I wanted it to be the perfect moment—which, clearly, my planning sucks." He paused again. "I'm going to give you one more chance to give me the right answer."

Tears filled my eyes and I nodded as I smiled down at him. "Ask me again."

"Will you marry me, Luna Truly?"

I stared at him as tears fell down my cheeks. Oliver Hart was the absolute love of my life. I would never experience another love like him and I never wanted to. He was all I wanted and nothing would ever change that.

Not fate.

Not life.

Not even death.

"Yes."

Acknowledgments

A few years ago, on a hot summer day, one of my closest friends and I sat and watched our two children playing together. We sat and dreamed about a future for my goddaughter, who walked and talked like a typical child, yet required medical care around the clock. She was tethered to a ventilator that assisted her breathing, yet my son never once looked at her as if she were any different from him.

We sat and pondered about what a future would look like with two little best friends growing up together and one day falling in love, despite their differences.

And that was when the story of Luna and Oliver was born.

The seed was planted in my brain and over the years, it blossomed into this unforgettable journey. And over the years, my goddaughter managed to shock all of us, soaring past the bleak odds she was given. By an absolute miracle, her body has began to heal itself. Long gone are the days of toting around a ventilator and all her medical equipment. I'm typing this with tears still in my eyes from the video her mother sent me two weeks ago of her telling me they're hoping to to remove her tracheostomy tube in the near future.

Like Luna Truly… you are fearless and limitless, little L.

I will never forget the day you came into my life and I will never be able to express how grateful I am for that moment and the ones that came after. Love you always.

To O—it has been an honor to be your friend and to watch you these past nine years. The mountains you have moved, the distances you have gone. I aspire to one day be a fraction of the woman and mother you are.

To my husband—thank you for keeping the children and I fed and watered while I worked on this labor of love. Thank you for your love and for always believing in me and my dreams.

To my children—my love for the two of you knows no limits. I never imagined I would have the biggest cheer-leaders bugging me for snacks. And even if I may take away your electronics, I still love you.

Cat—637.

To everyone from behind the scenes: Maddy, Carnold, Lauren Brooke, M, Ashley, Alix and MJ—Each of you have played such an important role in this book and the production of it. Forever grateful for each of you!

To my readers—you all decided to take a chance on me and on my stories. I wouldn't be where I am now without you all reading and showing your love and support!

About the Author

Cali Melle is a USA Today Bestselling Author who writes sports romance that will pull at your heartstrings. You can always expect her stories to come fully equipped with heartthrobs and a happy ending, along with some steamy scenes.
In her free time, Cali can usually be found living in a magical, fantasy world with the newest book or fanfic she's reading or freezing at the ice rink while she watches her kids play hockey.

Also by Cali Melle

<u>ORCHID CITY SERIES</u>

Meet Me in the Penalty Box

The Tides Between Us

Written In Ice

Dirty Pucking Play

The Lie of Us

<u>WYNCOTE WOLVES SERIES</u>

Cross Checked Hearts

Deflected Hearts

Playing Offsides

The Faceoff

The Goalie Who Stole Christmas

Splintered Ice

Coast to Coast

Off-Ice Collision

<u>ASTON ARCHERS SERIES</u>

Make Your Move

Make Your Play

Make Your Save

Make Your Change

Make Your Shot